RECKLESS
HEART

RECKLESS HEART

Amy Clipston

ZONDERVAN.com/
AUTHORTRACKER
follow your favorite authors

ZONDERVAN

Reckless Heart
Copyright © 2012 by Amy Clipston

This title is also available as a Zondervan ebook.
Visit www.zondervan.com/ebooks.

Requests for information should be addressed to:
Zondervan, *Grand Rapids, Michigan 49530*

Library of Congress Cataloging-in-Publication Data
CIP applied for: ISBN 978-0-310-71984-7

Cover design: *Thinkpen Design*
Cover photo: *iStockphoto*
Interior design & composition: *Greg Johnson/Textbook Perfect*

Printed in the United States of America

12 13 14 15 16 17 /DCI/ 20 19 18 17 16 15 14 13 12 11 10 9 8 7 6 5 4 3 2 1

In loving memory of James G. "Jimmy" O'Brien,
February 11, 1967–March 7, 1977.
Forever in our hearts.

Note to the Reader

While this novel is set against the real backdrop of Lancaster County, Pennsylvania, the characters are fictional. There is no intended resemblance between the characters in this book and any real members of the Amish and Mennonite communities. As with any work of fiction, I've taken license in some areas of research to create the necessary circumstances for my characters. My research was thorough; however, it would be impossible to be completely accurate in details and description since each community differs. Therefore, any inaccuracies in the Amish and Mennonite lifestyles portrayed in this book are completely due to fictional license.

Glossary

aamen: amen
ach: oh
aenti: aunt
appeditlich: delicious
Ausbund: Amish hymnal
bedauerlich: sad
beh: leg
boppli: baby
bopplin: babies
bruder: brother
bu: boy
buwe: boys
daadi: granddad
daed: dad
danki: thank you
dat: dad
Dietsch: Pennsylvania Dutch, the Amish language
    (a German dialect)
dochder: daughter
dochdern: daughters
Dummle!: hurry!
Englisher: a non-Amish person
fraa: wife
freind: friend
freinden: friends
froh: happy
geb acht uff dich: take care of yourself
gegisch: silly
gern gschehne: you're welcome
grank: sick
grossdaadi: grandfather

grossdochdern: granddaughters

grandkinner: grandchildren

grossmammi: grandmother

Gude mariye: Good morning

gut: good

Gut nacht: Good night

haus: house

Ich liebe dich: I love you

kind: child

kinner: children

kumm: come

liewe: love, a term of endearment

Mammi: grandma

maedel: young woman, girl

maed: young women, girls

mamm: mom

mei: my

mutter: mother

naerfich: nervous

narrisch: crazy

onkel: uncle

Ordnung: the oral tradition of practices required and forbidden in the Amish faith

schee: pretty

schpass: fun

schtupp: family room

schweschder: sister

Was iss letz?: What's wrong?

Willkumm heemet: welcome home

Wie geht's: How do you do? or Good day!

wunderbaar: wonderful

ya: yes

Kauffman Amish Bakery Family Trees

(boldface are parents)

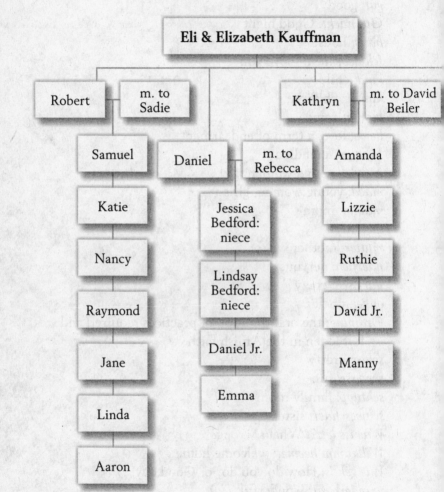

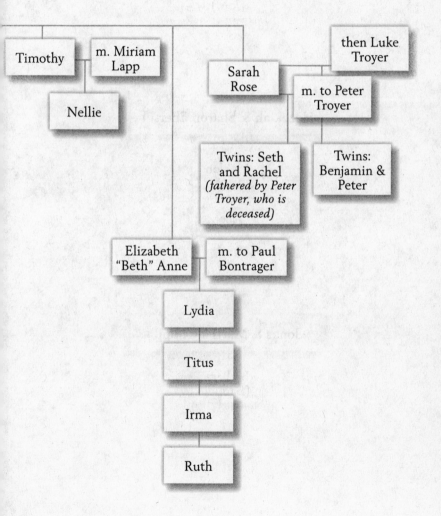

Timothy — m. Miriam Lapp
Nellie

Sarah Rose — m. to Peter Troyer — then Luke Troyer

Twins: Seth and Rachel *(fathered by Peter Troyer, who is deceased)*

Twins: Benjamin & Peter

Elizabeth "Beth" Anne — m. to Paul Bontrager

Lydia

Titus

Irma

Ruth

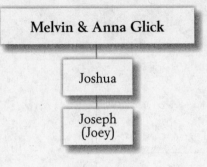

Melvin & Anna Glick

Joshua

Joseph
(Joey)

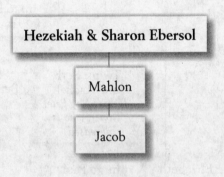

Hezekiah & Sharon Ebersol

Mahlon

Jacob

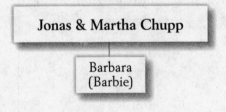

Jonas & Martha Chupp

Barbara
(Barbie)

L ydia Bontrager gripped the banister on the porch steps and heaved a deep breath. Closing her eyes, she willed the darkened farmland surrounding her to stop spinning. She groaned while touching her prayer covering, which had somehow come undone from her hairpins and hung crooked from atop her hair. The disheveled prayer covering seemed a fitting symbol for how she felt.

So this is what it means to be drunk.

Sunday evening had started out so innocently. She'd gone to a youth gathering at her mother's insistence, but her cousin, Amanda Beiler, hadn't attended. According to her other cousin, Nancy Kauffman, Amanda was still a bit under the weather after a bad case of the stomach flu. The group sang hymns in a barn on the farm owned by another member of their church district. But without Amanda there, Lydia found the gathering wasn't as much fun. It didn't help that Nancy spent most of the night flirting with her new boyfriend. Lydia had considered leaving, especially since Joshua Glick hadn't shown up either.

But it all changed when Mahlon Ebersol approached her.

Amanda had once said that fast-talking Mahlon was bad news. With his penetrating ice-blue eyes and sandy blond hair, he only had to smile to get all the girls in the church district to swoon. When he asked Lydia to join him and his friends out by the far barn, Lydia agreed before her brain engaged.

With a nervous giggle, she followed him and his usual entourage of boys and a few girls to the other side of the pasture. After a few prompts and dares, she took a swig of her first beer. Although it tasted worse than old milk, she didn't stop drinking it until the bottle, and the one that followed, was empty. Mahlon and his group seemed so cool and she wanted to fit in.

Opening her eyes, Lydia studied the front door of her white house. She knew in her heart the truth about her behavior this evening. She didn't really yearn to fit in with Mahlon and his wild friends. She even knew she could have resisted his smile if she'd wanted to.

What she'd really craved was to drink away the pain caused by what lay beyond that front door — her baby sister's mysterious illness, which had gripped her family for the past month. Four-year-old Ruthie had been fighting to shake a cold for weeks. Their mother tried all of the herbal remedies that had helped Lydia and her middle siblings, Titus and Irma, in the past. But little Ruthie's body refused to heal. Her fever had persisted, along with mysterious bruising, aches, and pains.

The doctor's visits increased, and her mother's stress level had heightened late last week. Usually sweet and patient, she had become almost militant, barking orders and snapping whenever the smallest mistake was made. Though she knew it was wrong, Lydia was relieved and secretly happy when her mother was in another room.

Taking another deep breath to steady herself, Lydia slowly started up the front steps and wrenched open the door. The large kitchen was dark since her parents always snuffed out the gas lamps when they went to bed. She'd returned home in the dark after attending youth gatherings in the past, but for some reason the kitchen seemed darker and larger than it ever had before.

If I were English, *I could flip a switch and banish this darkness*. But she knew it was an idle thought — propane- and battery-operated lamps were all her Amish tradition would allow. Lydia's only beacon of light would have to be the dim glow from the woodstove.

Lydia trudged across the kitchen, bumping into the table and stumbling twice as she moved through the family room and reached the bottom of the staircase. She leaned against the banister for balance and absently wondered why anyone would want to get tipsy. What was the purpose aside from feeling sick and nearly falling down?

At the top of the stairs, the glow of a propane lamp cast a faint light in the upstairs hallway. One of her parents was up with Ruthie! How could she possibly sneak to her room without being discovered?

Guilt rained down on her. Her mother and father thought Lydia had been singing hymns and talking with friends, and now she was sneaking into the house drunk. How could she betray her parents this way? They'd always believed the best of her. She'd never once given them a reason to doubt her. And now she'd managed to risk ruining that trust in just a few hours.

She gazed up the stairs, and for a moment she was convinced the house was swaying. She had to get up those stairs and to her room before she was discovered. Her legs buckled, and she wished she'd never met Mahlon Ebersol.

She shook her head and silently berated herself.

Tipsy or not, you can climb these stairs, just like you have every night.

With her eyes focused on the light glowing from Ruthie's room at the top of the steps, Lydia did her best to tiptoe up, tripping over her black sneakers only twice. When she reached the landing, she bit her bottom lip and silently debated if she should tell her mother that she was home. Of course *Mamm* would worry, but she also trusted her daughter to get home safely.

Lydia gritted her teeth at that word again. *Trust.*

She knew the right thing to do was to alert her mother that she was home. But if her mother saw her crooked prayer covering or if she caught a whiff of her breath . . . No, her mother didn't need this stress on top of Ruthie's unending illness.

What have I done?

She cupped her hands to her face and sucked in yet another deep breath. She then leaned over and peeked through the crack in the doorway, finding her mother, Beth Anne, rocking Ruthie in her arms. The only sounds in the room were the hiss of the lantern, the rhythmic creak of the chair, and her mother's soft, sweet voice singing a hymn to her baby in High German.

Tears filled Lydia's eyes as she took in the scene. How could she have been out drinking while her mother was up late consoling Ruthie?

Pushing those thoughts aside, Lydia knew she had to get to her room and climb into bed. Work would come early in the morning, as her parents always said. Lydia would have to help handle nearly two dozen spirited scholars at the one-room schoolhouse where she served as a teacher's assistant on Mondays and Wednesdays. *How I hope they behave tomorrow.*

She did her best to straighten her prayer covering and then walked past the room, pretending not to see her mother in the rocking chair.

"Lydia?" *Mamm's* voice called in a stage whisper through the hallway.

"*Ya?*" Lydia's heart pounded as she stood outside her bedroom, which was right next door to Ruthie's.

"Come to the door," *Mamm* whispered.

Lydia bit her lower lip and moved to the door, standing just outside the flood of light. "How is she?" she asked.

Her mother's pretty face was tired. Lydia had recently noticed the lines and dark circles under *Mamm's* eyes; it seemed as though she had aged ten years in only a few weeks.

"She was fussy earlier," *Mamm* began, "so I decided to rock her. Now that she's so comfortable, I hate to move her."

"She looks peaceful." Lydia's strangled whisper felt riddled with guilt. She cleared her throat. "*Gut nacht.* Call me if you need help." She turned to go, losing her footing and then regaining her composure before tripping on her own feet. She almost snorted with sarcasm at her offer of help. How could she possibly rock Ruthie if she couldn't even stand up straight? Lydia would injure both her sister and herself.

"Wait," *Mamm* called. "Did you have fun?"

"*Ya,*" Lydia said from the other side of the door.

"*Gut,*" *Mamm* said. "Get to bed now. It's late, and work comes early in the morning."

"*Gut nacht,*" Lydia repeated, trying not to walk into the doorway as she stepped through the darkness into her room.

She flipped on the battery-operated lantern sitting on her nightstand and its dim light flooded her small room, casting shadows on the plain white walls. Lowering herself onto her bed, she wished the room would stop spinning. *If I feel this bad, how is Mahlon feeling? He drank at least as much as I did.* Though, when she thought about it, he didn't seem to have any problems steering the horse when he drove her and a few other friends home in his buggy. Perhaps he was experienced at this sort of thing and alcohol didn't bother him as much anymore. But Lydia didn't want to ever get comfortable with this feeling.

She struggled when she got up to change into her nightclothes and stumbled while hanging her simple blue dress and apron on the peg on her wall. Crossing back to her bed, she stopped at the window and moved the green shade, revealing the dark, shadowy pasture. Her eyes settled on Joshua's house, focusing on his room, which was located at the center of the bank of upstairs windows. She wondered what had kept him away from the youth gathering tonight, and a melancholy feeling settled in her stomach.

Lydia had known Joshua her whole life. When they were younger they'd played during recess at the one-room schoolhouse where Lydia now taught part-time. Not only was he handsome, with dark brown hair and warm blue-green eyes, he was always nice to her. When the other boys teased her for tripping on the playground, Joshua defended her. When her father needed assistance repairing the pasture fence after a bad storm, Joshua and his father lent a hand. And when Lydia needed someone to talk to after arguing with her middle sister, Irma, Joshua would listen, helping her to clear her head so she could go back into the house and apologize.

Joshua was there for her, ready to give her a smile or a good word of advice when she needed it most. She'd always hoped that, when she turned sixteen, she and Joshua would date and possibly even get married after a few years. He was her idea of the perfect husband—honest, hardworking, and handsome. Now that she was sixteen-and-a-half and he was seventeen, maybe her dream would become a reality.

She involuntarily swayed and clutched the windowsill for balance. Joshua would be appalled if he heard about her behavior tonight. Although he and Mahlon had been good friends when they were younger, Joshua stopped socializing with him soon after Mahlon and his entourage of boys became rowdy.

What if Josh finds out I drank with Mahlon tonight? Would his opinion of me change?

Lydia grimaced and pushed the shade back in place as the question swirled through her already-swimming mind.

Climbing into bed, Lydia silently prayed, trying her best to ignore the sickening feeling that the bed was spinning. She begged God to forgive her for her sinful behavior tonight and she also asked to keep her actions a secret. Although she knew she should be punished for her indiscretions, she also dreaded the pain the news of her behavior would cause her family.

She closed her eyes and, while still deep in prayer, fell asleep.

2

"Are you feeling okay?" Barbie Chupp balanced a pile of primers in her arms while studying Lydia with a concerned expression in her dark brown eyes. Though only five foot two, Barbie's presence filled the room. "You've been awfully quiet all day. Did the *kinner* get on your nerves? They were a bit wild, but I think the warm weather gives them spring fever."

Trying to ignore the monster headache that had haunted her since she'd woken up this morning, Lydia forced a smile and rubbed her forehead. "I'm just a tad bit tired today."

Barbie grinned. "Did you go to a youth gathering last night?"

"*Ya.*" Lydia snorted with sarcasm. "*Ya*, I did."

"I remember those days," Barbie said with a nostalgic expression, missing the sarcasm and absently twirling a brown strand of hair that had escaped her prayer covering. "I still recall when I first met my Stephen. It was as if we were the only ones in the barn that night. He looked at me and I melted."

Lydia couldn't help but grin. Her mother always called Barbie a hopeless romantic. Her mother was very wise.

Barbie's expression was expectant. "Do you have a sweetheart yet?"

Lydia shook her head, but when her temples throbbed in response she regretted the motion. "Not yet."

"Oh, you will," Barbie said. "You're so *schee* and sweet. There's someone out there for you. And when you meet him it will be the most *wunderbaar* feeling you'll ever experience."

Lydia forced a smile, wondering if she really ever would experience something like true love. If so, would it be with Joshua? Or had she ruined that love story before it could begin? Her hand involuntarily returned to her pulsing temples.

She scanned the desk, searching for something to change the subject. She spotted a pile of art projects and pointed to them. "Do you need help grading these? I can take them home and bring them back Wednesday."

"Oh, don't be *gegisch*," Barbie said, waving off the comment with a hand she freed from the pile of books. "I can handle that. I don't expect you to take work home. You run along." She gestured toward the door. "I'll finish straightening up and lock up for the night. You look tired. Go on home and get some rest."

Lydia hid a wry smile at the suggestion that she'd get rest. Lately, she didn't know what rest was until she fell into bed.

"I'll see you Wednesday," Lydia said, hoisting her heavy tote bag over her shoulder. "Have a *gut* day tomorrow." As she had every week since qualifying to be a teacher's assistant following eighth grade, Lydia worked at her grandmother's bakery each Tuesday, Thursday, and Friday to help provide a steady income for the family. Fortunately, she enjoyed both jobs.

"You have a *gut* day too," Barbie said, placing the books on her desk. "I hope you're feeling better soon. Oh, and tell your *grossmammi* I said hello. *Geb acht uff dich!*"

"I will. *Danki.*" Lydia stepped out of the schoolhouse and lifted the skirt of her plain purple dress while negotiating the steps. She breathed in the warm spring air as she moved down the rock path toward the road.

Birds chirped and a horse clip-clopped in the distance. Lydia's black apron absorbed the warmth of the bright sunshine, and she wished she had a pair of sunglasses to stop the glare from exacerbating the pain in her already aching head.

As she walked toward home, she noticed a large moving van parked in the driveway of an *English* farmhouse that had been empty since the Fitzgerald family relocated last year. A couple of men in matching dark work uniforms carried boxes from the truck toward the large brick home while a little girl with blonde pigtails ran around the yard with a puppy following close behind her.

Lydia smiled at the sight as she continued past the house toward her farm.

"Bitsy!" a little voice hollered. "Bitsy, come back here right now!"

Lydia stopped and turned back just as the puppy and little girl bounded toward her.

"Lady," the little girl shouted. "Can you please stop my dog? Bitsy! Get back here!"

Dropping her bag on the ground, Lydia squatted. When the dog approached her, she scooped up the little fur ball that, in turn, showered her with kisses all over her face.

"Hi there, little one." Lydia laughed as the puppy slobbered on her cheek. "You must be Bitsy."

Out of breath from her trot, the little girl huffed and

puffed as she sidled up to Lydia. "Thank you so much. I thought for sure she was going to run away and never come home. We're new here so she wouldn't be able to find her way back if she got lost."

Lydia handed the puppy over and then swiped her hand down her soaked cheek. "I'm glad I could help. Bitsy is a cute little puppy."

"Yeah," the girl said, frowning at the dog. "But she doesn't listen. My dad says that it's revenge because I don't listen, but I don't know what that means. How is that revenge? I thought revenge was bad."

Lydia stifled a laugh. "I'm Lydia. What's your name?"

"My name is Michaela," the girl said. "When you spell it, it's Michael with an *A* at the end. I'm named after my grandfather. He died before I was born. My daddy was really sad when he died, so he made sure I was named after him. If I'd been a boy, I would've been named Michael. But I'm glad I'm a girl."

"Michaela is a very nice name," Lydia said. "How old are you?"

"I'm four." Michaela looked proud as she shared this information. "I'm going to start kindergarten in the fall. I can't wait to go to school. My mommy says the teachers don't know what they're in for."

Lydia chuckled at the statement. "I think the teachers will enjoy having you in their classes." While looking at the pretty little girl, Lydia couldn't help thinking of Ruthie and wondering if she would ever be well enough to run around the yard and play with a puppy. Lydia leaned over and hefted her bag to her shoulder. "It was very nice meeting you, Michaela."

Despite the puppy licking her face, Michaela scrunched her nose, tilted her head, and stared at Lydia quizzically, sizing her up with her blue eyes. "Aren't you too hot in those heavy clothes?"

"I'm used to it. I've always dressed this way, so it's normal to me." Lydia pointed toward Michaela's denim jeans trimmed in pink. "It's sort of like how you wear jeans. I wouldn't feel comfortable in pants or jeans because I've never worn them."

Michaela's eyes rounded. "You've never worn jeans?"

Lydia shook her head. "No."

The little girl gasped. "Ever?"

"Never ever," Lydia said with a smile.

"How come?" Michaela's nose scrunched again and her little forehead puckered with curiosity. "I only wear dresses when I go to church on Sundays. I wouldn't like wearing them every day. I like to play in the mud, and Mommy says that—"

"Michaela!" a masculine voice called.

A tall boy who looked approximately Lydia's age loped down the driveway toward them. His dark brown hair fell below his ears and was styled similarly to the sloppy style she saw on the teenage *English* boys Lydia had seen come into her grandmother's bakery.

Approaching them, he smiled. "Hi. Is my little sister harassing you?"

"Tristan, I'm not bothering her," Michaela retorted with her free hand on her little hip in defiance. "I was just thanking my new friend for stopping Bitsy from running away. She'd never find her way back if she got lost. Don't you care about Bitsy?"

With a shake of his head, Tristan met Lydia's gaze and held out his hand. "I'm Tristan Anderson, and this is my shy little sister, Michaela."

24

"I'm not shy," Michaela chimed in. "And I already told her my name."

Tristan grinned as he continued to hold out his hand to Lydia. "I'm pretty sure she knows you aren't shy, Michaela."

Lydia took his hand and gave it a quick shake. "It's nice to meet you. I'm Lydia Bontrager." She pointed down the road. "My family's farm is a few houses down. Welcome to Lancaster County."

"Thank you," Tristan said.

"You live on this street?" Michaela asked.

"Yes," Lydia said. "I also teach at the little one-room schoolhouse up the road."

"Wow." Michaela's eyes were wide. "I wish I could go to your school. My mommy says my school is a few miles away."

Lydia smiled. "I bet you'll enjoy your school."

"I've never seen a one-room schoolhouse," Michaela said. "I thought they only had those in the olden days, like on that TV show Mommy and I watch called *Little House on the Prairie*. My mommy said she loved that show when she was little. She's old."

Trying to hold in her laughter, Lydia nodded. "I bet that's a nice show. We don't have a television, but I've read the books by Laura Ingalls Wilder."

Michaela's eyes looked as if they might fall out of her little head. "You don't have television?"

"No," Lydia said. "I don't."

"But how come—" the little girl began.

"Michaela," Tristan interrupted with a stern tone. "You know what Mom and Dad have told you about asking too many questions. It's very rude to put Lydia on the spot like that. You need to stop."

"Okay. Fine." Michaela sighed. "I'm sorry for being rude."

"You're not rude," Lydia said. "You're just curious. I'm certain you've never met an Amish person before."

Michaela shook her head. "We didn't have them in New Jersey. Everyone there had a TV and went to a big school and they all wear jeans." She glanced toward the house. "I'm going to go see if Mom needs help. See you later." Michaela trotted up the driveway.

"Sorry about that," Tristan said with a smile. "She's a little overwhelming."

"She reminds me of my younger sisters," Lydia said. "I love listening to children talk. They say the funniest things sometimes."

"They do say funny things, and sometimes it's at the worst opportunity," he agreed. "How many brothers and sisters do you have?"

"Three, and they're all younger," she said while adjusting her bag on her shoulder. "A brother and two sisters."

"That's a big family," Tristan said. "I only have Michaela to deal with." He hooked his thumbs in the pockets of his shorts. "So you teach? Are you old enough to be a teacher?"

"*Ya*," Lydia said. "We graduate from our schools when we're fourteen. For the last two years I've worked as an assistant teacher. How old are you?"

"Seventeen," he said. "I'll be a senior this year."

"Do you like school?"

He shrugged. "I do. My dad's a college professor."

"A college professor," Lydia said. "That sounds really interesting." She couldn't help but wonder what Tristan's life was like. It was so different than living on a farm and never moving from the house in which she was born. "Was it hard to move away?" she asked. "I always wondered what it would be like to have to pack up everything you own and start over somewhere new."

Tristan folded his arms over his blue T-shirt and looked at her with a thoughtful expression on his face. "Moving is never easy. I really didn't want to leave my friends before senior year." He frowned a little. "And I had to leave my girlfriend behind. That was really difficult. We're going to try surviving a long-distance relationship. I won't see her until later this summer, but we talk almost every day."

"What's her name?" Lydia asked, trying to imagine what his girlfriend would look like.

"Lexi," he said.

"Lexi?" Lydia said. "That's an unusual name."

"I guess it is," he agreed. "It's short for Alexis."

"Alexis," Lydia repeated. "I like that name. How long have you known her?"

He grinned. "I'd say nearly all my life. We grew up near each other and went to the same schools."

Lydia couldn't stop her smile. *Like Josh and me.* "So you must have a lot in common."

"We do," he said. "We've gone through just about everything together. She knows me better than anyone else."

"Tristan!" another masculine voice hollered. "Come help carry boxes!"

"I better go," Tristan said. "It was nice meeting you. Stop by to visit sometime."

"I will," Lydia said. "Nice meeting you too."

While Tristan followed Michaela up the driveway toward the house, Lydia continued her trek home. Despite her continuing headache, she smiled while contemplating Michaela's funny conversation. The little girl was a very sweet and precocious child. She would certainly liven up a classroom. And she'd enjoyed talking to Tristan too. It seemed like they might have some things in common.

Turning to her left, she looked toward the big white farmhouse where Barbie's aunt Deborah lived. She saw Deborah on the porch and waved to her as she continued walking home.

Reaching the long rock driveway leading to her house, Lydia sent up a silent prayer for Ruthie, asking God to make her well so she could someday meet Michaela and her adorable puppy.

ɔ8

"They seem really nice," Lydia said to her mother while washing the dinner dishes in the kitchen sink.

"Michaela is four, like Ruthie, and she says the funniest things. She told me everyone in New Jersey has a television, and she can't believe I teach in a one-room schoolhouse."

"Uh-huh," *Mamm* said while wiping the table.

Lydia wondered if her mother wanted to discuss something with her, but she'd remained reticent while Lydia yammered on and on about the new neighbors in hopes of inspiring her mother to talk. Instead of giving Ruthie a bath, her mother had asked Irma to watch Ruthie so she could help Lydia in the kitchen. Lydia assumed there was a reason behind her mother's sudden interest in kitchen cleanliness, but she hadn't really spoken since they began their cleanup.

"Tristan seems really nice," Lydia continued as she scrubbed a pot. "He seemed interested in what I said. Plus, I'm just happy to see someone move into the Fitzgeralds' house. It's such a pretty brick home. I've always wondered how many bedrooms are in it."

"Uh-huh," *Mamm* repeated, still running the washcloth over the table.

Lydia faced her mother while leaning against the sink.

Mamm's face was twisted into a frown as she worked. Her hand continued to swipe the cloth over the table in a methodical motion, hitting the same clean spot several times.

"I was thinking that I should take them a cake or something," Lydia said, hoping to get her mother to stop and look up. "I'd like to welcome them to the community."

"Uh-huh," *Mamm* said again. Her tone was flat, uninterested. She seemed to be in her own world. Was she thinking of Ruthie? Maybe praying for her?

"*Mamm*?" Lydia asked. "Are you listening to me?"

"*Ach!*" *Mamm* looked up at Lydia, startled. Her expression transformed back into a frown as she lowered herself into a chair. "I'm sorry, *mei liewe*. I have a lot on my mind. Sit with me, please."

Tossing the washcloth into the sudsy sink, Lydia joined her mother at the table and sat across from her. "*Was iss letz?*"

Her mother blew out a deep sigh and her blue eyes filled with tears. "The doctor called today."

Dread filled Lydia. "What did he say?"

"He wants to meet with your *dat* and me tomorrow morning." She paused to wipe a tear that had trickled down her cheek. "He has news to tell us, and he wants to share it in person. I fear that it's not *gut* news."

"Oh no." Lydia cleared her throat, hoping to stop the lump forming there from getting any bigger. "Do you want me to stay home from the bakery and take care of Ruthie for you?"

Mamm shook her head and reached for Lydia's hands. "No, but *danki*. The doctor wants us to bring Ruthie with us. He said he needs to do another exam and possibly talk about some procedures. He has some brochures geared to children that we can read to her, and we may have an opportunity to share them with her in the office. I appreciate your offer though, Lydia."

"But do you need me to go with you?" Lydia pressed on while holding her mother's hands. "Ruthie may be fussy if she's tired. We all know how she gets when she's tired. If she's having a bad day, she'll want to be home. I could help you keep her quiet and even take her outside to walk so you can talk to the doctor without interruption."

The tears in her mother's eyes glistened. "I haven't been working for weeks now, and your father is pulling extra hours installing kitchen floors. I don't need to tell you that money is tight, and we don't know what God has in store for us with Ruthie's illness."

"So, you need me to work," Lydia whispered as the gravity of the situation gripped her.

Her mother nodded. "The driver is going to pick us up early since the appointment is in Hershey."

"Oh." Lydia cleared her throat again. Changing the subject for just a moment, she asked, "Would it be all right if I brought home some pastries tomorrow for the Anderson family?"

Her mother looked confused. "The Anderson family?"

"The family I was telling you about," Lydia said. "You know—the little *maedel* with the puppy and the *bu* who's my age."

"Oh. Right," *Mamm* said. "*Ya*, you can take them some desserts tomorrow night. Maybe Titus and Irma can walk up with you before supper. That would be *wunderbaar gut*."

Lydia studied the dark circles under her mother's eyes and wondered when she had last slept. "Why don't you go to bed early tonight, and I'll make sure Ruthie is okay."

Mamm smiled and squeezed Lydia's hand. "You're sweet, but no. I'm certain I'll be awake all night anyway, praying and worrying. I can handle Ruthie. You worry about getting your sleep for work. You look tired today."

"I'm fine," Lydia said. The headache that had haunted her all day paled in comparison to her mother's exhaustion. Renewed guilt about her misbehavior at the gathering nipped at her.

A wail sounded from the family room, and *Mamm* jumped up from the table. "I better go check on her. She had a bad day. I noticed more bruising on her *beh*, she's still running a low-grade fever, and she looks so pale. I know we have to trust in the Lord, but I can't stop worrying."

Before Lydia could respond, her mother was gone, leaving Lydia to the task of finishing the dishes. As a yawn stole her breath, she wondered how much the meeting with the doctor would impact her family, and what it would mean for her own life.

3

How was Sunday night?" Amanda leaned closer to Lydia while they plopped chocolate chip cookie dough onto a large cookie sheet early the following morning. "Did you have fun?"

To buy some time before answering, Lydia looked around the large, open Kauffman Amish Bakery kitchen, which was owned by their grandmother, Elizabeth Kauffman. The sweet aroma of freshly baked bread filled her senses. Lydia's aunts and cousins bustled around them, chatting in Pennsylvania Dutch and preparing treats to be sold to tourists during the day. Lydia could see the propane-powered lamps, and the ovens, aligned in a row, which were run by gas.

Due to the May warmth, Lydia, her aunts, and her cousins did the bulk of the baking in the early morning to keep the heat to a minimum. But despite five fans that ran through the power inverters and gave a gentle breeze, Lydia often felt the heat radiating on her cheeks throughout the day.

Still trying to buy some time, she studied the familiar tools, plain pans, and ordinary knives and cutlery on the long counter in front of her while she silently debated what to share with her cousin. While she wanted to tell Amanda the truth about what happened Sunday night, she didn't want to disappoint or upset her. Due to being born six months apart and the oldest children in their families, they'd been best friends almost since birth.

"Lydia?" Amanda asked, moving closer and whispering in her ear. "Are you all right?"

"*Ya.*" Lydia forced a smile and looked up at her favorite cousin.

While Lydia had her father's light brown hair and matching deep brown eyes, Amanda was blonde and blue-eyed like her mother, Kathryn. When Lydia was younger, she envied her cousin's beautiful golden hair and sky-blue eyes, which mirrored Lydia's mother, Beth Anne, and the rest of the Kauffman daughters. Lydia used to wish she'd wake up one morning and find herself blessed with the same eyes and hair.

She gave up that silly dream, however, when her father told her she was just as pretty as the rest of her cousins and she should concentrate on being a good person on the inside instead of worrying about how she looked on the outside. He also reminded her that vanity is a sin. If only her father knew about her indiscretion on Sunday. Then he'd know that she wasn't such a good person on the inside.

"Well?" Amanda asked, her angelic face displaying annoyance. "Are you going to tell me about Sunday night?" A smile turned up her lips. "Did something really exciting happen between you and Josh?" she whispered.

Lydia sighed. "If only it was as simple as that."

"What does that mean?"

"Josh wasn't even there." Lydia dropped the last bit of dough onto the cookie sheet. *But if he had been, maybe I wouldn't have been so stupid.*

"Oh." Amanda seemed to study her. "So, how was it?"

"Awful," Lydia said. "You weren't there, and Josh wasn't there. There was no one to talk with."

Amanda gestured toward Nancy, who was icing a cake on a counter on the other side of the kitchen. "What about Nancy?"

"She was with her boyfriend," Lydia said in a low voice. "I always feel like I'm intruding if I bug her when they're together, you know?" She hoped Nancy had been so occupied with her sweetheart that she hadn't seen her take off with Mahlon and his friends and had missed the whole embarrassing scene.

"*Ya*," Amanda said. "I know what you mean. Who did you wind up socializing with?"

Lydia shrugged and wiped her hands on a rag. "Oh, you know. Just the usual crowd."

"Including . . . ?" Amanda raised an eyebrow. "Why aren't you telling me?"

"Because there isn't much to tell." Lydia lifted the cookie sheet and started toward the oven.

"Come on, Lydia." Amanda's voice transformed into a whine. "You know I hated missing it. I begged my *mamm* to let me go."

"There's nothing to tell." Lydia opened the oven door, slipped the cookies in, and set the small timer sitting on the counter.

Their grandmother approached them, wiping her hands on her apron. "What are you two discussing?"

Amanda folded her arms while scowling. "I've been asking Lydia to fill me in on Sunday night's youth gathering, but she won't tell me anything. I missed it because my *mamm* was certain I was still sick."

"You were sick, Amanda," Kathryn called from the other side of the kitchen without turning around from cutting out sugar cookies. "I didn't need you infecting all the members in your youth group. Their mothers would give me a piece of their minds for certain. That was a nasty virus."

Amanda rolled her eyes. "*Ya, Mamm.*"

Lydia stifled a chuckle at her cousin's expression as their grandmother moved over to the sink and began washing a pile of dirty bowls and utensils.

Nancy sidled up to Amanda and touched her arm. "You didn't miss much. The usual groups socialized together." Leaning forward, she lowered her voice. "I even saw Mahlon take a group out behind the barn."

Lydia froze, and she felt the color drain from her face.

"I'm certain they were drinking," Nancy whispered.

"*Ach,*" Amanda said with a gasp. "That's so wrong and it's also sinful. If their parents only knew …"

While the color came back to her face and her cheeks started to burn with embarrassment, Lydia held her breath and studied Nancy, who was oblivious to Lydia's reaction while she conversed with Amanda.

"Oh yes," Nancy said, nodding for emphasis. "They're out of control. If Mahlon's *dat* knew what he was doing, he'd—"

"What was that about Mahlon?" *Mammi* asked, facing them again and wiping her hands on a dishtowel.

Lydia felt sick. *Surely Nancy hadn't seen me Sunday night. If she had, she'd have said something by now.*

"We were just talking about a few of our friends," Nancy said quickly. "Some of them left the singing to do their own thing."

"Oh." *Mammi* gave them a little smile. "*Maed,* you know gossiping is a sin, *ya?*"

"*Ya, Mammi*," Amanda and Nancy said in unison before moving back to the work counter.

Lydia fiddled with the ribbons hanging from her prayer covering while crossing the kitchen. She hoped to disappear into the bathroom to allow her cheeks to cool down without having to explain why she was blushing.

"Lydia." *Mammi's* voice sounded above the conversations swirling and the fans humming. "Lydia, please slow down."

Lydia swallowed hard and faced her grandmother. "*Was iss letz?*" Her voice cracked a little, but she hoped she sounded normal.

"Let's go for a walk, *mei liewe*." *Mammi* looped her arm around Lydia's shoulders and steered her out the back door to the parking lot.

While they walked, Lydia surveyed the familiar property she'd known since birth. Out behind the bakery was a fenced-in play area where a few of her young cousins ran around, playing tag and climbing on a huge wooden swing set that had been built by her uncles. Her cousin Jane, Nancy's younger sister, looked up from the bench where she sat watching the children and waved as Lydia and her grandmother started across the parking lot. A few cars were parked in the lines, and Lydia knew the lot would be full before noontime. The tourist season was settling in on Lancaster County, and the bakery was a favorite spot for visitors to purchase goodies and souvenirs.

Beyond the playground was a fenced pasture with three large farmhouses. And four barns were set back beyond it. All of the property was owned by Lydia's grandparents, Elizabeth and Eli Kauffman. The dirt road leading to the homes was roped off with a sign declaring "Private Property—No Trespassing." One home was occupied by her uncle Timothy, aunt

Miriam, and their daughter, while her aunt Sarah Rose, uncle Luke, and their children lived in the second house. The last and biggest home was where Lydia's mother and her five siblings grew up and where her grandparents still resided. Lydia and her family lived a few miles away in the house in which her father and his older brother had grown up.

Lydia and *Mammi* crossed the vast parking lot and sat on a bench together, facing the white clapboard farmhouse that served as the bakery.

"*Wie geht's?*" *Mammi* asked with her arm still resting on Lydia's shoulders.

"Fine," Lydia said with a shrug. "How are you, *Mammi*?"

"I'm well, but you seem to have something weighing on your mind. I want to be sure you are okay." *Mammi* rubbed Lydia's shoulder while she spoke. "I know Ruthie's illness is taking a toll on the family. I spoke with your *mamm* yesterday afternoon, and she sounded very worried. If you need to talk, you know you can always open up to me, *ya*?"

"*Danki*, but I'm *gut*," Lydia said, her voice sounding thick. She absently studied the tall sign with "Kauffman Amish Bakery" in old-fashioned letters that hung above the front door.

"One of my favorite Bible verses comes from Psalms," *Mammi* said. "I ran across it last night during our devotional time."

"Oh?" Lydia looked up at her.

"It's from Psalm fifty-nine," she said, folding her hands over her black apron. "'But I will sing of your strength, in the morning I will sing of your love; for you are my fortress, my refuge in times of trouble.'" She gave Lydia a little smile. "Does that give you any comfort?"

"*Ya*, it does," Lydia said. "It makes sense. We need to lean on the Lord during the rough times."

"That's exactly right," *Mammi* said, squeezing Lydia's hands in hers. "I know it may seem like God has forgotten you, your parents, and your sister. But he hasn't."

Lydia forced a smile. "I know."

Mammi looked at her with concern. "Is there anything you'd like to talk about while we're out here alone?"

Lydia shook her head. "No. Everything else is okay." She knew lying is a sin, but how could she admit that she had behaved inappropriately Sunday night? Besides, Nancy didn't spot her, so she'd gotten away with the drinking. She didn't need to worry about it anymore.

A few more cars pulled into the parking lot and steered into spaces.

Still holding Lydia's hands, her grandmother stood and pulled Lydia up. "Let's head back inside. It's going to get busy soon." Looping her arm around Lydia's shoulders once again, *Mammi* steered her toward the back door. "If you ever need someone to listen, you know you can always talk to me, *ya*?"

"*Ya*," Lydia said. "*Danki, Mammi*."

"*Gern gschehne*," *Mammi* said. "Don't you forget that," she assured Lydia again. "I'm always available to listen if you need an ear, and our conversations will remain private if you would like them to, as long as I'm not breaking any rules with your parents."

Lydia gazed up at the clear blue sky, hoping her parents were receiving good news so their lives would become normal again.

4

Later that afternoon, Lydia balanced a box full of pastries while Titus schlepped along beside her and Irma raced on toward the Andersons' house.

"I don't see why we have to do this," Titus muttered, crossing his arms in front of his thin body. "I know they're new in the neighborhood, but why do we have to take them dessert?"

"Because it's the right and proper thing to do," Lydia said. "Irma! Slow down before you fall." She looked back at her brother. At twelve, he was the spitting image of their father, with light brown hair and matching eyes. "Why are you so glum?"

"Why do you think?" He kicked a rock as he walked. "Didn't you see *Mamm* and *Dat's* faces tonight? They aren't saying it out loud yet, but it's bad news about Ruthie."

Lydia sighed, thinking back to when she'd entered the kitchen after work. Her mother's eyes were red and puffy, evidence that she'd been crying. Her father's eyes were filled with despair. Seeing her parents that way was hard to bear. Lydia had put on a brave face, but she was falling apart inside.

When she asked what the doctors had said, her father asked her to take Titus and Irma to meet the new family and deliver the baked goods she'd brought home, as planned. He promised they would talk later.

"*Ya*, you're right, Titus," Lydia admitted. "It has to be bad news about Ruthie. I was hoping I'd imagined their moods, but it's definitely bad."

Looking up at her, Titus's eyes were full of worry. "What are we going to do?"

She shrugged, not knowing the answer. "I guess we'll find out what it is and then support *Mamm* and *Dat* in any way we can."

"Do you think I can quit school and get a job?" he asked. "Maybe that would help since *Mamm* isn't working. I could see if *Grossdaadi* would hire me at the furniture store. I once helped him make a chair, so I know I can do it."

Lydia smiled down at her brother, impressed by his self-lessness. "I think we should wait and see what *Dat* says. I believe he'll want you to finish school before you start working. You only have two years left. Maybe you can take on more chores or even go to work with *Dat* if he has to work on a Saturday, *ya*?"

"That sounds like a *gut* plan," Titus agreed. "I'll ask if I can do more."

Irma reached the path leading to the front door of the Andersons' house, and she gave them an impatient wave. "Come on! Hurry up!"

"We're coming," Lydia said. "If I run I may drop this box, and we'll have a mess." She and Titus caught up with Irma, and they walked to the front porch together. "Now remember," she began as they climbed the steps, "use your manners. Be respectful and smile." She looked at Titus. "You need to smile too. I know it's difficult, but *Mamm* and *Dat* would want us to be welcoming."

Titus nodded, but his expression remained stoic. "*Ya*, I know."

Irma hurried to the door. "I'll ring the bell!" She pushed the button and grinned up at the door. With her light hair and blue eyes, her middle sister probably mirrored their mother at the age of seven.

The bell rang out on the other side of the door, and soon they heard footsteps. The door slowly creaked open, revealing a beaming Michaela. "Hi!" she said. "Mommy, it's my Amish friend! Come meet her."

"Michaela!" a feminine voice called. "I asked you to wait for me before you opened the door." A woman who looked about Lydia's parents' age came around the corner and smiled. "Hello."

"Hi, Mrs. Anderson," Lydia said, holding out the box. "I'm Lydia Bontrager, and this is my brother, Titus, and my sister Irma. We want to welcome you to the neighborhood. I brought you some treats from my grandmother's bakery."

"Oh, my goodness," Mrs. Anderson said, taking the box. "That is so kind of you." She made a sweeping gesture toward the inside of the house. "Please come in."

"Thank you," Lydia said, motioning for her siblings to follow Mrs. Anderson into the home.

Stepping into the foyer, Lydia peeked into the spacious front room, which she assumed was the family room. Boxes of all shapes and sizes were strewn about the room, and a flat television was sitting on a pedestal in the corner. They passed an open staircase on their way to the large kitchen, where more boxes sat stacked on the counters, center island, and floor. Utensils, gadgets, and dishware clogged the counters that were not covered in boxes. A small dinette set positioned in a nook was the only clean space Lydia could see.

"Please excuse the mess," Mrs. Anderson said. "As you can see, we're still working on getting situated. Moving takes so much time. I told my husband this is the absolute last move. We've moved six times since we were married, and I'm not doing it again. He can bury me at this house." She smiled at them.

"I imagine moving is a hassle," Lydia offered as she stood by the refrigerator. She could see Irma smiling at Michaela, who babbled on and on about her new room.

"Mommy," Michaela said, turning toward her mother. "May I take Irma upstairs to see my new room?"

Mrs. Anderson looked at Lydia. "Would it be okay if your sister followed Michaela upstairs for a tour?"

"Yes," Lydia said with a smile. "That would be fine."

Grabbing Irma's arm, Michaela pulled her toward the stairs. "You have to meet my puppy, Bitsy. She's locked in the bathroom right now so she doesn't get into boxes. She's in time-out after pulling out all of my socks and chewing holes through them."

Lydia couldn't help her grin. She enjoyed hearing Michaela prattle on about her puppy.

"My daughter is a bit of a chatterbox." Mrs. Anderson motioned toward the table. "Please, have a seat."

"Thank you." Lydia looked toward the table and waved an encouraging hand at Titus. "Go ahead and sit." She followed him to the table, where they sat across from Mrs. Anderson, who opened the box and gawked at the cookies and pieces of cakes and pies. "I hope you like desserts," Lydia said. "I brought a variety of our best sellers."

Mrs. Anderson pulled out a butterscotch macaroon

cookie and took a bite. "This is fantastic, Lydia. Thank you so much."

"You're welcome," Lydia said. "As I said before, we want to welcome you to the neighborhood."

The back door swung open and Tristan crossed into the kitchen, wiping his hands on a rag. "Dad ran to the—" He stopped speaking when he saw Lydia and Titus. "Lydia! How are you?"

"I'm doing well," Lydia said. "This is my brother, Titus. Titus, this is Tristan."

"Hi," Titus said with a quick wave. "Nice to meet you."

"You too," Tristan said. His eyes moved to the box on the table. "What do you have there, Mom?"

"Goodies from Lydia's grandmother's bakery." Mrs. Anderson tipped the box toward him. "Wash your hands and come try one of these cookies. They are absolutely mouthwatering."

"Oh, wow." Tristan crossed to the sink, where he scrubbed his hands. "Thank you, Lydia."

"You're welcome." Lydia absently fiddled with a napkin. "I tried to choose a variety for you."

"It's really cool that your grandmother has a bakery," Tristan said. "Is it close by?"

Lydia nodded. "It's not far at all. I usually walk there on the days I need to work."

"My grandmother and aunts make the best desserts in the world," Titus chimed in.

"Really?" Mrs. Anderson smiled. "Tristan, would you please grab those disposable plates and utensils left over from lunch?" She pointed to the counter. "Would you like a cookie or piece of cake, Lydia?"

"Oh, no, thank you," Lydia said. "I'm really not hungry

right now. I guess I ate too much at lunch." In truth, seeing her parents so upset had stolen her appetite.

"Titus!" Irma's voice rang out from the stairway. "Come meet Michaela's puppy!"

Titus looked over at Lydia, his eyes asking for permission.

"Go on," Lydia said.

"Excuse me," Titus said to Mrs. Anderson before trotting out of the kitchen and disappearing up the stairs.

"Would you like a drink?" Tristan asked. "My mom picked up a gallon of iced tea this morning at the store."

"That would be nice," Lydia said. "Thank you."

Tristan delivered three glasses of iced tea to the table. He then sat across from Lydia and placed plates, napkins, and utensils on the table that bore the logo for a local sandwich shop. He peeked into the box of goodies and grinned. "Wow. This looks amazing. Thank you so much."

"You're welcome," Lydia said before sipping the sweet tea. "I picked out my favorites too."

"You said your dad ran somewhere?" Mrs. Anderson asked Tristan.

"Yeah." Tristan bit into a whoopie pie. "He left to get more parts for my car. Hope we can get it running tonight. I found Dad's tools while we were unpacking, so I asked him to look at the car. The sooner it runs, the sooner I can get my license. And before you ask, Mom, I did find the papers that prove I took driving lessons back in Jersey."

"That's great. But shouldn't you finish unpacking first?" his mother asked.

"Yes, but I can't go looking for a job without a car," he said with a gentle smile. Tristan gave Lydia a sideways glance that seemed to say "aren't parents cute sometimes?" and she suppressed a giggle.

"Very true." Mrs. Anderson turned to Lydia. "Your grand-mother is a wonderful baker."

"Thank you," Lydia said, running her fingers over the con-densation on the glass. "She has taught me a lot. My mother has too."

"Lydia teaches at the one-room schoolhouse a couple of blocks up the street." Tristan pointed as if directing her to the school. "You teach there on the days you aren't at the bakery, right?"

"That's right," Lydia said. "Assistant teaching is only a part-time job, so all of the Amish assistant teachers have other jobs too."

"Really?" His mother looked fascinated. "How interest-ing." She smiled and then picked up a pecan delight cookie. "How many students do you have?"

Lydia sipped her drink. "We have twenty-five."

"And the school is really only one room?" Tristan asked as he pulled a couple of butterscotch macaroon cookies from the box.

"That's right," Lydia explained. "It's truly just one room with outhouses outside."

"Outhouses." Tristan shook his head. "That's wild. I'd love to see the inside of the school sometime. It's so differ-ent from what we experience in public school."

Lydia smiled. "Maybe I can show you if you're nearby one afternoon when we're locking up. I can't let you in during the school day because it would be too disruptive. But I think it would be okay with the teacher if I gave you a quick tour after school sometime. She's very nice."

Mrs. Anderson continued to look impressed. "How does the teacher manage without you when you're working at the bakery?"

"The children are mostly well behaved," Lydia explained while fiddling with the napkin again. "We just have a few rambunctious boys who get into mischief sometimes."

Tristan grinned as he finished the butterscotch macaroon cookies. "I was known to get into some mischief when I was younger, right, Mom?"

His mother chuckled. "Yes, you gave your father and me a few gray hairs." She took one more cookie and then closed the box. "I'm going to ruin my dinner if I keep eating these. This was so nice of you, Lydia. I would love to meet your parents sometime. Maybe we can come up for a visit."

"Oh," Lydia said, touching the ties on her prayer covering while she considered the offer. *I don't think* Mamm *and* Dat *would enjoy that right now.* "That would be very nice, Mrs. Anderson. But I don't think this is the best time to visit. My youngest sister has been ill for a while. Her name is Ruthie, and she's four, like Michaela. She's seen quite a few doctors, and it's been really difficult to handle at our house. I know that my parents would enjoy meeting you, but I think we need to wait until we know what's going on with my sister."

Mrs. Anderson and Tristan both frowned.

"I'm so sorry to hear that," Mrs. Anderson said. "Do the doctors know what's wrong with her?"

"My parents took her to see a specialist today, and I think they finally got an answer." Lydia stared down at the frayed napkin on the table. "They haven't told me what the doctor said yet. I think they want to wait until later when my siblings are in bed." She dreaded that conversation with her parents but knew she would have to endure it.

"I'm really sorry, Lydia," Tristan said. "That has to be really difficult for everyone in your house."

Lydia met his kind expression and smiled. "Thank you. It's really difficult for all of us."

"Maybe once your sister is better we can have you and your family over." Mrs. Anderson looked around the kitchen. "Of course, it'll have to be after this mess is sorted out."

"That would be nice. Tristan told me your husband is starting a new job here in Lancaster, right?" Lydia asked, in an attempt to change the subject from her family.

"Yes, that's right. My husband took a job as a professor here," Mrs. Anderson explained. "We're making a new start in Lancaster. He'd been on sabbatical for a while."

"Doesn't school end in June for you?" Lydia looked at Tristan.

"Yeah," Tristan said. "But I finished up my finals early, so we were able to move before the end of the year. Even though I didn't have any real classes left, my parents are making me finish out the year here anyway." He had an annoyed expression on his face, and Lydia swallowed her laughter.

"We decided to come early before the start of next semester so my husband could get organized." Mrs. Anderson gave Tristan a little smile. "This one wasn't happy about the move at all, so his father had to bribe him."

"Bribe him?" Lydia was confused. "What do you mean?"

"He gave me a car as a way to make the transition easier," Tristan explained. He folded his hands on the table and frowned. "I wasn't happy about leaving my friends — especially my girlfriend. But I already told you that. Anyway, since he gave me a car, I can drive down and visit them every once in a while."

His mother looked at him with serious eyes. "As long as your grades don't suffer."

"Yes, Mom." Tristan rolled his eyes at Lydia, and this time she laughed.

They discussed the weather until the children came trotting into the kitchen with Bitsy in tow.

"You should see the upstairs, Lydia," Irma said while puffing to catch her breath. "They have a television in every room! Michaela turned hers on, and we saw a program with talking penguins in a city zoo!" She laughed, hugging her arms to her stomach. "It was so funny. Can you imagine talking penguins? Do you think they really talk when humans aren't around? That's silly, *ya*?"

Titus frowned with frustration. "I told her it was a cartoon, but she doesn't get it."

Lydia smiled and then stood up. "We best get home. *Mamm* and *Dat* are going to wonder where we've been. Thank the Andersons for inviting us inside to visit."

"Thank you," her siblings said in unison.

Irma squatted and rubbed the puppy's head. "Good-bye, Bitsy."

"Thank you so much for the treats," Mrs. Anderson said as she followed them to the door. "It was wonderful meeting you."

"You too," Lydia said. She opened the front door with a *whoosh* and Irma and Titus scampered out, waving as they started down the porch steps.

Mrs. Anderson touched Lydia's arm. "I hope everything works out with your sister. Let us know if you need anything. I'd be happy to help your family in any way I can. I can always bring a meal or babysit your siblings if you need to go to the doctor with your parents."

"Thank you," Lydia said. "That's very thoughtful and kind."

Tristan sidled up to Lydia as his mother walked back toward the kitchen. "I hope your sister is okay too. Can you let me know once you hear the news?"

"I will," Lydia said as she hugged her arms to her chest. "I appreciate your concern."

"It was great seeing you again." He leaned against the front door. "Thanks for coming by and bringing great desserts. I had no idea Amish food was so delicious."

"The tourists love it," Lydia said. "My grandmother's bakery is a well-known place to visit."

"I can see why." He grinned.

"You'll have to come by and see it one day while I'm working," Lydia offered. "It's called the Kauffman Amish Bakery. I could introduce you to my family members who work there and you could get some treats. I bet Michaela would enjoy it too. You could bring her along."

"That sounds like a plan." He glanced toward the street. "I guess I better let you go catch up with your brother and sister. See you soon. I'll expect that tour of the schoolhouse too."

"I look forward to it." Lydia said. "Good night." She followed Irma and Titus down the street. She was thankful for the brief distraction with her new friends before she had to face whatever news was waiting for her at home.

5

She's asleep," *Mamm* said as she entered the kitchen later that evening after dinner.

Lydia held her breath while sitting quietly between Irma and Titus at the kitchen table. The only sound was her mother's soft footsteps and the scrape of the wooden chair when she pulled it out from under the table. *Mamm* sank into the seat next to their father, Paul, and her eyes filled with tears.

"We have some news," *Dat* began, his voice soft and thick. "And it's not *gut* news."

Oh no. This is very bad. Lydia felt her eyes fill with threatening tears.

Mamm swallowed a sob, and then Lydia couldn't hold back her own hot tears, which trickled down her face.

"Your sister has ..." His voice broke and he paused to clear his throat. "She has," he began again in a raspy whisper, "leukemia."

Lydia gasped as more tears flowed.

"Lu-kee-meeeeee-a?" Irma asked, trying to sound out the name. "Is it bad?"

"*Ya*," *Dat* said, wiping a tear from his cheek before placing his arm around their mother. "It's cancer, and cancer is bad."

"Cancer?" Irma asked. "That means she's very sick."

"That's right," *Dat* said. "It's cancer of the blood. She has something called acute lymphoblastic leukemia, and the doctor told us it's the most common kind of leukemia in children."

Lydia tried to understand what her father was saying. It sounded like a foreign language. "What does it mean exactly?" she asked. "What is acute lymphoblastic leukemia?"

Dat cleared his throat. "Leukemia affects the blood and bone marrow. That's why she's very sick with fevers, has bruising, and is so weak."

Irma's face began to crumple.

Lydia sniffed and pulled her little sister toward her. Grief and worry rained down on her. *How can this be happening to us? This has to be a bad dream.*

Titus wiggled in his chair, his face grim and his eyes shiny from developing tears. "Are they sure she has this cancer? Could they be wrong?"

Their father pulled *Mamm* closer while she continued to cry. "They aren't wrong," he said. "They are absolutely certain. We were hoping they would give us *gut* news today, but the Lord didn't see fit for that."

"What happens now?" Lydia quickly wiped a tear from her cheek. "What can they do for her?" She hoped to hear a happy answer that would cause all of her worry to disappear.

"She has to undergo treatments," *Dat* said. "She'll have to travel to the hospital and stay there for a while. Your *mamm* will go with her and stay there."

Lydia's eyes rounded as panic and questions surged

through her. Mamm's *leaving? Where does that leave me?* "What do you mean? How long will she be gone?"

"Who is going to take care of us?" Irma's eyes filled with shock and she mirrored Lydia's worry.

"We don't have an exact date yet, but it will be soon." *Mamm* sat up straight and wiped her eyes. "*Dat* and Lydia will take care of you, and you know that your *aentis* and *mammi* will help out too. You'll be taken care of."

Lydia rubbed Irma's back in an effort to soothe her sister, even though she still felt unsure of their future. *How am I going to get through this? It's too much to digest so quickly.*

"Will Ruthie be okay with the treatments?" Titus chimed in.

"The doctor said she should do just fine." *Mamm's* voice was a ragged whisper, audible only because the room was deathly quiet. "Most children survive."

Most children? Lydia bit her lower lip and wondered if she were having a horrible nightmare. *How is this happening to my family? Why us? Why now?*

"I don't want her to go," Irma said with a sniff. "I want her and *Mamm* to stay right here in our house. Maybe the doctor can come here and make her better."

"We'll be okay," Lydia whispered to Irma. She felt the need to calm her sister even though she felt as if she were falling apart inside. While Lydia wiped her eyes, her mother's eyes searched hers as if asking if she believed little Ruthie would be okay.

"Things are going to be stressful," *Dat* said. "Your *mamm* and Ruthie are going to be gone for a while, and we're all going to have to do our part to keep this household running." His voice sounded with authority, and that strength seemed to permeate the room as Titus sat up straight and *Mamm* wiped her remaining tears.

"How can we help?" Lydia asked. The question seemed to bubble forth before her brain registered it. But the question gave her a feeling of control despite the chaos of this news.

Reaching across the table *Mamm*'s father had made as a wedding present years ago, *Dat* took Lydia's hand in his. "You're such a *gut kind*." He looked with love at his other children, his eyes shining with fresh tears. "You all are *gut kinner*, and we love you very much. But you're right, Lydia. Your *mamm* and I are going to need you to do more at home. I'm going to have to work more hours and ask for more jobs. The doctor bills are going to pile up quickly." His eyes focused on Lydia. "I'm going to need you to take on more chores in the house. You may need to take over the cooking, but your *aentis* and *mammi* may also bring us meals. We're going to share our news with the community, and I assume they will reach out to us and help us in any way they can."

"How long will *Mamm* be gone?" Lydia asked, her voice a strangled whisper.

"It looks like it will be several weeks." He paused and turned to *Mamm*, and they shared worried expressions. "If she has complications, then she'll have to stay in the hospital longer."

Lydia nodded. "I understand."

Dat gave her a quick smile, telling Lydia that he was proud of her and causing tears to form in her eyes again. The weight of her parents' request both frightened and saddened her. *Am I strong enough to do all they're asking? What if I let them down?*

"What about me?" Irma asked. "What can I do?"

Mamm smiled. "You can help Lydia as much as possible."

Lydia touched her sister's prayer covering. "Maybe you can sweep the kitchen floor every night after supper."

Irma looked encouraged. "I can do that."

"I'll take care of the animals," Titus said. "You don't worry about it, *Dat*. I can feed and water them, and I'll also collect the eggs."

"*Danki*," *Dat* said.

Mamm's eyes moved to the clock on the wall. "It's very late. We better get to bed. I have to get up early in the morning to take Ruthie back to the doctor."

"Let's pray before we go to bed," *Dat* said. "We have to ask God to hold little Ruthie in his loving arms and give her doctors strength and wisdom."

Lydia bowed her head and tried to swallow the lump in her throat while silently praying for her sister. When she heard her father's chair push back, she knew it was time for bed.

As she walked past her mother, Lydia stopped and touched her arm. "I'm sure everything will be okay." Her weak voice betrayed her words. In her heart, she knew there was a chance things wouldn't be okay.

Her mother nodded, but her eyes didn't echo her agreement. "You go on to bed, Lydia. Tomorrow will be a long day."

"I'll tuck Irma and Titus in, and you go on to bed," Lydia insisted. "You will be tired in the morning."

Mamm cupped her hand to her mouth to stop a yawn. "I think I'm going to sleep in Ruthie's room again tonight. I worry that she'll wake up and cry for me."

Seeing the worry and exhaustion in her mother's eyes caused Lydia to protest. "No." She touched her mother's arm again. "I'll listen for her. If I can't handle it, then I'll come for you."

Mamm looked surprised. "Are you certain?"

"*Ya.* I can handle it for you." Lydia kissed her mother's cheek. "You just take care of yourself."

"*Danki, mei liewe,*" *Mamm* said softly. "You're a *wunderbaar gut dochder.*"

Unable to speak, Lydia moved toward the door.

"Wait," *Mamm* called to her.

Lydia turned and found her mother holding up a small booklet. "What's that?"

"I thought you might like to read a little bit about Ruthie's illness." *Mamm* stood and brought it over to Lydia. "This has some information on the disease, and it's fairly easy to understand."

"*Danki.*" Lydia took the booklet and headed for the stairs. Once upstairs, Lydia placed the booklet on her bureau, changed into her nightclothes, and headed out into the hallway to tuck in her siblings. She found Titus sitting up in his bed and staring at a book.

"It's bedtime," Lydia said gently. "*Mamm* and *Dat* are talking downstairs, so I thought I would come and tuck you in for them."

Titus met her gaze and his big brown eyes were glassy where tears had collected. "Do you think Ruthie is going to live?"

Lydia forced a smile and hoped it was convincing. She couldn't let her brother know how scared she truly was. "*Ya,* I do. According to the doctors, most *kinner* live and the treatments do their job. You have to trust that the doctors know what they're doing, and they're going to make her better. It just might take some time."

He snuggled under the covers. "I'll pray for her, and I'll do my chores too."

"*Gut,*" Lydia said, touching his hair. "I'm going to need

your help, so I'm glad you're going to do your chores." She kissed his head. "*Gut nacht, mei bruder.* Don't forget your prayers tonight. Try your best to sleep and don't let your worries take over your rest."

"I won't," he said with a yawn. "*Gut nacht*, Lydia."

She left his room, gently closing the door behind her, and padded over to Irma's room. Peeking in through the cracked door, she found Irma on her knees while silently praying. With her eyes shut tight and her hands clasped together, Irma looked deep in concentration. Leaning on the door-frame, Lydia waited for her to finish.

After several minutes, Irma opened her eyes. "*Aamen,*" she said before standing up and crawling beneath the sheets.

Lydia stepped into the room, and Irma looked up at her.

"Where's *Mamm?*" Irma asked. "She's hasn't come up to tuck me in yet."

Lydia stood over her. "She asked me to do it since she and *Dat* need to talk. Is that okay?"

"*Ya.*" Irma gave Lydia a questioning look. "Do you think God will answer our prayers?"

Lydia sank onto the bed, which creaked under her weight. "I do. Why do you ask?"

"I'm just hoping my prayers for Ruthie will help." Irma ran her fingers over the colorful quilt her grandmother Elizabeth had made for her when she was born. "I know God listens to us and he answers the prayers that are in his plan. Do you think he has a plan for Ruthie's illness?"

"I do believe he has a plan for Ruthie as he has a plan for all of us." Lydia brushed Irma's long blonde hair back from her face. "We have to trust God and let him take care of Ruthie. You can pray and think of her all the time. I know that will help."

Irma moved under the covers. "I'll do that."

"*Gut nacht,*" Lydia said before kissing her head. "Sleep well."

"You too," Irma said.

Lydia exited Irma's room and closed the door before stepping over to Ruthie's room. She gently pushed open the door and found Ruthie on her side, sleeping with her blonde curls framing her pale face. Although she looked like a sleeping angel, it was clear she was ill. She looked frail and tiny, sleeping in her crib since she'd never outgrown it.

Moving to the crib, Lydia peered in, tempted to touch her sister's head. But she feared her touch might wake her, and the girl needed her sleep.

She looked at the single bed across from the crib, next to the rocking chair. Her mother had slept in that bed many nights since Ruthie had become ill. Lydia considered sleeping there, but her room was just on the other side of the wall, and she knew she would hear Ruthie if she cried out. Lydia had lain awake many nights in the recent past, listening to Ruthie cry.

Turning back to her baby sister, Lydia remembered the day Ruthie was born. She would never forget the excitement of waiting in the family room for the news while her mother delivered her in her bedroom with the help of Lydia's father and a midwife. Lydia was ecstatic to hear she had another sister, while Titus had frowned and bemoaned being the only boy.

Lydia smiled at the memory and couldn't resist lightly touching one of Ruthie's little feet. "We're going to take *gut* care of you," she whispered. "You just rest and keep up your strength."

She quietly returned to her room and flipped on the battery-operated lantern by her bedside. After getting ready for bed, she retrieved the booklet her mother had given her from her bureau and began to read it, trying to absorb as much information as she could about the disease and the treatment. She discovered that bone marrow is the spongy center of bones where blood cells are formed. Leukemia is caused when the blood cells produced in the bone marrow grow out of control. She read about the chemotherapy and the different ways medications are administered.

Most of the concepts were completely foreign, but she found herself staring at one sentence:

Most children with acute lymphoblastic leukemia are cured of their disease after treatment.

Most.

The word rolled around in Lydia's mind. It was a short word, but it held so much meaning. It meant that Ruthie could be cured.

She *could* be. But there were no guarantees.

That's where God comes in.

The words seemed to bubble forth from deep in her heart.

"*Ya,*" she whispered. "That's where God comes in."

Lydia placed the booklet on her bedside table, set her alarm clock, and flipped off the lantern. While she stared up at the dark ceiling, she tried to make sense of the evening. It seemed as if her world had been turned upside down in just a few hours. How could her baby sister have leukemia?

It didn't make sense. How could God take such a perfect baby and give her a horrible, frightening illness? Why was Ruthie the only one of the four children to contract it?

A soft knock sounded on her doorframe and, after turning the lantern back on, she crossed the room. Pulling the door open, she found her father frowning in the doorway. Worry settled in her gut.

"Is *Mamm* okay?" she asked.

"*Ya*," *Dat* said. "She's rocking Ruthie."

"Oh." Lydia wound her fingers through her long, light brown hair. "I told *Mamm* I would take care of Ruthie tonight, but I never heard her cry. I was only sitting here quietly reading the booklet." She pointed to her nightstand. "I don't know how I missed it." She started for the door. "I'll take over."

He shook his head. "No, you don't need to. Your *mamm* and I were talking, and she said she needed to hold Ruthie. She went into her room and picked her up even though she was sleeping."

"Oh." Lydia was confused. Why didn't her mother want her to help out tonight? It didn't make sense at all, but maybe nothing made sense when your child was diagnosed with leukemia. Still, Lydia wanted to help her mother in every way she could. She felt the need to do something to help her sister too. If she just sat in her room, she'd feel lost with her life spinning out of control. "Is *Mamm* going to need help?"

He shrugged. "I think she'll be okay, but I wanted to just speak to you alone for a moment."

Lydia opened the door and motioned for him to come in. "What's on your mind, *Dat*?"

"I want to thank you for being so strong earlier," he began, stepping through the door. "I'm certain it tore you apart to see your *mamm* so upset. I know it was difficult for me. Things are going to be stressful, and there will be a lot of stress put on you. But I know you're a hardworking *maedel*."

She nodded even though she didn't feel very strong. At the moment, she felt as if everything she'd known was slipping away and a new, scary life was about to begin.

"I believe the Lord is testing us somehow through this,

and we need to be ready to take this on." He fingered his beard.

"Today *Mammi* quoted a verse from Psalm fifty-nine," Lydia said. "I can't remember all of it, but I know that it said 'for you are my fortress, my refuge in times of trouble.'"

Dat smiled. "That's right." He touched her arm. "We'll get through this with the Lord's help."

"*Ya*." Lydia forced a smile. She wanted to believe him, but doubt was swelling within her. *Am I as strong as my parents think I am?*

"*Gut nacht*," her father said. "I'm going to go check on your *mamm* and Ruthie."

Dread slithered in Lydia's stomach as she watched her father disappear into the dark hallway. Tears filled her eyes. How was she ever going to cope with taking care of the family while her mother was gone? It didn't seem fair that this was all landing on her so quickly. Why was this happening to her?

Suddenly a thought occurred to Lydia, and it filled her room like an ominous storm cloud. If the Lord was testing her family, he must have a difficult lesson waiting for them.

6

During the church service, Lydia sat next to Amanda and among the other young unmarried women while she sang along with the familiar German hymns in the *Ausbund*. It was the Ebersol family's turn to host the three-hour service, which was held in the home of one of the church district families every other Sunday. Lydia was always amazed at how the living room and bedroom movable walls in each member's home could create such a spacious meeting area. From the time she had been a little girl she'd become accustomed to sitting on the backless benches that were lined up for the district members and would later be converted to tables for lunch.

Lydia had once walked by an *English* church in town and noticed that the doors were open. Able to see inside the sanctuary, she found they were much different than what she was used to. Unlike the English churches, Lydia's worship area didn't have an altar, nor cross, nor flowers, nor instruments.

Today's service began with a hymn. Lydia joined in as the congregation sang slowly. Her uncle Daniel Kauffman had been chosen as the song leader before the service began. He began the first syllable of each line and then the rest of the congregation joined in to finish the verse.

While the ministers met in another room for thirty minutes to choose who would preach that day, the congregation continued to sing. Lydia saw the ministers return during the last verse of the second hymn. She spotted them hanging their hats on the pegs on the wall, symbolizing that the service was about to begin.

The chosen minister began the first sermon, and his message droned on like background noise to the thoughts echoing in Lydia's head. Although she tried to concentrate on the preacher's holy words, she couldn't stop looking over at the spot where her mother and Ruthie were sitting.

Amanda leaned over to Lydia and touched her hand. "Are you all right?" she whispered.

Lydia smoothed her apron over her legs. "*Ya*. Just thinking about things."

"The Lord will take care of Ruthie," Amanda said softly. "I can feel it."

"*Danki*," Lydia whispered. Although she appreciated Amanda's words, they did little to comfort Lydia. She felt a tiny twinge of jealousy toward her cousin. Amanda had no idea the worry Lydia felt since Amanda and her siblings were healthy. Their family was normal and had nothing to fear.

The first sermon ended, and Lydia knelt in silent prayer along with the rest of the congregation. After the prayers, the deacon read from the Scriptures, and then the hour-long main sermon began. Lydia stared at her lap and willed herself to concentrate on the sermon, which was spoken in German.

She swallowed a sigh of relief when the kneeling prayer was over. The congregation then stood for the benediction and the closing hymn was sung.

When the service was over, Lydia moved toward the kitchen with the rest of the women to help serve the noon meal. The men converted the benches into tables and then sat and talked while waiting for their food. As she had headed for the kitchen, she had smiled and greeted friends and relatives. Now she made small talk while filling coffee cups for the crowd of men.

Once the men were finished eating, Lydia filled a plate with food and followed Amanda to a corner to eat with friends. They joined other young people in the community, and Lydia sat quietly while everyone discussed their plans for the evening. These special weekly youth get-togethers were the events Lydia and her friends looked forward to all week long.

Lydia was sipping her cup of water when someone sank onto the bench beside her.

"Hi, stranger," Joshua said with a grin as he lowered his plate and lifted a piece of homemade bread. "I haven't seen you in a while."

"Hi, Joshua." Lydia absently touched her prayer covering, hoping it was still straight. "It's been busy at our house."

"Busy, *ya*?" he asked, his eyes still accentuating his smile. "Too busy to walk across the field to my house? Remember when we were about seven and we tried to count how many steps it took to get from your porch to mine?" He bumped her with his elbow as he'd always done since they were in school together.

"*Ya*." Lydia chuckled. "I think I lost track around three hundred."

"We were lucky we counted that high." He grinned. "Now, Lydia. What's your excuse for not coming to see me these days? Are the scholars wearing you out at school?"

"Why are you blaming this all on me? Why do I need to do all of the walking toward your house?" She crossed her arms with feigned annoyance. "Last I heard, the boy was supposed to do the walking toward the girl's house. Isn't that how it works?"

Josh held up his hands as if to surrender. "You're right. I should be doing the walking. It's my fault." His teasing expression faded as if he read the worry in her eyes. He always seemed to know how she felt before she opened up to him. "You don't seem like yourself today. Is something wrong?"

Lydia paused, wondering how much she should share in front of the group, even though she knew news of her sister's illness would spread through the community like wildfire. Although they knew gossip is a sin, not many of the ladies in the church district were very good at keeping secrets. Nancy had shared that her mother and her mother's friends were known in the community for sharing gossip during quilting bees.

"Ruthie is very sick," she said, careful to keep her voice low. "My parents took her to specialists in Hershey and they—"

"Lydia," Mahlon interrupted, dropping into the seat across from them. "How are you feeling?" His grin was wide, and Lydia's cheeks flamed in response. "Are you coming to the youth gathering tonight?"

Lydia stared down at her homemade bread smothered in jam, and her stomach seemed to twist. "I don't know."

"I hope you do," Mahlon said with a small chuckle. "It'll be fun."

Lydia cleared her throat. She wished she had the strength to stare him down and tell him no, but his handsome face and wide grin somehow sapped all of her resolve. What was wrong with her?

"Mahlon," Joshua began with an annoyed tone, "can't you see you interrupted us? Don't you have any social skills at all?"

Mahlon snorted. "What made you so uptight?"

Someone called Mahlon's name across the room.

"I'll see you all later," Mahlon said as he stood. He looked at Lydia and smirked. "Hope to see you later, Lydia." With a wink, he was gone.

Lydia wished her cheeks would stop flaring as she lifted a roll from her plate. She was certain Joshua would suspect something was going on between Mahlon and her, and it could ruin her hopes of Joshua's asking her to be his girlfriend.

Joshua leaned in close, and she could smell his clean, soapy scent. His eyes were full of suspicion. "What was that about?"

"I don't know," she said softly, hoping she was a good liar. "I saw him last week at the youth gathering, and he said hello. That was it." She stared at the uneaten roll in her hand to avoid his eyes.

"He has absolutely no manners," Joshua muttered. "I can't believe we used to be best friends. Anyway, what were you saying about Ruthie?"

Lydia took a deep breath and looked up at him. "She has leukemia."

His blue eyes were full of shock. "Oh no. I'm so sorry."

She ran her fingers over the edge of the table. "She starts treatments in a few weeks, and she'll have to stay in the hospital up in Hershey for a while. Apparently the treatments are rough."

"Lydia," he said with eyes full of sympathy. "I'm so very sorry. I had no idea."

"I know," she said. "I assume word will get around fast, so you will hear it soon anyway."

"How are your parents?" he asked as he angled his body toward her.

"My parents are taking it very hard," she said. "It was really difficult the night they told us. I've never seen my mother so upset and worried before. It was scary."

"If there's anything I can do, please let me know, okay?"

He touched her hand, and her skin warmed at his touch.

"*Danki*, Josh." She gave a sad smile. "How's your family?"

"Fine," he said, lifting his cup of water. "The dairy has been busy. Joey's been helping my *dat* and me more, which is nice. My *mamm* is doing fine." He gestured across the room toward a group of women talking. "You should go say hello to her. She's asked about you."

"I looked for you at the youth gathering last week," Lydia said, hoping that she didn't sound too eager. "I was surprised you weren't there."

He frowned. "Remember that stomach flu that was going around the district?"

"Oh." She grimaced. "You got it."

He gave a sheepish smile. "*Ya*, unfortunately our house wasn't spared."

"I'm sorry to hear that." She ran her finger over the wooden table. "Will you be at the gathering tonight?"

"Probably." He shrugged. "I don't have any other plans."

A few of the young men at the table stood and started toward the door.

"I guess it's volleyball time," Joshua said as he stood. "I'll see you later." He gave her a smile that told her he looked forward to seeing her later, and her pulse leapt. There was something about Josh's smile that always made her feel safe. It was as if that special smile was meant only for her.

"Okay." Lydia's eyes were glued to him as he disappeared through the doorway. He headed toward the kitchen while walking with the swagger she'd learned to admire over the years.

Mahlon came up behind Joshua. Glancing over at Lydia, he grinned and waved before he disappeared outside with the rest of the young men.

"Lydia, I think Mahlon likes you." Amanda's voice was low in her ear. "It's obvious. Did you see that smile and wave?"

Lydia frowned. The attention Mahlon paid to her could possibly ruin her chances with Joshua. "I'm certain he doesn't like me, Amanda."

"Oh, I think he does. I heard him say he wants you to come to the youth gathering tonight and he kept smiling at you." Amanda gave a determined nod. "You did something to catch his eye."

Lydia swallowed a groan. Amanda had no idea how true that statement was. "If I did, then I wish I could take it back." And that was the truth.

"You may have a suitor whether you like it or not." Amanda scooped a spoonful of potato salad into her mouth.

"There's only one suitor I want," Lydia said. "I just wish he'd realize that I'm waiting."

"*Buwe* don't think like we do," Amanda said. "My *mamm* said it took my *dat* two months to ask her out. Josh will probably ask you out when you least expect it."

"Or never." Lydia sighed.

Amanda looped an arm around Lydia. "Don't lose your faith. As *Mammi* says, God is with us, and he will guide and protect us, even when we think he's forgotten us." She pointed toward Lydia's still-full plate. "Aren't you going to eat?"

Lydia shook her head while thinking about Mahlon's sudden interest. She had no desire to finish her lunch. "I've lost my appetite."

"You want to go?"

"*Ya*," Lydia said.

Amanda gathered up both plates. "Let's help in the kitchen and then go outside for some fresh air."

C3

Later that afternoon, Lydia and Amanda sat on a small hill and watched the young men play volleyball. Lydia studied Joshua, who jumped and set the ball easily, as if he were a professional volleyball player.

Amanda shucked her sweater and placed it on the grass beside her. "Isn't the weather *schee*? I can't remember a nicer spring."

"*Ya*." Lydia said while pulling up blades of grass. "The scholars had spring fever this week in class. The *buwe* were even more rambunctious than usual."

Amanda chuckled. "I bet teaching is a challenge, *ya*?"

Lydia shrugged. "It's not so bad."

"Are you going to become the teacher when Barbie gets married?" Amanda tented her hand over her eyes to shield them from the sun while gazing toward the boys on the makeshift volleyball court.

"I don't know," Lydia said. "I haven't really thought about it."

"You should think about it." Amanda lifted a peanut butter cookie from the napkin beside her. "I would imagine she'll get engaged this summer and married in the fall.

I think she and her sweetheart are very much in love. I've heard my *mamm* talking to her *mamm*."

Lydia flicked a few stray blades of grass off her purple dress. She knew there was a possibility that the parents might ask her to become the teacher, even though most teacher assistants often went to serve as teachers in neighboring districts. She wasn't certain, however, that she wanted to be a full-time teacher. The women in her family seemed to always work full-time at the bakery, and part of her wanted to follow in their footsteps and keep with the family tradition.

Amanda handed Lydia a cookie, and Lydia bit into it.

"Do you want to talk?" Amanda offered.

Lydia yanked up more grass. "I'm just worried about what's going to happen with Ruthie. I remember when Bishop Chupp's daughter died of leukemia. Weren't we about twelve?"

Amanda shook her head. "Just because the bishop's daughter died of leukemia doesn't mean that Ruthie will."

"I know," Lydia whispered. "But I can't stop thinking about her. The side effects of the treatments are terrible. I was reading about them last night. She can have mouth sores, hair loss, rashes, diarrhea, vomiting, and nausea. Her life is going to be terrible." Her voice trembled with her worries. "She's only four, Amanda. How will she understand what's happening to her? She's going to wonder why God has done this to her."

With tears glistening in her blue eyes, Amanda touched Lydia's hand. "You know we will all pray for Ruthie, and we'll have faith that she'll get through this. *Mammi* tells us to always have faith, even in things we don't see, *ya*?"

"*Ya*," Lydia said before clearing her throat in hopes of stopping the lump that threatened to form.

They sat together in silence for a few moments while watching the volleyball game. Joshua and his friends laughed while the ball flew over the net and bounced off Mahlon's head. Lydia's eyes lingered on Joshua's handsome face. When his gaze met hers, he winked, and she smiled.

Her thoughts moved to Tristan, and she realized that she hadn't told Amanda about him or the Andersons.

"I met the new family that moved into that vacant *English* farmhouse last week," Lydia said while picking at more blades of grass. "The family is really nice."

"Oh?" Amanda raised an eyebrow and then bit into her cookie.

"The son is seventeen, and then there's a daughter who is four," Lydia said. "The father is starting a new job at one of the nearby universities. The son's name is Tristan, and he's going to be a senior in high school in the fall. And the sister is Michaela." She smiled. "She has this adorable little puppy named Bitsy, that is so funny. The other night, Titus, Irma, and I took a box of pastries over to the family, and we had a nice visit. Michaela took Titus and Irma upstairs to see her room and meet the puppy."

Amanda's expression transformed to concern, but Lydia continued her story without acknowledging it.

"While Michaela took Titus and Irma upstairs, I spoke with Mrs. Anderson and Tristan," Lydia began, while fingering the ribbons hanging from her prayer covering. "They were very interested in our one-room schoolhouse, and Tristan said he'd like a tour sometime."

Amanda shook her head. "You aren't going to give him one, *ya?*"

Lydia shrugged. "I don't know. I might sometime if he happens to stop by. It's not like I'm going to plan it."

"Lydia," Amanda began, lowering her voice and glancing around at the friends sitting close by before continuing. "You know it's not wise to get involved with an *English bu*. The bishop frowns upon it, and your parents will too. Just keep your distance before you wind up in trouble."

Lydia squelched the urge to roll her eyes. "I know that, Amanda. He's just a friend. We're allowed to have friends."

"Don't play with fire." Amanda lifted the last cookie from her napkin, broke it in half, and handed a piece to Lydia. "You don't want to be lured into the *English* life. It would break your *mamm's* heart."

Lydia did roll her eyes at that comment. "You're only sixteen, like me. Why do you talk like you're forty?"

Amanda laughed. "*Mammi* says I'm wise beyond my years too. I guess it's a gift."

"Or a curse."

Amanda swatted her arm. "That's not very nice."

"You deserved it for misunderstanding me. I don't like Tristan that way," Lydia said. "Besides, Tristan has a girlfriend back in New Jersey. I just think he and his family are nice. That's it. Nothing more."

Amanda looked unconvinced. "You went on about him and his sister."

Lydia stared across the pasture at Joshua and finished the cookie. "You know who I have my heart set on. There's only one *bu* for me. I just wish he'd realize it."

"He will," Amanda said as she popped the last piece of cookie into her mouth. "It'll happen in God's time."

"I know." Lydia sighed, and leaned back on her hands.

L ydia," her father called from the family room late Sunday evening a week later. "Please come back in and sit with us."

Lydia sucked in a deep breath while placing a glass in the sink. She knew it wasn't good news if her parents wanted to speak to her alone after her siblings were in bed. Then standing in the doorway to the family room, she saw her parents sitting next to each other on the sofa, while holding hands and frowning toward her.

"I know it's bedtime," *Dat* continued, "but we need to speak with you."

She sank into a chair across from them and looked back and forth between their grim expressions. They seemed to be the only expressions they wore since Ruthie had visited various specialists last week. The dark circles under her eyes were a stark contrast to the powder blue of her mother's eyes, and the crow's feet outlining her father's chocolate eyes seemed more prominent. It seemed as though her parents were aging right before her, and it scared her.

"Is this about Ruthie?" Lydia asked, her voice in the same

strangled whisper as when she first heard about Ruthie's illness.

Her parents exchanged worried glances.

"How are things at the schoolhouse?" her mother asked with a forced smile.

"School is fine," Lydia said, looking back and forth between them again. "You don't have to sugar coat this, *Mamm* and *Dat*. I know things are bad. Please just tell me the truth. I promise I'll be strong."

Dat blew out a sigh. "Your mother is leaving tomorrow to take Ruthie to the hospital to start her treatments. We knew this was coming, but we didn't think it would come so soon. She's going to stay there at least a few weeks."

"She's leaving tomorrow?" Lydia voice rose and her mother immediately gave a warning glance telling her to keep her voice down. "I thought we might have some time before this happened. She has to leave tomorrow?" Panic shot through her.

"The doctor said we have to go as soon as possible," *Mamm* said. "He had to schedule the treatments, and they start this week. We have to stay in the hospital for a while. The treatments have many risks, but the risks are less if she is at the hospital instead of at home. Also, the drive back and forth can be expensive. It's just better for us to be there." She sniffed and dabbed her eyes with a tissue she fished from the pocket of her apron. "I'm going to stay with cousins who aren't too far from the hospital. It will save us a little money."

Lydia let the words soak in. Although she'd read about the treatments, she was still taken by surprise to hear this news. She had no idea her home life would face this upheaval so quickly. "So you and Ruthie will be gone for a few weeks?"

"That's right," *Dat* said. "That means you'll need to run

the household and also work. I'll help as much as I can, but I'm going to take on more flooring jobs to try to help with the bills."

Lydia felt her shoulders droop as if the weight of this turn of events were physically causing her to hunch. *This is all happening too fast.* She studied her mother's sad face. "I'm going to miss you."

Mamm sniffed again. "I'll miss you, Titus, and Irma, but this is how it's going to be for a while. I thought you could come and visit us on Saturdays. I'm not certain if Ruthie is allowed to have visitors, but we'll figure that out as we go along."

Dat squeezed *Mamm's* hand. "We'll get through this with God's help."

"I know, *mei liewe*," *Mamm* whispered. "I keep telling myself that."

Lydia watched her parents and wondered when life was going to be normal again. How long would this dark cloud of Ruthie's illness stay in the house? It was almost too much to bear.

Mamm met Lydia's gaze again. "I think your *mammi* is going to travel with me and stay for a while. Your *aenti* Kathryn is going to take over running the bakery. I know she's capable. She definitely is *gut* at giving orders." For a mere moment, Lydia was comforted by her mother's brief smile.

"I wish I could go with you," Lydia said, her voice thick. "Maybe I could help with Ruthie."

"I need you here," *Mamm* said while dabbing more tears. "Irma and Titus need you, and we also need you to keep working."

"You told us you were strong, so I am simply going to tell you. Things are bad for us financially," *Dat* said, his expression pained. "I need to ask you to contribute your entire paychecks to the household fund for a while. Unfortunately it may be for a long while."

This is worse than I ever imagined! Lydia took a deep breath in an effort to calm her frayed nerves. "I understand."

"And, again, I'm going to pick up as many extra shifts as I can," he said. "It still won't be enough, however. The cost of these treatments is overwhelming. There's no way we can possibly pay it all off, and making payments is going to be a burden."

Mamm cleared her throat. "We're going to speak to the bishop about the medical bills, but most likely we'll have to apply for state support because the cost is so high."

My parents need to ask for assistance? There isn't enough money to pay the medical bills and the household bills? How can this be happening? "I'll do all I can," Lydia said, her voice still thick. "I'll work as much as possible. I can ask for more hours at the bakery." She felt as if the walls were closing in around her.

Mamm shook her head. "No, I can't have you away for more hours. I need you to keep up with the chores at the house. I'm sorry that it's going to be a lot of pressure on you, but you're the oldest. We need to just get through these treatments and then see where God leads us with the illness."

"I know," Lydia whispered, folding her arms across her chest. She wondered if she was as strong as her parents believed her to be. Could she handle both working and running the household?

"*Ach*," *Dat* said as he stood. "We better get to bed. Tomorrow will be a long day."

Mamm wrapped her arms around Lydia as she headed toward the stairs. "We'll get through this, Lydia. God will see to it."

"When are you going to tell Irma and Titus?" Lydia asked as they stood on the bottom step.

"Tomorrow morning at breakfast." *Dat* snuffed out the propane lamp and switched on a battery-powered lantern before stepping over to join them at the stairs. "We only found out this evening when we received the message from the doctor."

Dread flooded through Lydia. "This is all happening so fast. I don't know if I'm ready for it all."

"We'll all get through this somehow. Go on now, Lydia," *Mamm* said with a gentle push. "You must get some sleep. We'll rise early tomorrow so we can deliver the news to Irma and Titus. We wanted you to know first so you can help us tell your siblings."

Lydia pressed a hand to her neck and wished the tension that knotted there would release. After wishing her parents good night, she disappeared up the stairs and into her room, gently closing the door behind her. She flipped on her portable lantern and then studied the plain white wall where ominous shadows seemed to taunt her.

With tears filling her eyes, Lydia climbed into bed. Her eyes moved to the ceiling while worry, anguish, and confusion swirled around her, much akin to the night when it felt as if her bed were spinning out of control.

Now it was her life that was spinning out of control. Her mother and baby sister were leaving in the morning, and Lydia would now be surrogate mother to her middle siblings. Her life wouldn't be her own anymore. What did that mean for her involvement in youth activities? She knew the answer to that question—she would no longer be able to participate. In less than twenty-four hours, she would go from being a normal sixteen-year-old Amish girl to being a mother to her siblings and a breadwinner for her family.

Will this spinning ever stop?

She covered her face with her hands while tears flowed from her eyes. Rolling to her side, she sobbed until she fell asleep.

Cʒ

The following morning, Lydia jumped out of bed thirty minutes early, dressed, and rushed downstairs to start making breakfast. She dreaded how Titus and Irma would take the news, and she hoped she could lighten her parents' load by doing extra chores.

When she reached the kitchen, she turned on the propane lights and surveyed the counters while considering what to serve for breakfast. She would make her father's favorite— eggs and fried potatoes.

Pulling on her sweater and grabbing a portable lantern, Lydia rushed out to the hen house and loaded up her apron with eggs. Back in the house, she quietly pulled out the supplies she needed and began cooking.

Her mother appeared in the doorway several minutes later and gave Lydia a surprised look. "What are you doing?"

"I thought I'd get started on breakfast so you and *Dat* can figure out what you want to tell Irma and Titus," Lydia said, placing a platter full of fried potatoes onto the table. The enticing aroma caused her stomach to growl.

"Your *dat* went outside early to start on chores so we can talk to Titus and Irma and let them digest everything before they leave for school." *Mamm* grabbed a pot lid and placed it over the potatoes to keep them warm. "You're very thoughtful, Lydia. *Danki.*" She glanced at the table. "I'll get the dishes and utensils."

"It's okay," Lydia said, cracking an egg. "I can set the table while the eggs are frying. You can go check on Ruthie."

"All right," *Mamm* agreed.

Lydia continued to cook. She pulled a fresh loaf of bread from the cabinet and found two jars of homemade preserves in the refrigerator. By the time Irma and Titus came downstairs, breakfast was served.

"*Gude mariye,*" *Mamm* said to the children. "Please have a seat. We'll wait for your *dat* to come in and then we'll have our blessing."

Titus and Irma sat and exchanged surprised glances. Lydia knew they would be confused, since they were used to taking care of chores before eating breakfast.

The door opened, and her father came in from completing his chores in the barn. He spotted the food set out on the table and smiled. "That smells *appeditlich.*"

"Lydia cooked," *Mamm* said with a sweeping gesture. "She was cooking when I got downstairs this morning."

"*Danki*, Lydia," her father said, shucking his coat. "You did a *wunderbaar gut* job." He washed up at the kitchen sink and then took his place at the head of the table.

After silent prayer, Lydia passed the platters around the table, and they filled their plates with eggs, potatoes, and bread. Her mother kept the conversation going, asking questions about what the children thought they would do in school today.

Lydia felt as if she were holding her breath, waiting for her parents to share the news of *Mamm's* plans to leave for the hospital with Ruthie today. It was almost torture to listen to the chitchat, knowing a more important issue was hanging over them, like a dense fog smothering the air in the room. At one point Lydia almost asked her mother to just tell Titus and Irma the news. But she knew that she would be punished for speaking out of turn.

After they finished eating, Irma started to stand up to help clear the table.

"Wait," her father said. "We need to discuss something."

"I thought so," Titus said. "Something fishy was going on when breakfast was ready when we came downstairs." He turned to Lydia, and she forced a smile in an effort to reassure him that things would be okay.

Irma sat back down. "*Ya.* I did too."

"You're right," *Dat* began, pulling on his beard while he chose his words. "There is something going on. Your mother and I have some news to share, and it's going to be difficult to tell you. We wanted you to eat early so you can think it over before you go off to school today."

Irma's eyes widened. "Did something happen to Ruthie last night?" She turned to Lydia. "You said prayers would help! Why didn't they help?"

"It's okay," Lydia said. "Nothing happened to Ruthie last night. She'll be fine."

"Calm down," *Mamm* said, taking Irma's hands in hers. "Listen to your *dat.*"

Irma sucked in a breath and Lydia rubbed her back.

Lydia swallowed a sigh. *This is going to be much more difficult than I thought.*

"Remember when we told you Ruthie was going to need special treatments from the doctor?" *Dat* began.

"*Ya,*" Titus said, folding his napkin and turning to *Mamm.* "And you said she'll have to be in the hospital for a while, and *Mamm* will have to go with her."

Irma looked back and forth between her parents, and her mouth gaped. "You're leaving us? You're going to the hospital with Ruthie?"

"Only for a short time," *Mamm* said, patting Irma's hand. "I will be back."

"And I will take *gut* care of you while they're gone," Lydia chimed in. "You don't have to worry about that." She tried to keep her tone light, even though the task of acting as her siblings' mother felt like a huge mountain she'd never be able to conquer.

"Are you going too, *Dat*?" Titus asked, looking confused.

"Only your *mamm* and Ruthie are going," *Dat* said, still fingering his beard. "Your *mammi* Elizabeth is going to go too, to help your *mamm*."

"When are you leaving?" Titus asked, his frown deepening.

"Today," *Mamm* said. "A driver is going to pick us up after you leave for school. We're going to pick up *Mammi* on the way."

"Today?" Irma's lip began to tremble as she stared at *Mamm*. "I don't want you to go. I'm going to miss you." Irma jumped up, came around the table, and hopped into *Mamm's* lap.

Mamm held her close and kissed her head. "You will be fine, *mei liewe*. We'll talk on the phone, and you can even write me letters. It will be just fine. I'll be home before you know it. I need you to be strong and to behave for Lydia and *Dat*. You need to do your best in school and help out with the chores at home. Can you do that for me?"

Irma looked up at *Mamm* and nodded while sniffing. Tears splattered her pink cheeks.

Lydia wished she could wake up from this surreal nightmare. How could she possibly take the place of their mother?

She'd never be able to comfort Irma like their mother could. Her mother was the woman who kept the household running without any flaws. She knew just what to do in any situation. Why would Lydia's parents put this pressure on her? It was just unfair. It was impossible for Lydia to achieve that at sixteen.

"We're going to be okay," *Dat* said, and Lydia wondered if he was trying to convince himself as much as the rest of them.

Irma wrapped her arms around *Mamm*, and Lydia hoped her mother wouldn't cry. Seeing her mother shed tears would make this situation even more painful.

Unable to take any more of this sadness, Lydia stood. "I'll take care of the dishes while you all talk." She carried the plates and glasses to the sink and started the hot water. Her parents continued to reassure Irma and Titus that everything would be fine, and she hoped they were right.

After she finished the dishes, she prepared lunch for herself, Irma, Titus, and her father. Glancing at the clock, she found she had ten minutes before she had to leave for school. Since her parents were still deep in conversation with Titus and Irma, Lydia slipped through the family room and up the stairs.

Lydia rushed to her room, grabbed something off a shelf in the corner, and dropped it into the pocket of her apron. She walked down the hallway and gingerly pushed open Ruthie's door. She found her sister sitting up in her crib while hugging her favorite cloth doll that she'd named Hannah.

"*Gude mariye*," Lydia said with a smile. "How are you and Hannah today?"

"We're *gut*," Ruthie said, her voice small. "I smell breakfast."

"*Ya.*" Lydia lowered herself onto the rocking chair across from the crib. "I made breakfast this morning."

"You did?" Ruthie giggled. "I bet you burned the eggs like you did last week."

"That's not nice." Lydia laughed. "And I didn't burn the eggs."

"May I have some?" Ruthie moved to her knees. "I'm hungry."

"Of course you may," Lydia began. "But I'd like to talk to you first."

Ruthie looked surprised.

"You and *Mamm* are leaving on a trip today. You're going to see some really smart doctors who can help you."

"I am?" Now Ruthie looked confused.

"*Ya.*" Lydia stood and walked over to the crib. "You'll be gone for a little while. I have to go to school in a few minutes, but I just want to tell you that I love you."

Standing, Ruthie pulled Lydia into a hug. "*Ich liebe dich.*"

Lydia closed her eyes, trying in vain not to cry. She then pulled the small, worn stuffed orange cat from her pocket. "I want you to take this with you." She handed the toy to Ruthie. "This is Snuggles. *Mammi* gave it to me a long time ago."

Ruthie's eyes widened as she hugged the cat and her doll. "*Danki*! I'll take *gut* care of her."

Lydia smiled through her tears. "If you ever get scared, you just hug Snuggles and Hannah, and they will take away all your fears."

Ruthie smiled. "I'll hug them all the time."

"*Gut.*" Lydia touched her sister's nose.

"Lydia!" Her mother's voice sounded from downstairs. "It's time to go."

"We better get downstairs." Lydia hoisted her sister into her arms. She silently marveled how light Ruthie was as she carried her down the stairs. After depositing Ruthie on a bench at the kitchen table, Lydia brought her a cup of milk. She sat with Ruthie while Irma and Titus kissed their mother good-bye.

When her siblings moved over to say good-bye to Ruthie, Lydia retrieved the lunch pails from the counter.

The crunch of tires in the driveway alerted her that her father's ride to work had arrived. Keeping with tradition, her father paid a non-Amish driver to take him to work every day.

"It's time to go," *Dat* told *Mamm*, a frown turning down his lips. "I will try to call you later from the shop."

"*Ya*," *Mamm* said. "I'll leave you a message with my phone number." She cleared her throat, and Lydia saw tears in her mother's eyes. "I'll take *gut* care of Ruthie. You take *gut* care of the rest of the family."

"You know I will," he said.

They embraced and kissed, and Lydia felt as if she should leave the room. She turned back to her siblings and touched Ruthie's arm. "You take *gut* care of Hannah and Snuggles, *ya*? Promise me?"

Ruthie's little face beamed. "*Ya*. I'll take *gut* care of *Mamm* too."

"*Danki*." Lydia kissed her head. "I'll see you soon, Ruthie."

"*Kinner*," *Mamm* called. "You're going to be late for school. You have to leave now."

"Let's go," Lydia said to her middle siblings. "It won't look too good if I'm late since I'm the assistant teacher." Lydia motioned for Irma and Titus to hurry along. She hugged her mother good-bye. "I'm going to miss you, but I promise I'll do my best to take care of everyone."

"*Danki*," *Mamm* said. "*Ich liebe dich.*"

"I love you too," Lydia said. She handed out the lunch pails and said good-bye to her father. She waved to her mother and Ruthie one last time before stepping out onto the porch.

As Lydia eyed the van waiting for her father, she sent up a prayer that her life would be normal very soon and that she could go back to living like a normal teenager, not a surrogate mother for her siblings.

8

Danki, Aenti Rebecca," Lydia said Friday evening. "I appreciate all you did for us today and yesterday too."

Her aunt touched Lydia's cheek and smiled. "It's the least I could do, *mei liewe*. I wish I could do more." She pointed toward the stove. "I think you may have enough chicken and dumplings for leftovers tomorrow."

The aroma caused Lydia's stomach to gurgle, and she realized she'd hardly eaten anything since an apple at lunchtime. "You know that's my *dat's* favorite supper, *ya*?"

Rebecca nodded. "Irma shared that your *dat* wasn't in a very *gut* mood last night, so I thought this might help."

"*Danki*." Lydia touched her hand, resisting the temptation to ask her aunt to stay. It was a silly notion, since Rebecca had young children of her own to care for. "Give my love to Daniel Junior and Emma. I hope to see you again soon."

"You will." Rebecca hefted her tote bag over her shoulder. "I'm certain I'll see you Sunday. Bring me news of your visit to Hershey."

Irma and Titus entered the kitchen after washing their hands.

"*Danki* for supper," Titus said as he sat down in his usual spot at the kitchen table.

Irma hopped into the kitchen with a smile turning up her pink lips. "It smells *wunderbaar gut.*"

"*Gern gschehne,*" Rebecca said with a wave as she opened the door. "*Gut nacht.* Tell your *dat* hello for me."

Once Rebecca was gone, Lydia and Irma set the table and served the meal. After prayers, they began to eat the chicken and dumplings, homemade bread, and green beans Rebecca had prepared. The women in the community were taking turns bringing meals and helping Lydia's family through this difficult time. Kathryn had come by Tuesday and Wednesday to lend a hand, and Rebecca had helped the past two nights.

"This is *appeditlich,*" Irma said while shoveling more chicken into her little mouth. "*Dat* will love it."

"I hope so," Titus said.

"How was school?" Lydia asked before stifling a yawn.

While Irma rambled on about every incident that had taken place during the school day, Lydia nodded and feigned interest. Her thoughts instead wandered to the Hershey hospital and her mother and Ruthie. She'd wondered about her mother all day. Although she tried to reach her by phone, she'd only been able to briefly speak to her grandmother, whose cheerfulness sounded forced when she declared that things were going just fine.

"I'll help with the dishes," Titus said when their plates were clean.

Lydia looked at him with a confused expression. "What do you mean? I need you to go feed the animals."

Titus piled up the dishes and headed for the sink. "How about we switch up our chores tonight? You can take care of the animals, Irma."

Irma laughed while gathering up the glasses. "You're *gegisch*."

"I'm not joking," Titus said as he turned on the water and poured in dishwashing detergent. "Tonight I want to help out in the kitchen and you can take care of the barn."

"No!" Irma bellowed, pushing him away from the sink. "I want to do the dishes!"

"But I'm sick and tired of raking out the horse stalls and feeding the animals by myself," Titus snapped. "It's not my fault I'm the only *bu*. You can do the barn work and get dirty too. You're capable even though you're a *maedel*!"

"You two need to stop it right now," Lydia hissed. "You know better than to behave this way. I may not be *Mamm*, but you will treat me like *Mamm* beginning right now."

Lydia looked at Titus and Irma, who both stared at their shoes. Taking a deep breath, she counted to ten and touched the ties to her prayer cap while trying to get her temper in check. She'd survived a busy day at the bakery dealing with impatient *English* customers only to come home to squabbling children. She missed her mother so much her heart ached, and she also longed for the comfort and guidance of her grandmother's talks at the bakery. It didn't seem fair that Lydia had to deal with all of this stress by herself. At a time like this, she needed her mother ... and her grandmother.

Frustration surged through her, and she silently prayed for God to guide her words.

"Now, we will complete our chores without any further discussions," Lydia began, shaking a finger at each of them for emphasis. "Irma, do the dishes. Titus, get out into the barn before *Dat* gets home. He told you you'd better have your chores done or he is going to take you out behind the barn for a whippin'. You know how tired and upset he was last night and your blatant disobedience rankled him even further. Let's not have a repeat of that scene, *ya*?"

"But I'm sick and tired of doing the same chores all the time." Titus gestured toward the sink filled with soiled dishes and frothy soap. "You two get the easy work inside the house, and I have to do the real dirty work!"

Lydia rubbed her temples where a headache brewed. "Lord, give me strength," she whispered. This behavior was so out of character for her siblings that she was baffled. She'd never known them to argue or complain about their chores. In fact, she'd even witnessed Titus whistling while cleaning out the horse stalls in the recent past. Where had his sudden combativeness come from?

She glanced at the clock and realized their father would be home soon. He would most likely lose his temper if he walked into this scene, and she'd already experienced more than enough stress for one day.

Lydia needed to take control and make them mind. Mustering all of her emotional strength, she frowned at her brother and sister. "Titus," she began in her best authoritative voice, "this is how it works when *Mamm* is here, and it's how it will work while I'm in charge." She pointed to him. "You take care of the animals and the barn, and Irma does the dishes."

"You're not *Mamm*, you know," Titus seethed, anger in his eyes. "She's gone to Hershey with Ruthie. She'll probably stay away from us as long as she can. It's probably easier for her to just take care of one child. We all know Ruthie is the favorite."

"Is *Mamm* ever coming back home?" Irma asked with tears in her eyes.

The worry in both of their eyes stunned Lydia. She

touched Titus's arm, and he blanched. "Ruthie is not *Mamm's* favorite. She loves all of us equally, but right now Ruthie needs her the most." She turned to Irma and touched her little hand. "Irma, you know *Mamm* is going to come back. *Mamm* and *Dat* explained to you that this is only temporary. We just have to be patient."

"I know, but it's been so long." Irma sniffed and swiped her hand under her nose. "She's been gone since Monday, and now it's Friday. She needs to come home now. It's been too long."

Lydia blew out a sigh and then pulled Irma into a hug. "I miss her too, but she's taking care of Ruthie. The doctors are doing their best to make Ruthie well so she can be like us and live a normal life. Right now she's so sick that she can't go to school. Don't we want her to go to school when she's six? Don't you want her to help with the chores too?"

Irma nodded, and her long, blonde braids bounced on the shoulders of her blue frock.

Lydia touched Irma's head. "We have to trust God that the doctors are giving her the right medicine. And we have to do our best while *Mamm* is gone. That's what *Mamm* asked us to do, *ya*?"

"When is she coming back?" Titus asked, his expression softening.

Lydia realized why her siblings were so out of sorts—they missed their mother too.

"I don't know," Lydia said. "She said it may be a few weeks. We'll just have to make the best of it and try to get along. That's what she expects us to do. She would be very disappointed if she heard us arguing like this. We don't want to disappoint her, do we?"

Titus shook his head and sighed.

"Does she still love us?" Irma asked.

"Irma," Lydia said with impatience radiating in her voice. "You know the answer to that. Of course *Mamm* loves us. She'll never stop loving us. You need to stop asking *gegisch* questions."

Headlights shown through the window and an engine hummed outside, announcing the arrival of her father.

"*Dat's* driver is dropping him off," Lydia said as her heart pounded in her chest. "*Dummle*! Get to your chores now."

Titus rushed outside, and soon she heard his muffled voice greeting their father. Irma busied herself at the sink while Lydia pulled her father's dinner plate from the oven, where she'd kept it warm for him. She then wiped the table and straightened the counters.

The door opened with a bang, and *Dat* came through the door with a frown on his face. "*Wie geht's*," he said before placing his tool bag on the floor. "Supper smells *appeditlich*." He crossed to the table and studied the plate Lydia had heaped high with food.

"*Aenti* Rebecca and I made your favorite. She had a *gut* recipe I thought you'd enjoy." Lydia had hoped that perhaps the special supper would bring a genuine smile to his face, something she'd longed to see for the past few weeks.

"*Danki*, Lydia. That's very thoughtful of you." *Dat* turned to Irma and kissed the top of her head. "*Wie geht's*, Irma? How was your day?"

"*Gut*." Irma smiled. "I have to tell you about school today. I had a really *gut* day."

"Okay." *Dat* started toward the doorway. "Just let me wash up, and I'll listen to your stories."

Relief flooded Lydia at the nice exchange between her father and middle sister. *Maybe things can be somewhat normal after all.* Once her father disappeared toward the bathroom, Lydia looked at Irma, who was stacking the dishes on the counter. "I'm going to go check on Titus. I'll be right back."

"Okay," Irma said. "I'm going to talk with *Dat* while he eats."

Lydia stepped outside to the barn and gazed up at the crystal clear blue sky. *Is Mamm looking out the window, watching this beautiful sky as well?* She sank onto the porch swing and sucked in a deep, cleansing breath. She shifted and the swing moved back and forth while she rubbed the arms of her green dress. The early evening air was crisp, and she wished she'd fetched her sweater from the peg by the door on her way out to the porch.

She enjoyed the solace outside, which was a stark contrast to her day spent working in the busy bakery and the evening of dealing with her siblings. She longed for some time to herself, and hoped this situation would only be temporary— just as she'd promised Titus and Irma it would be.

Titus emerged from the barn, wiping his hands on his trousers as he walked toward the porch. "The animals are fed and watered," he said while climbing the stairs.

"*Danki*," Lydia said. "Please go get your bath so Irma can take hers."

"I will." He started for the door and then stopped in front of her and frowned. "I'm sorry about earlier. I shouldn't have yelled, and I don't mind my chores. I just—I just wish *Mamm* and—" He bit his lower lip and his eyes filled with tears.

"I miss them too," Lydia said with a gentle smile. "But we'll get through this."

He stepped toward the door, opening it with a loud creak. He looked back at Lydia once more. "Are you coming in?"

She yawned and hugged her arms to her chest. "In a few minutes. I just need some quiet."

"I'll tell *Dat*." He disappeared through the door.

Lydia rubbed her arms and moved back and forth on the swing. The sun was getting ready to set and the shadows were shifting on the dirt road, heading for the street. Her gaze moved across the pasture toward the Glick home. She wondered why Joshua hadn't come to visit this week. Was he too busy working on the farm? It seemed odd that he hadn't made time to come and check on Lydia and her family, especially since she'd told him of Ruthie's illness. She hoped he would stop by soon. An easy conversation with Joshua would do wonders for her frayed nerves.

Something out of her peripheral vision at the end of the driveway caught her gaze. Her eyes focused, and a figure on a bike moved swiftly up the drive. Since it was a real bike and not a scooter, Lydia knew it wasn't an Amish person. The figure was tall and lean and dressed in jeans and a T-shirt. It had to be an *Englisher*. She had *English* acquaintances that frequented the bakery, but not one had ever visited her at home. In fact, she couldn't remember the last time an *Englisher* had visited at all.

She stood and walked toward the door, ready to get her father outside in case the visitor had unethical intentions.

"Lydia?" a voice called.

Turning, she saw Tristan coasting up to the porch with a wide smile on his face. "Tristan?"

"Hey." He stopped short of the steps and hopped off the bike. "How are you?"

"I'm doing okay." She gave him a surprised smile. "What are you doing here?"

"I haven't seen you all week, so I thought I might take a

ride to try to find you." He hesitated. "Is it all right if I visit with you for a few minutes? I won't take up much of your time. But if it's better that I don't—"

"No, no. It's fine." She gestured toward the porch. "I can talk with you for a few minutes and then I need to get my sister ready for bed." Lydia sank back onto the swing.

Tristan parked his bike by flipping down the kick stand. He then sat on the top porch step while leaning his back against the railing. "How's your littlest sister?"

"She ... She has leukemia." Lydia drew in a shaky breath. "I would have told you, but I've been so busy, since my mother went with her to Hershey for chemotherapy. My grandmother went with them too, and when I talked to her, she said things are going well. We're going to visit them tomorrow."

"Oh," Tristan said after a moment. "I'm glad it's going well for your sister. I hope she's doing better soon. I'm sure it has to be hard for your whole family."

"Thank you," she said. "How was your day? You had to start school, *ya*? Or did you get to skip since you already completed your exams?"

"No, I don't get a free pass, but it's okay," Tristan said with a shrug. "I'm the new kid, so I'm trying to find my way. It seems like a waste of time since the year is almost over, but I have to get *acclimated* and all that." He motioned quotation marks with his fingers for emphasis.

"Have you heard from Lexi?" she asked.

"Yeah," he said. "She's having a hard time because she misses seeing me every day. But I promised her I'd come visit after school is over."

"I bet you've been busy since you're going to school and also unpacking the house, *ya*?"

He nodded. "I'm also studying for my driver's test. I guess you don't have to worry about that, right?"

Lydia shook her head. "No. Some kids get their license during their running around time, but it's not something I'm interested in doing. I don't think my parents would like it very much, and I don't want to be a bad role model for my younger siblings."

Tristan raked his hands through his messy dark hair. "I can understand that. How are things at home with your mom and baby sister gone?"

Lydia folded her hands over her apron and debated how much to share with her new friend. "Things are ..." She paused, trying to think of a word to describe how she felt, but there were no words. Her emotions were a conflicting and confusing mess ranging from fear to frustration. "I don't know how to describe it."

He raised his eyebrows. "If it's too personal, then you don't need to share."

"No, it's okay," Lydia said. "Actually, I think it might make me feel better if I talk about it. It seems like I'm so busy taking care of everyone else and working that I don't get much time for me anymore. I don't mean to sound selfish, but I'm afraid I'm going to lose myself with all this stress."

His expression was full of empathy. "That makes perfect sense. You're dealing with a lot. Just hearing that your baby sister is sick is a lot to handle."

"Thank you," Lydia said, absently smoothing her black apron. "You're right. We knew she was sick, but it was a shock when we found out she had leukemia." She looked out across the field.

"Well, how *are* you doing everything?" His expression was filled with compassion and empathy.

Lydia bit her lower lip. "I'm doing okay. It's hard though. I have to take care of Titus and Irma, as well as work my two jobs, and clean house and cook."

"That is a big burden to carry." His expression conveyed empathy for what she was going through. "Sounds like you're getting a crash course in adulthood."

"That's very true." She sniffed as her eyes welled up with tears. It felt strange to be confiding so much in a boy she barely knew, let alone crying in front of him. But Tristan was so easy to talk to. "I feel guilty for thinking this, but I keep wondering if I'll ever be able to go back to a normal life."

"I'm sure you will. You'll have to hang in there for a while, but God won't abandon you."

Lydia was speechless for a moment. *He's a Christian!* She cleared her throat.

"I think you're right," she finally said as she wiped her eyes.

The door opened with a bang, causing Lydia to jump. Her father stepped onto the porch and glanced back and forth between Lydia and Tristan as a scowl turned down his lips.

A chill skittered up Lydia's spine. *Uh oh. Dat's smile is gone.*

"Lydia?" *Dat* asked. "What's going on here?"

"*Dat.*" Lydia popped up from the swing. "This is my friend, Tristan. He's the *bu* who moved into the Fitzgeralds' house." She forced a smile, hoping his expression would relax. "Remember when Irma, Titus, and I took them treats from the bakery?"

Dat stared down at Tristan. "It's very late." He turned to Lydia. "It's time to get ready for devotions."

"Yes, *Dat.*" Lydia gave Tristan an apologetic look. "I need to head inside now."

Tristan stood and got his bicycle. "It was nice meeting you, Mr. Bontrager." He smiled at her father, who didn't return the gesture. "I was very sorry to hear about your daughter. I hope she's better soon." After pausing for a beat, he climbed onto the bike and looked at Lydia. "Take care, Lydia. I'll see you soon."

Before she could respond, Tristan took off down the driveway toward the road.

"What were you thinking, Lydia?" her father asked.

"It wasn't planned," Lydia said. "He appeared on his bike and asked if we could visit for a few minutes. I didn't invite him, but I thought it would be rude to send him away. He only wanted to know how Ruthie and our family are doing."

Dat shook his head. "Lydia, he's *English*. Do you know how this would look if the bishop stopped by and found him here visiting you alone on the porch at night?"

"We're just friends, *Dat*," Lydia insisted, her voice spiking up an octave. "He's our neighbor. Why can't I visit with my neighbor?"

"Seeing him at the market is one thing, but visiting alone on a dark porch is something else completely," he said. "How would this look to the parents of your students? How would they feel if they knew you were out meeting *English buwe*? This is not a habit they would like you to teach their *kinner*."

"I'm not out meeting *English buwe, Dat*." Anger swelled within her. "I was just talking to a friend. He's very nice, and so is his family."

Dat's scowl deepened. "You know this behavior is completely unacceptable. I advise you not to do this again." He opened the door. "Get inside. It's getting late."

Frowning, Lydia stepped through the door to the kitchen. She wondered what part of her life would fall apart next.

9

On Saturday morning, Lydia's heart flip-flopped as the van drove into the hospital parking lot. She'd read in the booklet that chemotherapy could have devastating effects, and she worried that Ruthie wouldn't be up to their visit, which would disappoint both Titus and Irma.

The van parked at the curb, and while her father spoke to the driver, Lydia gathered Titus and Irma on the sidewalk.

"Now remember," Lydia warned them. "We must behave in the hospital. We have to be quiet and respectful since many ill people are here. We can't be loud in the hallways."

Titus nodded and adjusted his coat over his best Sunday shirt and vest. Lydia had told him to look his best to make their mother happy.

"I know." A smile curled up Irma's little lips. "I'm excited to see Ruthie, *Mamm*, and *Mammi*." She held up a card she'd made with construction paper the night before. "I can't wait to give this to Ruthie. Maybe she'll hang it on her wall."

Lydia smiled and touched the top of Irma's prayer covering. "I bet she will love it."

"Let's go," *Dat* said, heading for the large glass door. "The van will be back here to pick us up at four." He held a small cooler that contained their lunch, which Lydia had packed before they'd left the house that morning.

Lydia took Irma's hand and held her back while the automatic doors opened.

"Wow," Irma whispered. "How'd that door open on its own?"

"They're electric doors," *Dat* said. "A lot of *English* buildings have them."

Irma's eyes were wide with wonder as she stepped through. She turned back to watch them close, and Lydia tugged her along.

"Keep moving, Irma," Lydia said with a smile. "Ruthie is waiting for us."

After checking in at the desk, *Dat* led them to a bank of elevators.

Irma stared again in wonder at another set of large doors. "What's this?"

"It's called an elevator," *Dat* said, an amused smile gracing his lips.

Lydia couldn't help but smile along with him and enjoy the excitement in her sister's eyes.

"*Elevator*," Irma repeated the word. "I can't wait to see what it does." She looked around the spacious lobby where people dressed in a variety of clothing styles moved about. "This place is so interesting! It's so different from our district. I've never seen so many people."

Lydia grinned. "*Ya*, it is interesting to see all of these different people at the hospital."

The elevator doors opened with a *whoosh*. *Dat* stepped on and gestured for them to follow. Holding Irma's hand, Lydia tugged her inside.

Dat pointed to the lighted numbers on the plate in front of him and told them the floor where Ruthie's room was located. "Would you like to push the number for the floor?"

Irma giggled and mashed her little fingertip on the number. The elevator took off, and Irma jumped back, gripping the handrail behind her. "This is *schpass*!"

Titus chuckled and shook his head. "You're so *gegisch*."

Lydia beamed as her family shared a laugh. She wished she could freeze this moment in time.

When they stepped off the elevator, Lydia took Irma's hand as they followed her father to a reception desk. A woman in bright pink scrubs sat surrounded by a computer and stacks of papers.

Irma tugged Lydia's hand and pointed to colorful paintings of animals on the walls. "Look at that," she whispered. "It looks like the pictures of Noah's ark we have in our books at school."

"*Ya*," Lydia said, leaning down to her. "You're right."

Irma pointed out a giraffe, a cow, and an elephant, while her eyes remained wide with wonder.

"*Kumm*," her father said. "We must go this way."

The nurse led them down a long hallway, and Irma pointed out the colorful images of animals and children on the walls during their journey. They stopped outside a closed door, and the nurse faced them.

"Hi," she said. "My name is Jenna and I'm a nurse here. I need you each to wear a special mask so you don't give your sister any germs." She pulled a blue facemask from a box on the wall and handed one to each of them, then explained how to put it on.

Irma giggled while Lydia helped her. Titus examined his mask and looked confused.

"Let me help you," *Dat* said, his voice muffled behind his own mask. He assisted Titus while Lydia put on hers.

"Now," Jenna said, addressing Lydia and her siblings. "Your sister may be very tired. She's been taking a lot of medicine, and sometimes it upsets her tummy. She may not want to talk, but I'm certain she'll be happy to see you."

Glancing at her father's apprehensive expression, Lydia's stomach seemed to turn over. How bad were things behind that door?

When the nurse opened the door, Lydia saw her grandmother. She was holding a small dishpan while sitting in a chair next to Ruthie's bed. When she looked over at them, her eyes widened with surprise, and she quickly placed the dishpan on the small table beside the bed. Although Lydia couldn't see her grandmother's mouth because of the mask she was wearing, the crinkles around her eyes illustrated her joy at their presence.

Irma looked unsure as she slowly stepped into the room with her eyes focused on Ruthie. She approached the bed with caution and then turned to her grandmother. "How is she?" she asked, her voice muffled behind the mask.

"She's doing okay, *mei liewe*. She's just very tired right now." *Mammi* touched Irma's head. "I'm certain she'll be very *froh* when she wakes up and sees you, your siblings, and your *dat*."

Lydia looked around the room, taking in the scenery her baby sister must have become accustomed to seeing daily. Her eyes moved to a television screen on the wall, which displayed an animated television program. It felt surreal to Lydia to hear noise from a television, though the sound was very low. She assumed the television served as background noise, a mere distraction to the worry and fear floating around the hospital room.

She stepped over to the bed and placed her hand on the cool plastic bedrail. As she'd feared, Ruthie's skin was pasty white, and her little body was almost bony. She touched her sister's thin blonde braids and suspected her hair may have started to fall out. Glancing over to the pillowcase beside her, she saw a few strands of hair, and her heart sank.

"*Ich liebe dich*," Lydia whispered. "You're in my prayers day and night, sweet Ruthie."

"Where's *Mamm*?" Irma asked while sitting on *Mammi's* lap.

"She went to get something to eat," *Mammi* said, hugging Irma close. "Tell me all about school." She gestured for Titus to come across the room. "Sit with us, Titus. You tell me about school too."

While the children talked to their *grossmammi*, *Dat* sidled up to Lydia. "She looks sick," he whispered. "Look at her pale face." He touched Ruthie's arm, and she shifted onto her side while continuing to sleep. "My poor *boppli*."

Lydia saw tears glistening in her father's eyes, and her lips trembled. She prayed he wouldn't cry. She needed him to be strong because her courage had begun evaporating when they stepped into the hospital room.

"Let's sit," he said, moving toward two chairs lining the wall. "She needs to sleep."

Lydia looked around the room again, taking in the bright paintings and pictures of children, animals, and rainbows. She wondered if the pictures gave her sister comfort and joy. She hoped so, as they seemed to be having the opposite effect on her. Lydia was sure she'd never see the primers in her classroom the same way again.

Did Ruthie even understand what was happening to her? Was she afraid? Did she believe God would make her well?

Lydia glanced back at her sister in the bed. *Sometimes I'm not even sure.*

Irma and *Mammi* continued to talk, while Titus gave one-word answers to *Mammi's* questions about school and their friends.

The door opened again, revealing their mother wearing a mask and holding a tray with six cups. She stepped into the room. "Hello," she said, her voice muffled like everyone else's and a smile around her eyes. "I was hoping you'd be here when I returned."

Irma popped up and rushed over to *Mamm*, causing her to stumble forward. "*Mamm!*"

Dat stood and took the tray from *Mamm's* hands, and she leaned down and hugged Irma. "It's so *gut* to see you. Come sit with me." She crossed the room and sank into a chair beside Titus while pulling Irma onto her lap. "*Wie geht's?*"

Irma began to repeat the same school stories she'd told *Mammi*, and *Mamm* listened with interest. She looked across the room and gave Lydia a smile with her eyes, and Lydia breathed a sigh of relief. It was so good to see her mother.

Mammi stood and motioned for Lydia to follow her. "Lydia and I are going to go for a walk. We'll be back soon."

Lydia followed *Mammi* out to the hallway. She pulled off her mask as they headed toward a sitting area near the nurses' station.

"I thought you might like to talk," *Mammi* said, looping her arm around Lydia's shoulders as she so often did.

Lydia sighed. "We're managing." She didn't want to tell her grandmother she was so exhausted that she feared she might not be able to get out of bed some days. Or that some nights she cried herself to sleep and prayed that life would be normal when she awoke in the morning.

"Sit. Tell me." *Mammi* motioned toward the sofa in the sitting area. "How are things at home?"

Lydia sank onto the leather sofa. "We've had some rough days, but, all in all, we're okay." She studied *Mammi's* eyes. "How is Ruthie? Is she okay? How's my *mamm*?"

Mammi sat beside Lydia. "Ruthie has been very ill from the chemotherapy. She's been sick, which is why I was holding the dishpan. I don't know if you noticed how pale she is."

"And her hair?" Lydia asked softly, her voice trembling.

"*Ya.*" *Mammi* pushed a stray strand of hair that had escaped Lydia's bun back from her cheek. "She's starting to lose her hair." Her expression brightened. "However, the doctors are optimistic that the medicine is doing its job. They said we should have *gut* test results soon."

"And my *mamm*?" Lydia asked, feeling hopeful. "How is she holding up?"

"She has moments when she's strong and moments when she's not so strong, which can be expected." *Mammi* gave her a gentle smile. "Your *mamm* is very courageous. You're just like her too. I'm very proud of you for taking care of your siblings. I spoke with your *dat* yesterday, and he said you are doing an outstanding job, despite the stress and worry in the house." She touched Lydia's nose. "You're a very *gut maedel*. Please keep it up."

"*Danki,*" Lydia said. "I promise I'll do my best." *But I don't know how much longer I can hold on without passing out from exhaustion and stress.*

"Lydia!" Irma called, running down the hallway toward them.

"Irma," Lydia said. "Slow down and don't yell. Remember what I told you about behaving in the hospital?"

"I know," Irma said, bending over in an attempt to catch

her breath. "Ruthie is awake and she's asking for you. You must come back to the room now."

Lydia followed Irma back down the hallway, putting on their masks before entering the room. Her heart swelled with hope when she saw Ruthie sitting up in bed and smiling at Titus, who was sharing a story about the stray kittens that lived in the barn. Although she looked so tiny and pale, her blue eyes were bright as she listened to him describe the colors of the different little kittens who'd been born just last week. Irma's homemade card sat next to her, along with Snuggles, the stuffed orange cat, and Hannah, her favorite cloth doll she'd brought from home.

Ruthie turned toward Lydia and raised her arms. "Lydia!"

"Hi, Ruthie," Lydia said. "How are you feeling?"

"*Gut.*" Ruthie pointed toward the stuffed cat. "I'm taking *gut* care of Snuggles. I'm so *froh* I have Snuggles and Hannah with me. They stay by me all the time, even when I get my medicine."

"I'm so *froh* that you have them too," Lydia said. "It's important that you keep your friends close by all the time."

"Lydia." Ruthie reached for her. "Sit by me."

Mammi tapped Lydia's shoulder and pointed toward a dispenser on the wall by the door. "Clean your hands with that foam before you touch her."

Lydia applied the cool foam to her hands and then sat on the chair by the bed.

Ruthie took Lydia's hand and held it tight while Titus continued to tell her all about the kittens.

Lydia surveyed the room again, this time taking in the various machines surrounding Ruthie's bed. She assumed the machines were used to dispense Ruthie's medicines and help them monitor her condition. She wondered how long it took the nurses and doctors to learn how to properly operate the machines.

They all shared stories about people at home while Ruthie listened with sparkling eyes. At lunchtime, a woman brought in a tray of food for Ruthie, and they watched her nibble without much interest.

Dat suggested they eat their packed lunches outside the room, and Lydia, her parents, and her middle siblings ate in the sitting area while their grandmother stayed with Ruthie. Lydia ate in silence while trying to digest her lunch along with her worried feelings for her baby sister. She was thankful for her gregarious middle sister, who kept everyone entertained while she prattled on about her assessment of the colorful pictures on the hospital walls.

After lunch, they sat in Ruthie's room and stared at cartoons on the television while she napped on and off. Lydia wondered if the medication was supposed to make her tired so she would sleep to help her heal or if it was a side effect.

At a quarter to four, *Dat* stood, and Lydia felt queasy. Although sitting in the hospital room was both tiring and dull, she wasn't ready to leave.

"It's time to go," her father said, his expression grim. "The driver will be here to pick us up very soon."

"I think I should stay here," Irma said, holding *Mamm's* hand. "*Mamm* needs us to stay and help take care of Ruthie." She looked at her mother. "Right, *Mamm*?"

Lydia also wished they could stay and keep their family together just a little longer.

Mamm touched Irma's prayer covering. "I wish you could stay and help, but your *dat* needs your help at home. Can you help your *dat* for me?"

"And I need your help too," Lydia chimed in.

Irma nodded, but her eyes sparkled with fresh tears. "I'll be *gut* and help Lydia and *Dat*. I promise." She wrapped her arms around her mother. *"Ich liebe dich, Mamm."*

Irma hugged *Mammi* and told her good-bye, and then touched Ruthie's hand and told her to get better.

Having just recently woken up from another short nap, Ruthie yawned in response. Lydia couldn't help but think that they should go back home and let her sleep in preparation for her upcoming treatments.

Titus said his good-byes and then waited at the door with Irma.

Lydia hugged her grandmother, again promising to do her best. Then she also touched Ruthie's hand and told her to feel better.

When Lydia hugged her mother, she felt *Mamm* grip her tightly.

"I'm so proud of you," *Mamm* whispered through her mask. "You're doing a *gut* job with the *kinner*. I promise I'll be home as soon as I can."

"Okay," Lydia said, her voice trembling. "Don't worry about anything at home. You just take care of Ruthie. Everything will be fine."

Mamm touched Lydia's cheek. "I'll see you soon."

"Ya, you will." Lydia turned to her father. "I'll take the *kinner* down to the lobby so you can say good-bye. Take your time."

"Danki," her father said.

She picked up the empty cooler, took Irma's hand, and then looked back at her mother and grandmother. *"Geb acht uff dich,"* she said before leading her siblings out of the room.

They deposited their masks in a trash can by the door and started down the hallway.

"She looks *grank*," Titus said as they approached the elevator.

Irma beamed. "*Ya*, but she liked my card."

Lydia looked around the hallway of the hospital, wondering how the nurses stayed happy and positive while surrounded by the patients' illnesses and families' sadness. *If I were* English, *I don't think I could work here and keep a positive outlook day after day.*

Irma mashed the button and clapped when the elevator door opened. She grinned and held onto the hand railing during the ride down to the lobby. They sat quietly in a sitting area and watched the people mill around. Lydia wondered how many of the people in the lobby had ill family members at that hospital. Did they feel helpless and lost like Lydia did? Or were they preparing to take home a family member who had been healed? She hoped she would see her sister come home very soon.

Her father appeared several minutes later. "Let's go," he said without stopping his trek to the doors.

Stepping out to the driveway, Lydia saw the van sitting at the curb. While her father climbed into the front passenger seat, Lydia helped Irma get in and buckle her seat belt before she took a place beside her in the center seat. Titus found a spot in the very back of the van and stared out the window.

During their silent ride home, Lydia listened to the low hum of the van's engine and the comforting rhythmic melody of the road noise. She closed her eyes and thought about their visit with Ruthie. Lydia wondered if she was as strong as her mother and grandmother thought she was. Could she possibly keep up with her house chores and continue working her two jobs? It seemed so unfair that all of the adults around her were expecting her to keep it all together. Didn't they know how much she was struggling to keep it all together?

Looking out the window, Lydia saw a car containing two teenaged girls, who appeared to be singing along with the radio without a care in the world. She wondered what it would be like to be happy and free of responsibility like those girls. What would it be like to enjoy a life of leisure and fun with her friends? Lydia had no idea. In fact, Lydia wondered if her friends even thought of her today while she sat at the hospital. Did Joshua even care about her anymore?

With a sigh, Lydia closed her eyes and swallowed a lump in her throat. The pressure her family had placed on her was almost too much to bear. And she'd never felt more alone in her life.

10

On Monday, over a week later, Lydia lifted one of her brother's blue shirts and pinned it to the clothesline that ran from the back porch to the barn. She glanced up just as Anna Glick, Joshua's mother, emerged from the house with another basket full of washed clothes from the wringer washer located in a small room off the kitchen.

"*Danki* for coming over to help me today," Lydia said. "I truly appreciate all of your assistance with the laundry. It's a big job to do alone."

"Don't be *gegisch*," Anna said while placing the basket on the porch. "It's only right to help a *freind* in need." She lifted another shirt belonging to Titus and held it out to Lydia. "How are you doing?"

Lydia took the shirt and pinned it to the line as she spoke. "I guess we're doing okay." She swallowed a yawn. The truth was that Lydia was so exhausted she felt as if she were sleep-walking through the day. Some days she wondered if she would make it through another hour without hitting the floor and snoring. She pushed on, however, and hoped that life would return to normal sooner rather than later.

"We went to see my *mamm* and Ruthie on Saturday," Lydia said in an effort to change the subject. "It was our second visit since they left."

"How did that go?" Anna pulled out another shirt and began to pin it after moving the line along.

"It was a little difficult to see *mei schweschder* so *grank*." Lydia thought back to the hopeless feeling that had engulfed her when she saw her sister, who'd looked so dwarfed in the huge hospital bed and by the machines that surrounded it.

Ruthie still looked so frail and pale. Her hair was even thinner, and her braids looked like they belonged on a cloth doll and not her little pink head. She'd even gotten sick in front of Lydia and her family, and her mother had held the little dishpan while she vomited. The sight was so upsetting to Irma that she'd burst into tears, and Lydia took her out to the hallway. It was a nightmare come to life for the whole family.

The whole situation remained the most overwhelming Lydia had ever experienced.

"I'm sorry, Lydia." Anna frowned while handing Lydia another shirt. She then pulled out one to pin herself. "Do you know when they'll be home?"

Lydia shook her head. "We don't know."

Anna patted Lydia's shoulder. "You don't need to worry. God will take *gut* care of your *mamm* and Ruthie, and they will be home just as soon as he sees fit." She held out a frock. "Until then, the community will take *gut* care of you and your family. In just a little bit, a few of the ladies from the church will be over with some food for you all. We'll make sure you don't have a thing to worry about." She handed Lydia the last shirt and then disappeared inside the house.

Lydia stared up at the laundry flapping in the gentle afternoon breeze and sighed. She was so sick and tired of receiving dismissive pats on the shoulder from well-meaning friends and family members. And if she heard one more person tell her that her mother and Ruthie would be home in God's time, she would scream. It seemed so easy for them to offer empty reassurances and send her on her way when they weren't the ones staring at the ceiling late into the night and wondering if her sister would come home at all.

The clip-clop of hooves drew her attention to the driveway where two buggies rattled toward the house. She met the first buggy in the driveway, and her lips formed a big smile when she saw her aunt Kathryn, her uncle David, Amanda, and Kathryn and David's other children in the buggy.

"We brought supper!" Amanda announced with a smile. "Hope you're hungry."

"It's so *gut* to see you!" Lydia said. "I'm so *froh* you came."

The second buggy came to a stop, revealing Nancy, her mother, Sadie, her father, Robert, and Nancy's siblings. The crowd climbed from the buggy and carried covered dishes into the house. Lydia grabbed a dish of warm noodles and followed her family into the kitchen, where her aunts began arranging the food.

Anna appeared from the laundry room and greeted the aunts and children. "Everything smells *wunderbaar gut*! I'm going to go gather up my family and dishes." She glanced at Lydia. "I'll be right back."

"*Wie geht's?*" Amanda asked, sidling up to her.

"Fine." Lydia opened a drawer and began pulling out serving utensils. "Anna helped me with the laundry today. How are you?"

"*Gut.*" Amanda grabbed a stack of napkins from the counter. "I missed you at the bakery today. It's not nearly as much fun when you're working at the schoolhouse."

"Let's have a blessing," Robert announced. "Everyone bow your head in silent prayer." After a few moments, Robert cleared this throat, announcing that the prayer was over. *"Aamen,"* he said. *"Danki* to everyone for this *wunderbaar gut* meal."

"Let's eat," Sadie announced. "Everyone, help yourselves."

Lydia helped her brother and sister fill their plates with potato salad, noodles, potato chips, cold cuts, chow-chow, and homemade bread. Once Irma and Titus were eating with their cousins at the table, Lydia prepared a plate for herself and followed Amanda out to the porch, where they sat side by side on the swing.

Lydia pushed her spoon through the hot, buttery home-made noodles and her stomach rumbled, reminding her that she hadn't eaten much all day. "This looks *wunderbaar.* Whose idea was this meal?"

Amanda grinned. "My *mamm* and I wanted to do some-thing nice for your family since we know you're going through so much."

Lydia ate a spoonful of noodles and sighed. The food was delicious and felt so good going down. She'd been starved and not even realized it.

Amanda recounted her run-ins with the customers at the bakery while Lydia ate. The hum of an engine caused her to look at the driveway where her father's van driver steered toward the barn. Once the van was parked, her *dat* emerged and looked startled. "Is there a party tonight?" he called as the van backed out of the driveway. His boots crunched on the rocks leading to the porch.

"Apparently so," Lydia said. "They surprised us with a *wunderbaar* supper."

"Isn't that nice." He smiled at the girls. "How are you, Amanda?"

"Hi, *Onkel* Paul," Amanda said with a smile. "I hope you like our supper. We thought you might like something different."

"*Danki*," he said as he climbed the steps. "I bet I will."

He disappeared into the house, and Amanda leaned over. "He looks *gut*," Amanda said. "How is he doing?"

"He's working very hard," Lydia said. "Most days he's very tired and he hardly speaks. I think he's having a difficult time without my *mamm*."

Amanda frowned. "I'm sorry to hear that."

"So, the bakery was busy today?" Lydia asked.

Amanda continued her conversation about her day. Soon Nancy emerged from the house and joined them, sitting in the chair next to Lydia. She chimed into the conversation, adding her own thoughts on the customers at the bakery. Her cousins droned on about their day, and Lydia enjoyed escaping into a conversation where the most serious problem discussed was a woman who spent twenty minutes deciding between macaroons and an apple pie. It felt good to sit and relax with friends after working at the schoolhouse that morning and doing laundry in the afternoon.

Lydia's heart fluttered when she spotted Joshua's family, including his father, Mel, his mother, Anna, and his twelve-year-old brother, Joey, crossing the pasture. Each was carrying a covered dish. She tried her best not to stare as Joshua sauntered across the pasture, but her eyes kept focusing on him.

In an effort to stop staring, Lydia turned back to Nancy and tried in vain to focus on her story about a rude customer while the Glick family continued toward the house.

"That smells *gut*," Anna said with a smile as she climbed the porch stairs. "I brought some hot dog surprise, pickles, and baked beans."

"*Danki*." Turning to Joey and Joshua, Lydia smiled. "*Wie geht's*. Did you come here to eat our food?"

"That's why I'm here!" Joey announced, causing everyone to laugh. "Where's Titus?"

"Inside," Lydia said. "Eating with his cousins."

As Anna and Joey disappeared through the door, Joshua smiled. "Good evening. I'm going to put this hot dog surprise on the counter, and then I'll be back to join you."

Amanda leaned over. "Do you want me to move so he can sit by you?"

Lydia swatted her cousin's shoulder. "No. Wouldn't that be horribly obvious?"

"Sometimes *buwe* need obvious," Nancy said while scooping more potato salad into her spoon. "I thought Andrew would never ask me out."

"How's Andrew doing?" Amanda asked between bites of her cold-cut sandwich. "You two looked *froh* Sunday night. I thought you might burst at the seams while you sat with him in the barn."

Nancy's cheeks blazed a bright pink. "He's doing fine. He's been working hard at his father's saddle shop. They're expanding and adding on a whole new section to the store. It's going to be very big when it's complete."

"Is that so?" Amanda wiped her mouth with a paper napkin. "That's really *gut* news. How's his *mamm*? I heard the flu was making its way through his house."

While Nancy discussed the details of Andrew's family and their health status, Lydia moved the remaining chow-chow around on her plate. She wondered what it felt like to have a sweetheart like Nancy's. Andrew seemed like a very nice boy, and his parents were always friendly at church services. A tinge of envy nipped at Lydia. She knew being envious is a sin, but she couldn't help the emotion from bubbling forth in her.

Lydia wished she could have a relationship with Joshua like the relationship Nancy had with Andrew. She'd been disappointed on Sunday when she only shared a passing hello with Joshua. While Joshua seemed to keep his distance from Lydia, Mahlon had come over three times to talk to her. He'd asked how she was, if she was going to the youth gathering, and if she wanted to get a ride home with him from the youth gathering if she decided to go. Why was she getting more attention from the boy she hoped to avoid than from the boy she hoped to date?

The door opened and banged shut. Joshua stood holding a plate almost overflowing with food in one hand and a plastic cup in the other.

Amanda shot Lydia a look that asked, *Are you sure you don't want me to move?* Lydia replied with a warning glance.

"What are you ladies discussing?" Joshua asked, moving past Lydia and her cousins.

"Andrew's family," Nancy said. "They're all getting over the flu."

"I'm sorry to hear they've been sick." Joshua settled into a seat beside Nancy and placed his cup on a table between them. "But they are better now?"

"*Ya*," Nancy said, picking up a potato chip from her plate. "Thankfully. His *mamm* was really sick for a few days."

"How are things on the farm, Joshua?" Amanda cut in. "Have you been busy?"

He nodded while biting into a sandwich. He finished chewing and wiped his mouth before responding. "It's been really busy. My father purchased a few more cows, so the barn is now full. Milk production has been *gut*, which is a blessing. We've also been helping out my grandparents a bit."

"That's nice," Amanda said, popping a chip into her mouth.

Amanda looked directly at Lydia as if to encourage her to talk, but Lydia was at a loss as to what to say. She didn't have much to share, except that she was exhausted and frustrated. Why would they want to hear about that?

"Did you have fun last night at the youth gathering?" Nancy asked Joshua. "I saw you and Andrew beating the other team at volleyball. They didn't seem to know how to play." She laughed. "Andrew said they spend more time retrieving the ball than hitting it back to your team."

Joshua snickered, and Lydia silently admired him. He shot her a warm smile and warmth filled her. Even though they hadn't talked much lately, Lydia was glad Joshua still had his special smile just for her. But she couldn't help wondering where he'd been for the past couple of weeks. Didn't he care about her?

"They weren't as good as usual," Joshua said as he again wiped his mouth with a napkin. "But I guess we all have our off days."

"That's for certain," Lydia muttered. She lifted her plastic cup and sipped the freshly mixed meadow tea, which her mother always picked up at the Amish bulk food store. The spearmint flavor was refreshing after hanging out the laundry.

Joshua seemed concerned. "How are you, Lydia? I haven't seen you in a while."

I've been working nonstop, have gotten almost no sleep because I'm worried my sister might die, and have been wondering why you haven't come near me in several weeks. Other than that, I'm fine. Instead Lydia said, "I've been busy taking care of the family." She gripped her cup. "I don't seem to get out much, but I'm thankful that people are helping me. Your *mamm* was a big help with the laundry. I appreciate the time she spent here today."

"How's Ruthie?" he asked.

"I guess she's okay. I don't really know." Lydia placed the cup on the little table in front of her so she wouldn't crush it in frustration. "My *mamm* left a message last night and said things are okay. I'm not really sure what that means. Ruthie didn't seem okay on Saturday, but I don't think my *mamm* wants to worry me more than she has to."

"We missed you last night," Nancy said. "You've missed the last two youth gatherings."

"I know," Lydia said quietly. "I heard it was at Lizzie Anne King's house last night."

"That reminds me." Nancy looked at Amanda. "Did you see Mahlon Sunday night? He and his group took off alone again. I am starting to wonder if they are doing drugs. Lizzie Anne said she smelled something funny behind the barn when she went out there to look for her cat."

"Mahlon's at it again, *ya?*" Joshua shook his head, and his eyes focused on Lydia. "I guess they never learn that drinking and drugs are bad and will get them in a lot of trouble."

Lydia's teeth gnawed on her lower lip as she studied Joshua's face. Had Joshua witnessed the attention Mahlon had bestowed upon her after church on Sunday? If so, did he suspect that Lydia and Mahlon were more than acquaintances? She swallowed a gasp.

Or is it worse than just a suspicion? Does Joshua know? Did Mahlon tell him I drank with them one night?

The questions echoed through her mind while Nancy

and Joshua continued to analyze Mahlon and his reasons for going wild.

"I don't understand why his friends go along with it," Nancy said while eating another potato chip. "You would think they would know better."

"I think it's because Mahlon can be so ... Oh, what's the word?" Amanda pushed the ribbons from her prayer covering over her shoulder. "You know what I mean. He can be mesmerizing with his blue eyes and sly smile."

"Mesmerizing?" Joshua snorted and rolled his eyes. "Please."

"Actually, Amanda is right," Nancy said. "Mahlon has a way about him. The girls really are taken by him if they don't know any better. He intrigues them because he knows just what to say. And he can be persuasive with just a mere look."

Joshua shook his head. "They must be naïve, because I see him for what he is—a sneak. He can't be trusted. He broke my confidence too many times before I just stopped talking to him altogether." He looked at Lydia. "What do you think, Lydia? Is Mahlon mesmerizing and intriguing? Can he persuade you with just a smile?"

"I don't know." Lydia shrugged and her cheeks burned with embarrassment. "I don't think so."

Joshua shook his head. "He's playing with fire. When he gets caught, his father will give him the worst whippin' of his life. His father is strict, stricter than most from what I've seen and heard."

"Where is the youth gathering going to be this week?" Nancy asked after finishing the last chip on her plate.

"I don't know," Amanda said. "Do you know, Lydia? Has anyone told you?"

Lydia shook her head. How could she possibly know?

She'd missed the last two because she had to care for the children. She was certain she wouldn't be able to attend the next one either. For all she knew, she'd miss them the rest of the year and Joshua would choose another girl to court. The thought caused her stomach to sour.

Her cousins didn't realize how difficult life was for her now. In fact, they sounded like spoiled brats discussing the upcoming youth events. Didn't they realize they were hurting her feelings?

She needed to excuse herself from the conversation before she said something she would regret later.

Lydia stood and gathered up her and Amanda's plates. "I'll take in our plates and grab some dessert for us. I saw that *Aenti* Kathryn brought some treats from the bakery." She turned to Nancy and Joshua. "Can I take your plates too?"

"*Danki*," Nancy said as she handed over her empty plate. "That was delicious."

Joshua shook his head. "*Danki*, but I'm still working on mine."

"I'll walk with you," Amanda offered as she stood. "I'll get a plate full of desserts to share too."

Lydia wished Amanda would stay behind and continue talking to Joshua and Nancy. She didn't want to be pressured to share her feelings right now.

The children raced out the door and headed to the field. Once they were gone, Lydia and Amanda stepped into the kitchen, where her aunts were cleaning up. Lydia dropped the dirty plates into the trash and then snatched a new one from the pile. She moved to the table and loaded up the plate with cookies, whoopie pies, and small pieces of cake.

"*Was iss letz?*" Amanda whispered while filling another plate. "You've been awfully quiet."

"Nothing is wrong," Lydia said, keeping her focus on the plate of goodies. "I'm just very tired. I haven't been sleeping much because of all my worry."

"You seemed very uncomfortable outside," Amanda pressed on. "It was like you didn't want to talk to us. Are you angry with me because I said you should sit with Joshua? I really didn't mean anything by it. You know I like to tease you about him."

Lydia sighed and met Amanda's concerned gaze. "Did you ever consider that maybe I feel left out?" She turned toward the sink and saw that her aunts and Anna were talking while working. They seemed completely oblivious to Lydia and Amanda's discussion.

"Left out?" Amanda's brow furrowed. "I don't understand. We were all talking to you. Even Josh asked how you were and how Ruthie's doing. How could you feel left out?"

"You just don't get it, do you, Amanda?"

"Get what?" Amanda frowned. "You're not making sense."

"I am making sense," Lydia said. "You, Nancy, and Joshua can go out and be with our friends while I'm stuck here taking care of Irma and Titus. I've missed two youth events, and I would imagine I'll miss a lot more. Perhaps it hurts my feelings when you talk about it so much."

"Oh." Amanda's eyes filled with hurt. "I'm sorry."

"Forget it." Lydia waved off the comment, headed out to the porch, and sank onto the swing.

"Is that for all of us to share?" Joshua asked, examining the plate on Lydia's lap.

"*Ya.*" She held it out. "Help yourself."

Amanda stepped onto the porch and scowled as she sat beside Lydia. Seeing the hurt on Amanda's face caused Lydia to regret her harsh words. How could she treat her best friend that way?

"I always love the treats from the bakery," Joshua said as he grabbed some chocolate peanut butter cookies. "I wish my *mamm* would work there so she could bring home treats every day."

Nancy chuckled. "Have you told your *mamm* that?"

"*Ya.*" He chewed a cookie. "I told her once, and she laughed. I told her I wasn't joking and she laughed even harder."

Nancy snickered and took a whoopie pie from Lydia's plate. When her eyes met Amanda's, she thought Amanda looked strange. "Are you okay, Amanda? You look upset."

"I'm fine," Amanda said, giving Lydia a sideways glance. "Everything is just fine."

Lydia stared down at her plate and was thankful when Nancy started a discussion on the weather and the upcoming summer. Joshua chimed in, discussing how nice his mother's garden looked.

Lydia sensed a tense air emanating from Amanda while Nancy and Joshua talked. She knew she needed to apologize, but she somehow felt justified for her ugly words. Why didn't her cousins realize how she was feeling? Didn't they know how much she wanted life to be normal again?

The kitchen door creaked open and then slammed with a loud bang as Amanda's mother came out to the porch. "I think it's time to head home," Kathryn announced. "Your *dat* wants to feed the animals and get ready for bed." She looked at Nancy. "Your *mamm* is packing up soon. Your *dat* is also ready to go."

Lydia stood and hugged her aunt. "*Danki* for everything. It was *wunderbaar gut.*"

"*Gern gschehne,*" Kathryn said, touching Lydia's prayer covering. "You know I'll do anything I can for you while your *mamm's* gone. Don't hesitate to ask."

Nancy's father stomped down the porch stairs and yelled to his children to pile into the buggy.

Nancy jumped up from her seat. "That's the signal to go." She gathered up Lydia and Amanda's empty plates. "I'll take these in and throw them away for you." She disappeared into the kitchen and emerged a few moments later followed by Joshua's parents and Lydia's father.

After saying good-bye, Nancy joined her family at the buggy. Lydia waved as they loaded up and started down the driveway toward the main road.

Joshua stood and stretched. "This was fun. I guess it's back to reality now. Tomorrow is another work day."

"That's right," Amanda said, standing. "I better get to the buggy before my *dat* starts yelling for me." She turned to Joshua. "It was *gut* to see you. Have a nice week." Then she spoke to Lydia with some hesitation. "*Gut nacht*, Lydia."

"Amanda—" Lydia began.

"What?" Amanda's expression was hopeful.

"*Danki* for dinner," Lydia said. The words were rushed, and there was so much more she wanted to say. An apology or the right words to smooth things over between them, however, didn't come to her.

Amanda bristled. "*Gern gschehne.*" Her tone was flat and void of true emotion.

Before Lydia could respond, Amanda was down the steps and climbing into her buggy.

Lydia was left on the porch with Joshua, wondering what she could possibly do to mend the rift she'd just created between her and her best friend.

"Is everything okay?" Joshua asked. "You were quiet tonight."

"I'm fine," Lydia said, even though she knew lying is a sin. "It's just been a long day."

"How's Ruthie, *really*?" he asked again.

"The doctors say the chemo is helping her, but she looks very sick," Lydia said. "She was very weak on Saturday."

"I'm sorry to hear that." He touched her shoulder. "I hope she's better and home soon."

"*Danki*," Lydia said. "I really want my family back and I want life to be normal again."

"I know you do," he said. "I hope the rest of the week goes well for you. Maybe I'll see you."

Her heart swelled with hope. Would he come and visit regularly?

"Joshua," his father called. "It's time to head home. We need to feed the animals."

"*Gut nacht*, Lydia," he said. "See you soon."

"*Gut nacht*," she said before waving to his parents and brother.

While the Glick family started across the pasture, Lydia's father climbed the porch steps. "What a nice surprise tonight, *ya*?" he asked.

"*Ya*, it was. I was very surprised too."

He wound his arm around her shoulder and led her to the door. "The Lord has blessed us with a very caring community."

She looked up and her heart turned over when she saw him give a true, genuine smile. "*Ya*," she whispered. "He has."

11

Wednesday afternoon, Lydia picked up the last of the primers and set them back on the shelf. Rain beat on the roof in the loud cadence of a thousand drums while thunder rumbled in the distance.

"I can't believe how much the *kinner* misbehaved today," Barbie said while packing up her bag. "I haven't seen them that out of hand in a long time."

Lydia grabbed the broom from the corner. "I guess it's truly spring fever." She moved the broom over the floor, and the *whoosh* of the bristles was barely audible above the rain.

Barbie frowned. "I am going to have to speak to Jacob Ebersol's father. He was out of control again today, and that's three days in a row. I can't tolerate that behavior."

"I understand." *He seems to be following in the footsteps of his older brother, Mahlon.* Lydia waved toward the door. "You should go ahead home. I'll finish cleaning up."

Barbie raised an eyebrow. "Are you certain? It's raining pretty hard. We should probably both head out before the roads start to flood. It will be a muddy mess when you walk home."

"I have an umbrella," Lydia said. "I won't melt in the rain. Go ahead and go, Barbie. I'll be fine."

"Fine, fine." Barbie pulled her sweater on over her blue frock. She gestured toward a nearby bucket into which water steadily dripped. "Remind me to tell the school board we need a new roof."

"I will," Lydia said. "The sooner they know, the sooner they can put it in the budget. Maybe they can even get it repaired in the first part of summer."

"I hope so," Barbie said, buttoning her sweater. "It's going to be raining inside if it gets much worse. Well, I better get out there and start my walk home. Be careful. I'll see you Monday."

"You be careful in the rain too," Lydia said while pushing the broom toward the front of the room. "*Geb acht uff dich.*"

"You too." Barbie pushed the door open, and the rain sprayed into the schoolhouse. "*Ach*," she said. "It's going to be a wet walk home!"

Lydia grimaced. "I hope it slows down some."

"I'm going to make a run for it," Barbie called. "Good-bye!" She disappeared out into the weather, slamming the door behind her.

Lydia continued to sweep. The rain beating above her seemed to represent her emotions. Aside from her frustrations with the children, she'd also been in a wretched mood after seeing her father break down in tears last night while talking with Titus about Ruthie. In her whole life, Lydia had never seen her father cry. The scene, which she'd witnessed in secret from the hallway outside of Titus's room, was just too much for Lydia to bear.

A rumble of thunder sounded in the distance, and Lydia decided she needed to get home before the storm worsened.

She stowed the broom and snuffed out the lanterns. After pulling on her sweater, she fished out her keys and umbrella from her tote bag and then hefted the bag onto her shoulder. She stepped out into the blowing rain and locked the schoolhouse door as the wind blew her skirt around her legs.

Lydia opened the umbrella and tried to hold it straight despite the angry wind. She lost her footing and began to slip down the steps, but she righted herself before falling down.

Biting her lower lip, Lydia started down the rock path toward the road. The cool raindrops sprayed her tights and the puddles soaked her black sneakers. She moved slowly down the road, gripping the umbrella with two hands while balancing the tote bag on her shoulder. The rain pounded the umbrella while the wind battled to blow it out of her hands. With the rumbling thunder growing louder above her, she pushed on through the storm, dodging muddy puddles as she headed down the road toward her home.

Lydia was nearly a block from her driveway when a gust of wind turned her umbrella inside out and knocked her backward. She tried to right herself, but instead, she tripped over a rock, stumbled back, and landed on her backside in a cold, muddy puddle. Her tote bag blew off her shoulder and splashed into the puddle beside her.

With tears filling her eyes, Lydia stood and stared down at the bag and her books floating in the mud.

Can this day possibly get any worse?

She heard the loud rumble of a car beside her, but Lydia kept her focus on collecting her wet and muddy papers and books that had escaped the protection of her tote bag. She heard a car door slam and she inwardly groaned, hoping no one had stopped to gawk at her.

"Can I give you a hand?" a voice asked.

Turning around, Lydia found Tristan giving her a concerned look. "Tristan," she said. "What are you doing here?"

"I was just passing by and I saw you." He picked up the rest of her books and motioned toward the car. "How about we continue this conversation in the warm, dry car?"

A flash of lightning lit up the sky before a loud crack of thunder sounded above her. Lydia jumped with a start.

"Come on," Tristan said, taking her arm and tugging her gently toward the waiting vehicle. "Before you get pneumonia or hit by lightning."

She climbed into the front seat of the two-door vehicle. Although she didn't know anything about cars, she guessed it was an older model due to the fading of the seat covers and dashboard. The engine boomed over the noisy racket of music blaring through the speakers.

Shivering from the cold, Lydia settled into the seat and smoothed her soaked dress over her legs.

Tristan climbed in next to her and turned off the radio. Glancing over, he frowned. "You're freezing."

"No," she said, her voice trembling along with her legs. "I'm fine."

He shook his head. "You're a terrible liar." He hit a few buttons on the dashboard and heat blasted at her through the vents. "How's that?"

"Much better." She crossed her arms over her chest. "I'm thankful that you came along when you did."

"Me too." Tristan put the car in gear and rolled forward through the pounding rain. The windshield wipers whooshed back and forth in a gentle cadence, barely keeping up with the drops. "Like my new ride?" He tapped the dash. "I got my license, and my dad got his old car running for me."

"Congratulations," she said. "It's wonderful that you passed the driver's test."

"Thanks." Tristan smiled. "How are you, aside from wet and cold?"

Lydia's lips trembled as all of the emotion she'd been holding inside came bubbling forth without warning. She sucked in a breath, trying in vain to stop herself from crying in front of him.

"Hey," he said, reaching over and touching her hand. "It's okay."

"I'm sorry," she whispered, wiping her cheeks. "It's just been a bad day. A really, really bad day."

He steered into her driveway and stopped the car. "Do you want to talk about it?"

"It's just ..." she began. "It's just everything." She sniffed and wiped her cheek. "I'm overwhelmed, and sometimes it feels like too much."

"I can understand that. You're going through a lot. I don't know how I could carry a load like yours."

Lydia studied his expression and found genuine concern and empathy. She wanted to tell him everything. She longed to share how seeing her father fall apart last night was too much and how she was exhausted from praying, worrying, and crying most of the night. But she couldn't form the words. Instead of speaking, she just nodded.

"My girlfriend, Lexi, always tells me that even when you feel all alone, you're not," he continued. "God is always there with us, even through the bad times."

"I know," Lydia said softly. "But sometimes I feel so alone I don't think I can stand it. All this pressure is overwhelming. I'm working two jobs, I'm acting as mother to my brother and sister, I'm keeping the household running, I've witnessed my father falling apart, and I'm exhausted. It's all just too much. It's just not fair that I have to handle all of this. Why do I always have to be the strong one in my family?"

"I'm sorry you have so much stress in your life. I can't even begin to imagine how difficult that is for you." He gave her a hopeful look. "But you're not alone. If you ever need a friend to talk to, don't hesitate to come find me." He tapped the steering wheel. "Now that I have a set of wheels, maybe we can go out for ice cream or something and get you away from it all—if your father says it's okay, of course."

She couldn't help but smile. "That would be nice."

He steered the car up the driveway and stopped in front of the porch. "I hope your evening gets better."

"Thank you," she said as she gathered up her drenched bag. "I appreciate the ride very much."

"Anytime," he said. "Take care."

"You too." Lydia hopped out of the car and trotted up the porch steps. When she reached the top of the steps, she waved as Tristan's loud car rattled back down the driveway toward the road. As he drove off, Lydia smiled while marveling at the deep faith Tristan seemed to have. She was so glad to have him as a friend. It was nice to not feel so alone for once.

The door opened, and her aunt Kathryn came out to the porch, looking in confusion at the car. "Who was that?"

"My *freind*," Lydia said, hoisting her bag on her shoulder and moving toward the door. "He rescued me from a mud puddle."

"He?" Kathryn asked. "Mud puddle? Lydia, what are you talking about?"

Lydia shivered as the wind blew through her soaked sweater. "Can we please discuss this inside? I'm drenched and cold."

"*Ach*, of course," Kathryn said, holding the door open for her. "You poor thing. You're shivering. Step inside and get out of this horrendous weather."

"*Danki*." As Lydia entered the house, the warm aroma of chicken potpie filled her senses, and she was thankful for her aunt's generous help with dinner after the long day. Irma and Titus looked up from reading books at the table and looked surprised by Lydia's appearance.

"What happened to you?" Irma asked, her blue eyes wide.

"You look like you fell in a pond," Titus chimed in with a toothy grin.

Lydia dropped her soaked bag on the floor with a thump and then peeled off her wet sweater. "I fell into a puddle, not a pond."

"It must've been a mighty big puddle," Titus said, and Irma cackled in response.

"Go wash up for supper," Kathryn ordered. "I need to speak with Lydia." Her expression was stern when she turned, and apprehension filled Lydia. She knew what was coming: another lecture about how inappropriate her friendship with Tristan was. She couldn't bear more stress today. "Could I possibly take a quick shower before we talk?" she asked, hoping to dodge the discussion.

"No," Kathryn said simply. "Let's talk now." She moved toward the table. "Have a seat."

Lydia held back a sigh and dropped into a chair across the table from her aunt.

Kathryn opened her mouth to speak, but stopped when Irma appeared holding a bath towel.

"Here you go, Lydia," Irma said with a smile.

"*Danki*," Lydia said, taking the towel and wrapping it around her shoulders.

"*Danki*, Irma," Kathryn said. "Now go wash up and then wait in your room until I call you. Please tell Titus to do the same."

"*Ya, Aenti*," Irma said before disappearing through the doorway.

"Now let's talk," Kathryn began as she lowered herself into the chair and stared at Lydia. "Who is this *bu* who drove you home?"

"He's a *freind*." She rubbed the towel over her arms. "He lives up the street. His family just moved into the Fitzgerald place a few weeks ago."

"He's *English*?"

"*Ya*," Lydia said. "His father is going to teach at a nearby university."

Kathryn frowned with disapproval. "Lydia, as the teacher's assistant you have a very important job."

"I know." Lydia ran the towel over her wet tights. "He's a nice Christian *bu*. Each time we talk, we discuss God. He's not a bad influence, and he doesn't have bad intentions."

"He may be a nice *bu*, but you have to consider how this looks to others. The parents look to you to set the example for their children. They would frown upon it if they saw you in a car with an *English bu*." She waved her arms as she talked. "And the school board would probably fire you. At least, they wouldn't approve of your becoming the teacher. We all know Barbie will most likely get engaged soon and then get married in the fall during the wedding season."

"He's just a *freind*," Lydia said, even though she knew it wouldn't help her case.

"That's fine if you see him on the street and you wave," Kathryn said, tapping her finger on the table for emphasis. "But riding in his car, especially alone, is something else entirely. I know that you're a *gut* girl, but still others' perception can be skewed to something that you don't want for yourself or for your family." She touched Lydia's hand, and her expression softened. "You understand, *ya*?"

Lydia gave a reluctant nod while hugging the towel close to her body. "*Ya*, I do."

"*Gut*." Kathryn popped up from the table. "Let's get out the dishes."

"*Ach*," Lydia said. "I'm soaked, remember?"

Kathryn chuckled. "That's right. Go get changed. Take a quick shower if you'd like. Please send Irma and Titus down to help set the table."

"*Danki*," Lydia said as she headed for the door. "And *danki* for supper. It smells *wunderbaar gut*."

"*Gern gschehne*," Kathryn responded while pulling dishes from the cabinet. "Go get warmed up and dry so you can eat."

While she stood in the doorway, Lydia's thoughts turned to Amanda and how rude she'd been to her Monday night. She faced her aunt and bit her bottom lip as guilt rained down on her once again. "*Aenti* Kathryn," she began. "How's Amanda?"

Kathryn looked confused at Lydia's tone. "Fine. Why do you ask?"

Lydia ran her finger over the doorway. "I've just been thinking of her."

"Oh." Kathryn smiled. "You can ask her how she is when she picks me up in a little bit. Go take your shower now."

"Okay." Lydia hurried up the stairs, gathered her clothes, and rushed back downstairs to the full bathroom, which was located off the kitchen. When she stepped into the shower, she allowed the warm water to soak her skin, and she wished the water would wash away all of her worry, frustration, and sorrow. Oh, how she wished her baby sister was well and that she and their mother were back home. She was so exhausted that her body ached. Her eyes felt like they were burning with exhaustion. What was even more frustrating was that she'd found a new friend, but she was forbidden to see him. She wished that her family would accept Tristan as her friend.

Closing her eyes, she stood under the water and silently asked God to restore her life to the way it used to be before Ruthie became ill.

cʒ

After supper, Lydia walked Kathryn outside to meet the waiting buggy. "*Danki* again for cleaning the house. Thank you also for making supper," Lydia said. "It was *appeditlich*."

"*Gern gschehne*," Kathryn said, opening the passenger side door.

Lydia walked around to Amanda, who sat in the driver's seat. "*Wie geht's?*" she asked.

"Fine," Amanda said without smiling. "How are you, Lydia?" The question was flat and void of emotion, just as she had sounded before.

Lydia looked at her aunt. "Could Amanda and I talk for a moment on the porch? I'll be sure to keep it quick."

"*Ya.* Just don't be too long," Kathryn said. "We have chores to complete at home."

Amanda handed her mother the reins and followed Lydia to the porch. Pushing the ribbons from her prayer covering behind her slight shoulders, she studied Lydia. "What do you want?"

Lydia took a deep breath and prayed that her words would be right. "I want to apologize. I'm very sorry for how I treated you." Her words trembled with her anxiety and guilt. "You're my best friend, and you're always there when I need someone to listen. I was horrible to you, and I hope you can find it in your heart to forgive me. Please."

Amanda's expression softened. "You know that I love you, and I would never do anything to hurt you."

"I know." Lydia blew out a sigh.

"Nancy and I would never, ever try to make you feel bad for missing youth gatherings." Amanda touched Lydia's hand. "We miss you when you're not there. I do, especially since I don't have a *bu* to spend time with."

"I should've thought before I lashed out at you," Lydia said. "I was just upset, and I took it out on you. It was wrong. You're the last person who deserves to be yelled at, because you're always thoughtful and considerate."

Amanda smiled. "I forgive you, but don't do it again." She hugged Lydia and patted her back. "I need to run, but we'll talk tomorrow at the bakery, *ya?*"

"*Ya,*" Lydia said. "*Danki.*"

"Amanda," Kathryn called. "We have to go or your *daed* is going to be upset with me."

"See you tomorrow," Amanda called as she hurried down the porch steps toward the buggy. "*Gut nacht.*"

"*Gut nacht.*" Lydia waved as they drove off, and she felt as if a small weight had been lifted from her shoulders.

12

The following Tuesday, Lydia iced a chocolate cake while her aunt Kathryn stood beside her. *"Wunderbaar gut,* Lydia. That's perfect."

"Danki." Lydia smiled.

The past week had flown by quickly, and she had found some peace ever since she'd prayed in the shower the night she'd fallen in the mud and accepted a ride home with Tristan. Even her visit with her mother and Ruthie had gone better than the previous one. Ruthie had smiled and laughed with Lydia and their siblings, and her mother seemed confident when she said the treatments were going well. When Lydia talked to her last night, her mother again sounded upbeat and positive, which lifted another worry from Lydia's mind.

Lydia believed God was carrying her and the rest of her family members. He was there for her, just like Tristan had said.

"I think that's your best chocolate cake yet." Her aunt lifted a knife from the counter. *"Ach,* I'm hesitant to cut it. It's so *schee* that I think we could sell it as a whole cake."

"I agree," Nancy chimed in while crossing the large

kitchen. "I think a customer would snatch that up. It would be perfect to take to a party."

"I agree," Amanda said. "It's perfect."

"*Danki.*" Lydia said.

"Let me help you put it in a box," Nancy offered, grabbing a cake box from the shelf behind the counter.

"You girls take care of the cake," Kathryn said. "I'm going to go check out front to see if we need to restock any of the peanut butter and oatmeal cookies. They've been disappearing quickly lately."

Nancy brought the box over and began folding it. "I bet this cake will sell quickly. You should start on another one."

Lydia laughed. "You're flattering me too much, Nancy."

Amanda sidled up to them. "You seem happier, Lydia. It's *gut* to see you smile again."

"*Ya,*" Lydia said. "I've been feeling better lately."

"That's *wunderbaar gut!*" Nancy said. "I was wondering if maybe your *dat* would let you come to the youth gathering Sunday night if things are looking up. It's been too long since you've been out with us."

Lydia gently lifted the cake and set it in the box, careful not to smudge the icing. The sweet aroma of the chocolate caused her stomach to gurgle. "I really don't know. I sort of feel guilty for asking."

Amanda touched her shoulder. "I think he would understand that you miss your friends. He was young once too. Didn't your parents meet at a singing?"

Lydia nodded and thought about her fantasy of riding home with Joshua. In her dream, he would tell her that he had a nice time and then ask if he could kiss her. She closed the box and looked up at Amanda. "Did Joshua make it to the last few youth gatherings?"

Amanda hesitated and shared a strange look with Nancy.

"What?" Lydia asked, feeling like she could be sick. "What did that look mean?"

"Nothing." Amanda frowned. "*Ya*, he's been there."

"Why do you say it like that?" Lydia looked at her with suspicion. "What are you keeping from me, Amanda? We never keep secrets, *ya*?"

"He's been there," Nancy chimed in. "I'll tell you the truth."

"Tell me what truth?" Lydia threw up her hands. "Would you please just tell me?"

"We've seen him talking to a girl," Nancy said slowly.

"Who is the girl?"

"She's someone from another district," Amanda said. "I think she's from Gordonville. Her name is Mary."

Lydia couldn't help feeling sick. "Oh."

Amanda touched Lydia's hand. "You should come Sunday night. You can get his eye off the other girl."

Shaking her head, Lydia lifted the box. "It's okay. It's just not meant to be." She started toward the front of the store with her cousins trailing after her.

"Don't say that!" Nancy insisted. "I bet he'd ask you out if you showed more interest."

"No, he wouldn't." Lydia stopped at the doorway to the front of the bakery and faced their empathetic expressions. "He told me a week ago that he'd stop by to see me, and he hasn't. If he were interested in me, he would've shown it by now."

"Maybe you can make him jealous," Amanda offered. "Mahlon has been asking about you at youth gatherings and I saw him talking to you at church last week. He seems to like you. Maybe if you came to a youth gathering and talked to him, Josh would see you together and realize how much he loves you."

Lydia glowered at Amanda. "You can't possibly be serious."

Nancy shrugged. "It might work."

"I don't have time for this," Lydia said, turning toward the counter filled with pastries for sale. "I have more important things to do than playing silly games, especially ones concerning Mahlon. If Joshua doesn't care, then so be it." Although the words were simple to say, their meaning stabbed at her heart. In truth, she wished he'd come by to see her. She missed him. Spending time with him could help ease some of the stress she'd been facing.

"You can't let go," Amanda said, her blue eyes filled with sadness. "He's always been meant for you."

Lydia shook her head. "Apparently not."

"Maybe you should talk to him," Nancy offered with a gentle expression on her face. "Ask him if he likes this other girl and where you stand in your relationship."

Lydia gasped. "That would be so forward."

"Hint around it then," Nancy said with a shrug. "See if you can say it without saying it."

"Girls," Kathryn called. "I need you back in the kitchen, please. We need some more peanut butter and oatmeal cookies. No more chatting for now."

Walking back to the kitchen, Lydia silently vowed to try to talk to Joshua on Sunday and find out if he was dating the mysterious girl from Gordonville.

C3

Later that evening, while putting Irma to bed, Lydia was still pondering the possibility that Joshua liked another girl.

She tried to smile while she and Irma knelt by the bed for prayers, but instead she grimaced.

When Irma was finished praying, she climbed into bed and studied Lydia's expression. "You're sad tonight, Lydia. Are you thinking of *Mamm* and Ruthie?"

Lydia shook her head. "Actually, I was thinking about something else. I try not to be sad when I think about *Mamm* and Ruthie. Instead, I try to think thoughts that are *froh*."

"You think about them coming home?" Irma hugged her cloth doll close to her chest. "I try to think about that every day."

Lydia brushed a lock of hair back from Irma's face. "I try to think about that too."

"When do you miss *Mamm* and Ruthie the most?" Irma asked.

Taking a deep breath, Lydia exhaled and stared at the plain white walls while she considered the question. "I guess I miss them the most at bedtime, because that's when I get the time to slow down. When I'm working or when I'm making supper, I don't have time to think about them. But when it's time for prayers, I have too much time to think about them."

"That makes sense. That's when I miss them the most too." Irma tilted her head. "Do you think Ruthie knows we pray for her every night?"

"*Ya*." Lydia said. "She's heard us pray for other people. When we have devotions with *Dat*, he always asks us who we're praying for, right? I'm certain she would know that we pray for her." She touched Irma's hand. "Now, it's time to sleep. No more talking, okay?"

Irma scowled. "You need to tell me why you're sad."

Lydia studied Irma's determined expression. How could she tell her little sister she was sad because she thought

Joshua was in love with another girl? How could her seven-year-old sister possibly understand that? "I'm not sad."

"*Ya*, you are," Irma said with emphasis. "Your eyebrows are pointed down when you're upset. Something has you worried."

She studied Irma's colorful quilt and considered her answer. "I'm upset about something very *gegisch*."

"What?" Irma's eyes rounded with interest. "Is it a secret? If it is, I promise I won't tell anyone, not even my best friend, Lillian."

"*Ya*, it sort of is a secret." Lydia couldn't help but smile at her sister's interest. She imagined that even at the age of seven, the girls liked to share secrets on the playground. "I heard something about a *bu* today that sort of made me angry."

"About a *bu*?" Irma scrunched her nose. "Which *bu*? Was it Joshua?"

Lydia chuckled. "You, Irma, are very perceptive."

"What does that mean?"

"That means you notice things." Lydia brushed back more of Irma's hair. "Nancy and Amanda told me they think Joshua likes a girl who lives in Gordonville."

"Oh." Irma frowned. "You're upset because you wanted him to like you, *ya*?"

"*Ya*," Lydia said. "But it's okay if he likes her. I guess I'm not meant to be his girlfriend if he chooses another, right?" She hoped she could convince herself to believe those words. "Maybe I'll meet another *bu* after Ruthie is well and I can go back to the youth gatherings. I'm young, right? It's not like I'm going to get married tomorrow. In fact, I'm not even baptized, so I can't really date. Why am I even worried about this?" She stopped talking when she realized she was rambling and only trying to convince herself that she shouldn't be upset about Joshua and the mysterious Mary.

"You want to marry Joshua?" Irma's mouth gaped. "Does he know?"

"No, he doesn't know." Lydia suddenly felt silly for sharing so much with her sister. Yet, it was a relief to get this off her chest and out in the open. "Listen, everything I told you is a secret. Please don't tell anyone, not even Lillian."

Irma looked serious. "I promise."

"*Danki. Gut nacht.*" Leaning over, she kissed Irma's forehead. "Sleep well. I'll see you in the morning." She stood and headed for the door.

"Lydia," Irma called. "I don't think Joshua loves that other *maedel.*"

"Why?" Lydia asked, leaning against the open door.

"Because I see him smile at you a lot," Irma said with a serious expression. "If he loved that other girl, he wouldn't smile at you so much. Lillian says that *buwe* only smile at girls they like. If they frown at you, then they don't like you."

Lydia couldn't stop a smile from turning up her lips. "You're right, Irma. They don't smile at girls they don't like."

Irma continued to look serious. "Have you ever thought about asking him if he likes you?"

"I don't know if I could do that," Lydia said. "*Mamm* says girls shouldn't be forward. It can give the wrong impression."

Irma shrugged. "It's just a question, *ya?*"

"*Ya,*" Lydia said. "It is." *But I could never ask it.* "*Gut nacht,*" she repeated.

"*Gut nacht,*" Irma said. "I'm glad you're here to take care of me and Titus while *Mamm* is gone. I miss her, but I really like talking to you."

An overwhelming feeling of love mixed with hope swelled

in Lydia's heart. "*Danki*," she said softly, as her voice quaked with emotion. "That's really, really nice. That makes me *froh* to hear you say that. Now, get to sleep."

"Okay," Irma said with a grin. "And your secret is safe with me." She then stuck her thumb in her mouth, closed her eyes, and rolled to her side while hugging her doll close.

13

"Can you possibly come in tomorrow and help with the class art projects?" Barbie asked as she packed up her bag the following day. "I could use an extra set of hands with the cutting and gluing."

"Of course," Lydia said, following her toward the schoolhouse door. "I can leave a message at the bakery tonight. My aunt has asked a few more bakers to come in and help us since we've been short staffed without my *mammi*. Since we're getting more help, I'm certain it will be fine for me to work here tomorrow."

Barbie pushed the door open. "*Danki*. I appreciate your—" She paused, and her expression turned to concern. "May I help you?" she asked, her voice filled with anxiety.

Lydia stood on tiptoe to see past her and saw Tristan sauntering up the rock path. "Tristan!" She waved, and he smiled in response. "I didn't expect to see you here."

"Hi, Lydia," he called as he approached the steps. "I thought I'd stop by and see if you were around. I got out of school early today." He looked at Barbie and held out his hand. "I'm Tristan Anderson. I recently moved here from New Jersey."

Silently, Barbie marched down the stairs and past him. Turning back toward the school, she shot Lydia a disapproving look. "It's time to go home, Lydia."

"I know," Lydia said. "How are you doing, Tristan?" She gave him a nervous smile.

"Fine," he said. "I was wondering if I could get that tour of the schoolhouse you promised me."

"Oh." Lydia looked at Barbie, who shook her head and continued to look concerned. "I'm going to give Tristan a quick tour. He's interested in seeing one of our schools since he's grown up in public *English* schools."

"I don't think that would be wise," Barbie said, hefting her bag farther up on her shoulder. "It's getting late. Isn't your *aenti* waiting for you to get home and take over with the *kinner*?"

"I'll make it quick," Lydia said, stepping back into the school. "Come on in, Tristan."

"Don't forget," Barbie called. "I need you here tomorrow."

"Okay," Lydia called. "Good night, Barbie." She led Tristan into the school. "This is our exciting school," she joked. "You can see it's just one room with a lot of desks, books, and a blackboard."

"Wow," Tristan said, stepping through the doorframe and glancing around the room. "It really is one room. Are you sure it's okay if I come in?"

"Of course it is." Lydia looked back out the door to find Barbie shaking her head and scowling at Lydia before walking back down the path. Lydia tried to ignore the uncomfortable feeling surging through her as she turned toward Tristan, who was standing in front of the blackboard and studying the math problems the students had worked on earlier. She dropped her bag by the door.

"This is incredible," he said, rubbing his chin. "You don't see an old-fashioned blackboard and chalk anymore."

"Old-fashioned?" Lydia stood beside him. "How is a chalkboard old-fashioned?"

"You don't see them in schools anymore," he explained. "My mom worked as a teacher's assistant in an elementary school last year, and every classroom there had those dry-erase boards."

Lydia shrugged. "I don't know what that means."

"It's where you write on it with special pens and then you wipe it off with an eraser, kinda like these." Tristan picked up the eraser from the little shelf below the chalkboard and held it in front of him. "You just wipe it off." He scrunched his nose. "The only disadvantage to those boards is that the pens smell awful. Sometimes they'll make you cough."

Lydia smiled at his exaggerated expression. "I've been known to cough from a dust cloud caused by the chalk, so it may be much the same."

He smiled. "I would imagine so." He gestured toward the chalkboard. "In the more high-tech classrooms, I've seen a board that's called a Smart Board."

"Smart Board?" Lydia crossed her arms. "Does it teach the class their math problems and correct their school work?"

Tristan rubbed his chin, pretending to consider the question. "No, I don't think they're quite *that* smart, but I believe the experts are working on the technology."

Lydia grinned. "So then what makes the board so smart?"

He pointed at the chalkboard as if it were the technologically advanced device he explained. "A Smart Board looks like a dry erase board, but it's really almost like a computer screen. It can be hooked up to a computer and then act like a keyboard, where you go to Internet pages. It's really cool. We had one at my high school last year. I used to wonder how the principal decided which teacher was important enough to get the hi-tech screen while the others only had dry erase boards."

"Wow." Lydia shook her head. "It seems to me like the new kinds of boards are just a waste of money when they do the same thing the chalkboard does. Why do you need to use it like a computer when you can simply write on the board and erase it when you're finished?"

"Very true."

She made a sweeping gesture toward the desks. "I assume the desks look the same in an *English* classroom?"

Tristan stepped toward the rows. "They are. Do the children sit in rows according to their grade like on *Little House on the Prairie?*"

"Yes." Lydia leaned back against Barbie's desk at the front of the room. "They do, with first grade in the front and the seventh graders in the back. We don't have kindergarten in our schools. The eighth graders sort of do an apprenticeship where they work in the community or at home and keep a journal of what they've learned. They only come in about once a week, depending on where they work and their schedules."

"That's fascinating." Tristan walked along the rows, studying them.

"You'll graduate next year, right?" Lydia asked.

"That's right," he said with a clap. "I can't wait."

"What will you do then?"

"I want to go to college. I may even follow in the family business, so to speak, and become a teacher, but I'm not sure yet. Hopefully, I'll figure it out when I'm at college."

"Will Lexi go to college too?" she asked.

"Yeah," he said. "We're going to apply to the same schools."

"That's wonderful."

He met her gaze. "How about you?"

Lydia fiddled with the ties of her prayer covering. "I'm not sure. I may see about becoming a full-time teacher or I may work in the bakery full time."

He grinned. "So you may follow in the family business too, huh?"

"I might." Lydia pushed her foot over the wooden floor. "I'm not certain quite yet."

Tristan looked around the classroom again. "Tell me something. How do you keep the other kids quiet when you're teaching one grade?"

"The children are mostly well behaved," Lydia said, hopping up and sitting on the corner of Barbie's desk. "Amish children have a very strict upbringing, and they know there will be serious consequences if they don't behave."

He looked impressed.

"For the most part, they all listen and are quiet when they need to be." She smoothed her skirt over her legs. "If they aren't doing what they're supposed to, then we warn them. Occasionally someone has to sit in the corner. If that doesn't work, the child knows we'll tell their father, which is the ultimate punishment."

"Wow." Tristan lowered himself onto a desk. "Have you had to do that?"

Lydia nodded. "We've had a couple of incidents with a few rowdy boys, but it's not very often. And usually it only happens once, if you know what I mean."

"Not many repeat offenders, huh?" He shook his head. "You wouldn't believe the behavior issues in my last high school. Some of the incidents were pretty violent."

"This is a different environment, a different culture. Comparing the two would be like comparing apples and oranges."

"I guess so." He glanced at the ticking clock on the wall. "I suppose I'd better let you go home. Barbie said your aunt is waiting for you?"

Lydia grabbed the handle of her tote bag and placed it on her shoulder. "My aunts and some other friends in the community have been helping us while my mother is gone with my baby sister. They help me cook, clean, and do the laundry."

"That's very nice." He started toward the door. "Your community truly helps one another."

"Yes, they do." She waited until he stepped through the doorway and then she followed, closed the door, and locked it. "We're very blessed to have so much help. It would be really difficult for me to do it all and do it well." Lydia followed him down the stairs.

"I've heard about those barn raisings," he said. "Have you been to one?"

"Oh yes, I have," Lydia said. "My grandfather's furniture store burned down a few years ago, and my father was one of the men who helped to rebuild it. We always help our friends and family members, and it's comforting to know that someone will always be there to help, especially when you need it most."

"It's really nice how all of your family is nearby," he said as they walked down the rock pathway toward the road. "My mom's family is in Florida, and my dad's is all over the United States—New Jersey, California, Maine, and some are even in Texas."

"Wow," Lydia said. "I guess you don't have family reunions often, *ya*?"

"No," he said, shaking his head. "I don't remember ever having one, really. We've visited some relatives, but I've never been to California to see my uncle."

"That's sad," Lydia said, adjusting her bag on her shoulder. "Does your uncle have children?"

"Yeah." Tristan pulled a pair of sunglasses from his pocket and slipped them on his face. "He has three sons I've never met. One is about my age."

"That's really sad," Lydia said. "My cousin Amanda is my best friend. I can't imagine not having her in my life." She adjusted the bag again.

"Is that heavy?" he asked. "Can I carry it for you?"

"No, thank you," she said. "I'm fine. Where's your car?"

He motioned toward his house as they walked past it. "I left it in the driveway. I thought I would walk over to the schoolhouse to see if you were still there." His happy countenance faded a little. "I guess I came at a bad time, huh?"

"You mean because of Barbie?" she asked.

"Yeah." He ran his fingers through his messy hair. "She wasn't too happy to meet me."

She frowned. "I'm sorry about Barbie. She's really a nice person, but not everyone is supportive of an Amish girl's being friends with an *Englisher*."

"An *Englisher*?" He laughed a little. "I've been called a lot of things but never that."

"Lydia!" A little voice hollered. "Wait up! Don't leave!" Michaela bounded down her driveway.

"Hi, Michaela," Lydia said as the little girl approached.

The little girl wrapped her arms around Lydia's waist. "I've missed you."

Lydia smiled down at her. "I've missed you too. We'll have to visit again soon."

"Lydia has to get home to her brother and sister," Tristan said. "We have to let her go for now, but maybe we'll visit again soon."

Michaela looked at Lydia with disappointment. "Oh. Bye, Lydia."

"Good-bye," Lydia said. "Give Bitsy a hug for me."

"Okay," Michaela said with a smile. "I promise I will."

"Good." Lydia turned to Tristan. "It was nice seeing you. Please tell your parents hello for me."

"I will," he said. "Thanks for the tour."

"You're welcome," Lydia said before starting back down the road toward her house.

Glancing toward the house where Barbie's aunt Deborah lived, she saw Barbie standing on the porch and talking to her aunt. As Lydia passed the house, she waved. While Barbie's aunt returned the wave, Barbie simply frowned. Lydia felt the muscles in her shoulders and neck tightening up with worry.

Walking up her driveway, Lydia wondered how long it would take for news of her schoolhouse tour to travel through the community, and what the repercussions would be.

☙

"I'd like to speak with you after school," Barbie whispered to Lydia as the children packed up their supplies at the end of the following day. "It's regarding what happened here yesterday."

Lydia swallowed a sigh as Barbie moved to the door and dismissed the children.

"We'll see you at home!" Irma passed by Lydia as she headed to the door. "*Gut nacht*, Barbie!"

"*Gut nacht*, Irma," Barbie said with a forced smile. While

Barbie said good-bye to each child as they left, Lydia began straightening up books and the desks that were no longer in a row. She was grabbing the broom when Barbie stepped back into the classroom.

"I'm very disappointed in you, Lydia," Barbie began. "It was inappropriate for you to have that *English bu* in this schoolhouse yesterday, especially since you were alone with him."

Lydia leaned on the broom. "Barbie, I know that it may have looked bad, but we're just friends."

"So you say." Barbie gestured with emphasis as she moved to the front of the classroom. "If the parents or the school board had been here and witnessed your taking an *Englisher* into this schoolhouse without a chaperone, they would have assumed you have loose morals and you are not the best role model for their children."

Not this discussion again. "I know, but—"

"There is no excuse, Lydia," Barbie continued with a stern expression. "There's nothing you could say to convince them otherwise. This behavior is no way to get the full-time teaching position."

Lydia bit her lip and stared at the toes of her black sneakers as doubt seeped through her. "What if I'm not sure about the teaching position?"

"What?" Barbie's voice was full of shock. "What did you say?"

Lydia met her confused gaze. "I said, what if I'm not certain I want the full-time teaching position?"

Barbie lowered her thin body onto one of the desks in the front row. "You can't mean that."

With a shrug, Lydia leaned the broom against the wall behind her. "I'm just not sure what I want to do. I like teaching just fine, but I also love working in the bakery. What if I want to work full time with my *mammi, aentis,* and cousins instead of teaching full time?"

"You're talking *narrisch* now," Barbie insisted. "You're meant to be the teacher. The scholars love you, and the school board is *froh* with your work. You would be ignoring God's call if you chose to work in the bakery instead of teaching here."

Lydia shook her head. "I don't feel God's call."

"Are you listening to your own words, Lydia?" Barbie stood up and spread her arms wide. "I'm very disappointed that you would consider not following me in this classroom. I've already heard the school board say they would seriously consider you. You belong here. This is what God wants for you. You need to serve the community here, not in the bakery. Your *mammi* has plenty of bakers."

Lydia studied Barbie's disappointed face and guilt surged through her, replacing the doubt. "How do you know I belong here?"

Barbie smiled. "Because you're very *gut* at teaching. You're a *gut* baker, but there are plenty of *gut* bakers around. We don't have many teachers. It would only make sense for you to replace me." She crossed the room and stood in front of Lydia, taking her hands. "You need to pray about this, and I think you'll see what I mean. We need you here. You need to remember your place, and it's not with that *English bu* with the handsome face and fast words. You belong with our people."

"You're right. I won't see him anymore."

"*Gut.*" Barbie began straightening the row of desks. "Let's get done so we can go home. It's been a long day."

Lydia grabbed the broom and began moving it back and

forth across the floor. While she knew she would miss talking with Tristan, she also believed Barbie was right. Lydia needed to focus on her community and the perception of her relationship with Tristan.

One thought kept nipping at her, however. How could an innocent friendship be wrong?

14

After the service the following Sunday, Lydia bit her bottom lip and stared across the pasture toward the boys playing volleyball. Her eyes were glued to Joshua's handsome face while he laughed and spiked the ball. He moved with a mixture of grace and masculinity, and she was mesmerized.

"Just go talk to him," Amanda muttered as if reading Lydia's thoughts. "You've been watching him so long that I'm surprised your eyes haven't fallen out of your head."

Lydia gave Amanda a playful swat. "I have not."

"*Ya*," Amanda said. "You have."

Nancy dropped onto the bench beside theirs. "What are you two talking about?" She held out a plate filled with raisin oatmeal cookies, and Amanda and Lydia each took one.

"I was just telling Lydia she needs to stop staring at Joshua and just go talk to him," Amanda said between bites of cookie.

Lydia elbowed Amanda, warning her to be quiet.

Nancy shrugged. "What's so difficult? Just go talk to him."

Lydia watched as the boys walked away from the net and started across the pasture toward the house. Joshua held the ball and tossed it up, setting it to himself while he walked and talked to a friend.

"Now is the perfect time, Lydia." Amanda looked toward the group of boys coming close to them. "Go on or I'll call him over and really embarrass you."

Lydia gasped. "You wouldn't dare."

"No, *she* wouldn't," Nancy said with a smirk. "But you know that *I* would." She stood. "Do you want me to call him over?"

"No!" Lydia gestured for her cousin to sit. "I'll go talk to him." She stood, smoothed her dress, and touched her prayer covering, hoping that she looked presentable and maybe even pretty.

Amanda and Nancy exchanged grins, and Lydia glared at them before she started toward the field where the boys were marching toward the house. As she approached the boys, Joshua glanced over, saw her, and broke off from the group. She breathed a sigh of relief when he headed in her direction. She'd dreaded having to talk to him in front of the group of boys. Although most seemed nice enough, she felt embarrassed around them.

"Hey, Lydia!" Mahlon called while waving from the other side of the field. "Missed you again last week. You need to come and hang out with the rest of us again."

Lydia's cheeks burned when Joshua looked at her with a confused expression. She kept her eyes on Joshua and hoped that Mahlon would get the hint and keep heading toward the house. She breathed a sigh of relief when she caught up to Joshua. "Josh," she said. "*Wie geht's?*"

"I'm doing fine." With a frown, he gestured in the direction of Mahlon. "He seems to always want to talk to you, *ya?* Every time I see him at church he's running after you. Why is that?"

She shrugged. "I don't know. So how are you?"

"I already said I'm fine," he repeated, tossing the ball up and down in his hands. His expression softened. "How are you?"

Lydia smiled. "I'm okay." She absently twisted one of the ribbons from her prayer cap around her finger. "Can you talk for a minute?"

"*Ya.*" He pointed toward a bench under a tree across the pasture. "Want to walk over there?"

"That sounds *gut.*" Falling in step with him, Lydia's heart fluttered. She wanted to follow Irma's advice and ask him about the girl from Gordonville, but her confidence had faded when she looked up at his smile. Why didn't she have the confidence her seven-year-old sister had? "How is your family?"

"Doing fine," Joshua said while still fiddling with the ball. "My *dat* dropped a tool and broke his toe last week, but he's doing much better. I'm glad Joey and I can help him with all the chores and take some of the load off him. We're also helping my grandfather with his farm on top of our chores." He looked at her cautiously before going on. "How are you doing? How's Ruthie?"

"I'm doing fine," she said with a shrug. "The visit with my *mamm*, Ruthie, and *Mammi* was *gut* yesterday. My *mamm* is very optimistic that the treatments are going well. Ruthie was a little weepy. She wanted to come home with us and didn't understand why she still had to stay at the hospital." A lump grew in Lydia's throat when she thought about how Ruthie had sobbed in their father's arms. She'd also seen tears in his eyes, which made the pain even worse.

"I saw your *mammi* earlier." Joshua pointed toward the house. "I guess she came home?"

"*Ya*," Lydia said. "She came back with us. My *aenti* Kathryn rode up to the hospital with us and stayed with my *mamm*. She tried to convince my *mamm* to come home and get some rest, but she couldn't leave Ruthie."

They reached the wooden bench, and Lydia lowered herself onto it.

"I can't blame her really," Lydia continued. "Ruthie is her *boppli*. How could she possibly leave her, right?" She sniffed. She hated feeling sorry for herself, but part of her wished her mother would come home.

"What's on your mind?" Joshua dropped the ball onto the ground and then sat on it while facing her. "You can tell me."

Wiping the tears that flooded her eyes, Lydia shrugged. "It's selfish and *gegisch*, but I wish my *mamm* could come home for a week to be with us. Just having her home for a few days would give me some relief from all of the pressure I have to deal with by myself."

He nodded. "I can see how you'd feel that way. You have a lot on you, and you all miss her."

Lydia smiled. "That's exactly right."

"But I think she'll be home soon." He rested his elbows on his bent knees. "You said yourself that she's optimistic, *ya*?"

She swiped her eyes with the back of her hands. "I did."

"There you have it." He smiled, and her heart turned over in her chest. "Do you think you'll be able to come back to youth gatherings again? I know that you're busy with your siblings, but maybe your *dat* would let you come every once in a while?"

She fingered the ties on her prayer covering. "I haven't asked because I've assumed he would say no, but maybe he will change his mind since things are looking up for Ruthie. I know he was *bedauerlich* to come home without her and

Mamm, but he also told me he believes they will be home soon."

"That's great news!" Joshua's expression brightened. "I'm so *froh* to hear it."

"*Danki*," Lydia said, letting her hands rest in her lap. Irma's suggestion echoed through her mind, and Lydia decided to try to broach the question of the girl in Gordonville in an indirect way. "So, you've been going to the youth gatherings?"

"I've actually made it to the last few. I missed quite a few, but I'm back." He rolled his eyes. "If I don't go, my father teases me."

"Teases you?" Lydia couldn't help but smile. "Why would he tease you?"

Joshua shrugged, and she thought she saw pink flush his cheeks. "He says I'll live with my parents forever and never marry if I don't go to the youth gatherings."

Lydia felt her own cheeks heat up. "Is that so?"

He gave a laugh that almost sounded nervous. "I told him I don't need to go to youth gatherings to find a *fraa*."

She swallowed, and her stomach fluttered. She wondered if he was referring to her or the girl from Gordonville, but she was too nervous to ask.

"I hope you can come back to the gatherings," he said. "I miss seeing you there with your cousins."

"I'll see what my *dat* says about it," she said, her voice a trembling whisper.

His expression darkened slightly. "I heard you have an *Englisher* friend."

Oh no! Lydia swallowed a gasp, remembering how Barbie had glared at her from Deborah's porch the day she gave Tristan a tour of the school. "Who mentioned that to you?"

He frowned. "So it's true?"

Lydia paused and glanced toward the house, wondering if Barbie or her aunt Deborah had told the community about Tristan. Or perhaps Deborah had told someone, and the rumor had spread through a quilting bee.

Lydia took a deep breath, mustering all the confidence she could find deep within herself. She was going to answer this question and give Joshua the whole truth, despite how her hands trembled in her lap.

"I'm not certain what you heard, but the truth is that I've become acquainted with a neighbor and his family, and they happen to be *English*. I consider him and his family *freinden*, and that's it." She studied his face, wondering if he was jealous or envious, but she couldn't read anything into his blank expression.

"How did you meet him?" he asked as he moved off the ball and sat beside it on the grass.

"I was walking by his *haus* the day he was moving in, and his little sister ran out to greet me while chasing her dog." Lydia smiled as she thought of Michaela and Bitsy. "Since then, I've taken pastries to their *haus* to introduce myself and my siblings, and Tristan has stopped by to see me a couple of times."

"Tristan?" Joshua looked confused. "That's his name?"

"*Ya*, he's Tristan, and his sister is Michaela."

"Those are unusual names." He lifted the ball and dropped it in his lap. "You like him?" The question was cautious.

"He's a *gut freind*," Lydia said simply. "He's easy to talk to."

He raised an eyebrow with curiosity. "Easier to talk to than your Amish *freinden*?"

Why would he make that assumption? She shook her head with annoyance. What rumors were spreading about her and

Tristan? She opened her mouth to answer but was cut off by a bellow from across the field.

"Joshua!" Mahlon shouted while standing by the volleyball net. "You need to give back the ball!"

Joshua stood. "I guess I'd better go. They may come for the ball and it could get ugly. You don't keep these *buwe* from their volleyball games."

Lydia rose and walked with him as he started toward the makeshift volleyball court. She wanted to defend her relationship with Tristan, but the opportunity was gone.

When they reached the outskirts of the volleyball court, Joshua gave her a smile. "Hopefully I'll see you tonight."

Lydia's pulse skittered. "I hope so." As he ran off, she contemplated all the questions he'd asked about Tristan. She wondered if Joshua was jealous of Tristan or if he was worried about her reputation. No matter the reason, Lydia knew one thing: she was intrigued by his interest.

☙

"Please, *Dat*," Lydia said, her voice a high-pitched whine. "Can't I go tonight?"

Dat shook his head, his face remaining a scowl. "No. I need you home."

"But why?" Lydia asked while standing in front of his favorite chair, where he sat every night after supper. "The kitchen is cleaned up, and the *kinner* are getting their baths." She glanced at the clock on the mantel. If she hurried, she might be able to catch a ride with Joshua, which would give her a chance to speak to him without any interruptions during the ride to the farm that was hosting the youth gathering.

Turning back to her father, she took a deep breath and willed her voice to be calm. "I promise I'll be back at a decent hour. I'll ask Josh to bring me back before it gets late so that I can be up extra early tomorrow to help the *kinner* get ready for school."

"I said no," *Dat* said, looking down at the open Bible in his lap.

Lydia seethed. It didn't make any sense. If all her chores were complete then why couldn't she go? She'd never known her father to be unreasonable, which made this all the more frustrating and difficult to understand.

"Why?" Lydia asked again. While she waited for an explanation, her body trembled with a mixture of nerves and anger. She'd been raised to never question her parents, but she couldn't stop herself from pushing the issue. She knew the repercussions of her disrespect could be devastating, but she didn't care. All she wanted was to be a normal part of the youth group tonight, instead of feeling like an indentured servant.

Looking up, he closed the Bible and removed his reading glasses from his face. "Lydia, I said no," he repeated, his voice even but stern. "I don't owe you an explanation. I'm your father, and you'll do as I say without questioning me or there will be consequences." He placed the glasses on his face and returned to the Bible as if nothing had happened.

With a gasp, Lydia dropped into the sofa beside his chair. While she'd been grounded in the recent past, she hadn't been spanked in years.

"I don't understand," she said softly in an attempt to keep her voice from quaking. "I've done everything that's expected of me, *Dat*. Why can't I go?"

Dat sighed and looked at her. The frustration in his eyes caused a shiver to slither up her spine. Her father rarely lost his temper, but when he did, his voice could rattle the walls.

"Are you trying to upset me, Lydia? I've already told you I had a tough day and I'm exhausted."

She prayed her voice would be full of confidence and not the anxiety that surged through her. "I know, but I'm almost seventeen. I feel I have a right to know why you won't let me go."

"You have a right?" He placed the Bible on the end table. "What does the Bible teach us about honoring our parents, Lydia? Are you aware of the Ten Commandments? What does the *Ordnung* say about obeying your parents? Are you above all those rules? Or are you *English* now that you have an *English freind*?"

Lydia felt like she'd been slapped. "No, I'm not *English*. *Ya*, I know I must obey, but I—I mean—I just ..."

"I said no, and that's the end of it." He shook his head and disappointment simmered in his eyes. "What's gotten into you? You know what we're dealing with here. This *haus* is under a lot of pressure, and I'm struggling to keep it all together without your *mamm*." His voice rose and vibrated with anger. "I can't believe you would be this selfish to think of yourself and your social life during a time like this. I thought you were more mature than that."

"I am mature," she said, sitting up taller on the sofa. "I'm working and giving you my entire paychecks to help pay the household bills."

"That's what families do," he retorted. "We take care of each other. It's your duty. You're to think of your family first, Lydia."

"I know that, *Dat*. You know I've always thought of the family first." She shook her head as hurt bubbled through her. Didn't he know how much she cared about the family? Didn't he see all she was sacrificing for the family? "How can you call me selfish? I'm almost seventeen! I want to be with my *freinden* too. I'm going to become an old maid if I stay home and miss these years. Is that what you want for me?"

He gave a sarcastic snort. "You think if you're forced to miss a few youth gatherings you'll be sentenced to a life as an old maid?"

She stood. "I can't believe you insulted me and then you laughed at me." She started for the stairs.

"Lydia!" he bellowed.

She faced him and swiped away impatient tears.

"You are to go to your room for the rest of the night," he said. "I'm very disappointed in you."

"And I'm disappointed in you," she said softly. "I miss *Mamm* too. She would've let me go. She would understand. I've done all that you've asked of me since she left. This isn't fair."

He stared at her for a moment, his scowl unmoving. "No, it's not fair to any of us." He then lifted his Bible and went back to reading without looking up again.

Lydia rushed up the stairs with frustration and anger surging through her. She stomped into her room and flopped onto her bed just as her tears began to flow. She sobbed into her pillow and then rolled over onto her back and stared up at the plain white ceiling above her.

She wished more than ever that her mother was home and life was back to normal. Her father's behavior didn't make any sense. Why couldn't she go out and be with her friends for one night? Was he determined to ruin her life? Didn't he want her to grow up?

After several minutes, Lydia stood, crossed the room, and opened the shade. Staring out at Joshua's house, she wondered if he was on his way to the gathering. Would he see the girl from Gordonville? Would he even notice that Lydia wasn't there? What would he think of her absence?

Sinking into the chair by her desk, Lydia closed her eyes and wiped her remaining tears. Her thoughts turned to her mother. How would her mother react to this situation?

She changed into her nightgown and crawled into bed. Taking a deep, cleansing breath, she rolled onto her side and prayed for patience and understanding when dealing with her father's confusing and erratic behavior. Although her father's behavior was difficult to bear, Lydia knew she had to respect him.

The prayers and questions echoed through her mind, keeping her awake most of the night.

∾

"Are you awake, Lydia?"

Lydia looked up and found her grandmother staring down at her while she sat on a bench outside the bakery the following Tuesday. Her younger cousins ran around and played on the swing set in front of her.

"You've been quiet all morning." Her grandmother sank down beside her on the bench. "Did you have a rough day at school yesterday?"

"School was okay. It was a usual Monday." Lydia cupped her hand to her mouth as a yawn stole her words.

"You look exhausted, *mei liewe*," *Mammi* said, looping an arm around her shoulders. "Tell me what's on your mind."

Lydia kicked a stone with the toe of her sneaker. "I haven't been sleeping much these days."

Mammi smiled at her. "Are you going to tell me what's bothering you or will I have to force you to eat Brussels sprouts for lunch to get the information?"

Lydia couldn't help but laugh. She'd always despised Brussels sprouts, and her disgusted facial expressions while eating them had become a family joke. "You don't have to pull out the nasty vegetables, *Mammi*. I'll tell you."

"Take your time, *kind*." *Mammi* rubbed her arm, and the gesture was comforting to Lydia's broken spirit.

"I'm tired," Lydia began, her voice thick. "I want my life to become normal again. I want my *mamm* and my baby *schweschder* home. I want my *dat* to become reasonable again."

"Reasonable?" *Mammi* looked baffled. "What do you mean?"

Lydia crossed her arms over her chest in defiance. "My *dat* won't let me go to any youth gatherings. I've missed all of them during the past month, and I asked him if I could go Sunday night. He said no, and he wouldn't tell me why. He's completely unreasonable."

Mammi looked surprised. "You questioned him?"

Lydia lowered her gaze to the green grass. "*Ya*, I did."

"I'm surprised at you," *Mammi* said. "You've always been a very respectful girl. What's gotten into you?"

"I know I was wrong. I've never talked back to him or my *mamm* before." Lydia shrugged. "I guess I'm frustrated because my life has changed so much. I'm missing out on time with my *freinden*." Her thoughts turned to Joshua. "They can all start dating and I'm stuck at home. I could miss my chance at finding a boyfriend."

Mammi chuckled. "Lydia, you have plenty of time to find a boyfriend. You can't rush that. It will happen in God's time."

Lydia sighed. "I know."

"Things are tough for you right now, but they are also tough for your parents." She touched Lydia's cheek. "Look at me, *kind*."

Lydia met her gaze.

"You have to start thinking about others and how this is affecting them."

"I know," Lydia said. "*Dat* told me I'm selfish. But no one is thinking about how this all affects me. I'm always told to think of everyone else, but where does that leave me? I have feelings too."

"I don't want to use a word as harsh as selfish, but there must've been a reason why he wanted you home Sunday night." *Mammi* glanced toward the playground. "Maybe he didn't want to be alone. Although your siblings were at home, maybe it gives him comfort when he knows you're home and he's keeping you safe. He can't control what happens at the hospital. He can't hold your *mamm's* hand if she needs comforting. He can, however, keep you, Titus, and Irma safe by knowing you're home and tucked in your beds."

Lydia's mouth gaped. "I never thought of that, *Mammi*."

"I know you didn't." *Mammi* smiled at her. "You're a sweet child, and you're doing a *wunderbaar gut* job keeping the *haus* running with your *mamm* gone. Before you lose your temper with your *dat*, please take a step back and think about what he's going through. He's been used to having your *mamm* with him and caring for him for close to twenty years. It's difficult for him too."

Lydia bit her bottom lip in an effort to stop the guilt from drowning her. "Okay. I'm sorry." But she still wondered when her family would think of her feelings. *Can't anyone see that I'm suffering too?*

Mammi hugged her. "You don't have to be sorry. Just do better next time."

"I promise," Lydia said softly. "I will."

"And your *freinden* won't abandon you, Lydia," *Mammi*

said. "They will always be your *freinden*. You're missing out on social gatherings now, but you'll be able to participate when your *mamm* and Ruthie are home and your life feels normal again."

"You think things will be normal for me again?" Lydia felt hope swell within her. "Really?"

"Of course," *Mammi* said. "The Lord will take care of you and the rest of your family. He's taking *gut* care of Ruthie and your *mamm*. I'm certain of it. But remember that it will all happen in his time, not ours. He determines when she'll come home and when things are back to normal."

"I know." Lydia sighed. "We have to wait for God's time." She wished people would stop saying that. Although she knew her grandmother meant well, the words felt empty and meaningless while she watched her world crumble around her.

Mammi's eyes seemed to study Lydia's expression. "You know you're not alone, *ya*?"

Lydia nodded.

"There's a psalm that gives me comfort when I feel alone or sad," *Mammi* said. "I'd like to share it with you. It goes like this: 'Trust in him at all times, O people; pour out your hearts to him, for God is our refuge.'"

The words soaked into Lydia's mind, and she felt as if a warm blanket had been wrapped around her shoulders.

Mammi stood. "I need to get back inside. You'll let me know if you need to talk, *ya*?"

Lydia smiled. "I will. *Danki, Mammi*."

15

Two weeks later, Lydia hurried down the street from the schoolhouse toward her home. Determined to keep her promise to Barbie, she hoped she would not run into Tristan or any members of his family during her two-block trek.

As she moved past Tristan's brick farmhouse, she did her best to keep her eyes on the sidewalk ahead of her. Curiosity won out, however, and she turned her head, spotting Tristan in the driveway, leaning against his car with a cell phone pressed to his ear. He turned and saw her, but she quickly looked away, quickening her steps with her heart thumping in her chest.

She was nearly trotting by the time she reached her driveway. She hurried up to the porch and stepped inside, and the aroma of hamburger casserole engulfed her. She hung her sweater on the peg on the wall and dropped her tote bag on the floor below it.

"*Wie geht's!*" her aunt Rebecca called as she stepped into the kitchen from the family room. "How was your day, Lydia?"

"It went well," Lydia said as she crossed the kitchen. "How was your day?"

"*Gut.*" Rebecca moved to the table. "Supper should be ready in a few minutes. I also cleaned the house and did a few loads of laundry."

"*Danki,*" Lydia said. "I appreciate all your help."

"*Gern gschehne.* Why don't you sit and talk to me?"

Lydia sank into a chair across from her aunt. "How are the *kinner,* Lindsay, and *Onkel* Daniel?"

"Doing well." Rebecca pushed the ties to her prayer covering back behind her shoulders and smiled. "Lindsay and the *kinner* asked about you the other day. You'll have to bring Titus and Irma by to visit."

"That would be nice." Lydia pointed toward her bag sitting on the floor across the room. "I'm going to start helping Barbie make lesson plans."

Rebecca's face brightened. "Is that so?"

Lydia forced a smile, hoping to convince her aunt that being a teacher was her choice. "I'm going to learn all I can in case Barbie does leave at the end of the year. I know the school board may choose a teacher from another district, but I can at least learn everything possible before then. And maybe if the school board wants someone else, I can still go to another district to teach." Lydia said the words with as much excitement as she could muster. She was only going through the motions, however, to try to please her family and Barbie. Her heart wasn't in the job.

"That is *wunderbaar gut!*" Rebecca patted her hands. "I'm so proud of you."

"*Danki.*" Lydia stood. "I'll fetch Irma and have her help me set the table."

"Not yet." Rebecca shook her head. "Wait. They're upstairs. I want to tell you something." A smile turned up her lips.

Lydia held her breath, anticipating what the news could be.

"Your *mamm* called today," Rebecca began. "And she had some news."

"What?" Lydia searched her aunt's eyes, hoping to find a clue there. "What is it?"

"She and Ruthie ..." Rebecca paused. "They're coming home tomorrow."

Lydia gasped. "They are?"

Rebecca nodded and sniffed.

Jumping up, Lydia came around the table and hugged her aunt. "It's a miracle! They're coming home."

"*Ya*, it is," Rebecca said. "But she asked me to keep it a secret."

"Oh?" Lydia dropped into the chair beside her. "Why would she do that?"

"She wants to surprise Titus and Irma." Rebecca ran her fingers over the table while she spoke. "Your *dat* is going to head up to the hospital tonight so they can leave as soon as possible tomorrow. They should be home when you get back from working at the bakery. In fact, she said you could leave early and meet Titus and Irma after school."

Lydia wiped joyful tears from her cheeks. "That sounds *gut*. I'll meet them by the school and walk them home."

"*Gut*." Rebecca stood. "I'm going to stay tonight and make sure you're all okay. I'll head home after you leave for work and the *kinner* leave for school."

"*Danki*." Standing, Lydia hugged her aunt again. "I'll call them down and then set the table." Walking to the bottom of the stairs, she smiled. Tomorrow her family would be back together, and life would be back to normal. "God is so good," she whispered.

෨

The following afternoon, Lydia stood at the end of the path leading to the schoolhouse while waiting for her brother and sister to be dismissed for the day. She couldn't wipe the smile off her face all day long at the bakery. Her mother and sister were finally coming home! Joy filled her soul at the thought of her family being together again. She couldn't wait to see Irma and Titus's reaction when they got home.

The door to the schoolhouse opened, and the children rushed out as if they'd been cooped up all week. They hollered, screeched, and laughed on their way down the stairs.

Irma and Titus emerged from near the back of the pack, and they both looked confused when they saw Lydia waiting for them.

"Hi, Lydia," Irma said. "Why are you here?"

"*Ya,*" Titus chimed in. "*Was iss letz?*"

Lydia chuckled, and the children exchanged more confused expressions. "Can't you two be *froh* to see me?" she asked as they started down the street. "I'm here to walk you home."

Titus stopped, his brown eyes studying Lydia. "Why?" A frown turned down the corners of his mouth. "Did something bad happen to Ruthie?"

Lydia touched his straw hat. "Why do you always assume the worst?" She took his elbow and gently moved him forward. "Let's go. There just may be a surprise waiting for you."

Irma's eyes lit up with excitement. "A surprise? Did we get a pony?"

Lydia laughed again. "No, silly, it's not a pony." She placed her hand on her sister's shoulder. "What did you do today?"

While Irma prattled on about her schoolwork and conversations with friends, the three of them continued down the road toward their home.

As they approached Tristan's house, Lydia thought about her friend, wondering how he and his family were doing. An ache developed in her heart. She missed her *English* friend and their easy discussions. She wished she could tell him her mother and Ruthie were coming home. She knew their friendship had repercussions, however, and she dreaded having to defend herself to her parents and the rest of the community, especially the school board.

"I wonder if Tristan and Michaela are home," Irma said, breaking Lydia from her trance.

"I don't know," Lydia said, increasing the speed of her gait. "We don't have time to stop now. We need to keep going."

"But I miss Tristan and Michaela," Irma said, slowing her steps. "Can't we go say hello? Just for a minute?"

"She said no," Titus snapped, taking Irma's arm. "There's a reason she wants us at home, so we need to go. Now."

Lydia looked with surprise at her brother. "*Danki*, Titus."

Frowning, he nodded.

Irma continued talking about her day while they hurried down the street toward the house. Lydia's heart fluttered as they made their way up the driveway. She couldn't wait to hug her mother and Ruthie. But she looked at Irma's small face and felt guilty for wanting to be the first through the door. Her little sister had cried herself to sleep many nights because she missed their mother.

When they approached the porch, Lydia slowed down, allowing Irma and Titus to go through the door first. She stayed back, taking her time as she entered after them.

"*Mamm!*" Irma shrieked.

Lydia smiled when she saw Irma wrapping her arms around their mother. *Mamm* sank into the chair behind her and held onto Irma. She looked at Titus and motioned for him to join them. She pulled him into the hug and closed her eyes.

Wiping her eyes, Lydia looked up at her father, who stood next to her *mammi*.

Dat stepped over to her and put his arm around Lydia's shoulders. "*Danki* for keeping it a secret," he said softly.

"*Gern gschehne*," she said. "Where is Ruthie?"

He frowned. "She's sleeping upstairs. She was completely worn out after the trip home. She looks a bit pale."

"Do you want me to go check on her?" Lydia offered.

"Lydia," *Mammi* called. "*Kumm*."

Stepping over to her mother, Lydia's eyes again filled with tears. "*Willkumm heemet, Mamm*."

Mamm opened her arms, inviting Lydia into a hug. "*Danki, mei dochder*."

"*Gern gschehne*," Lydia said, holding onto her mother. She closed her eyes, and silently thanked God for bringing her family back together.

"I made a special welcome home supper," *Mammi* said. "I thought you all would like my famous pot roast. Also, more guests are on their way." She glanced out the window. "Actually, it looks like they're here."

Lydia looked out the window and saw a line of buggies parking in front of the barn. She recognized her cousins Amanda and Nancy and their families.

"Everyone is coming to see us?" Titus asked.

"*Aenti* Kathryn and *Aenti* Sadie are here," Irma said with a grin.

While pulling dishes out of the cabinets, *Mammi* directed

them to go outside and help their cousins carry in the trays of food.

Lydia followed her mother into the family room, where she sorted through her luggage, which was strewn about on the sofa. She silently studied her mother, marveling at the dark circles under her tired eyes. She looked much older than she had before she'd gone to the hospital. She also thought she saw a couple of gray strands of hair sticking out from under her prayer covering.

"Are you okay?" Lydia asked softly.

Mamm gave her a tired smile and touched her cheek. "*Ya.* I'm fine. Why do you ask?"

"You look exhausted," Lydia said. "Can I do something for you? Would you like me to check on Ruthie? *Dat* said she's taking a nap upstairs."

Mamm paused, considering the question. "That would be nice. Would you carry up a couple of bags to her room? We have company arriving. I'll take my luggage to my room."

"Of course," Lydia said.

Her mother handed her a duffle bag and Lydia climbed the stairs, stepping as quietly as possible. When she reached Ruthie's room, she sucked in a breath. A mixture of joy and worry surged through her as she pushed the door open and peered in. Her baby sister was curled up in her crib.

Lydia placed the bag on the floor, careful not to make a sound, and padded across the room to peer in at Ruthie. Her sister looked even more tiny, thin, and pale than she'd remembered, and her beautiful golden curls had fallen out, leaving her with a little pink head.

Lydia reached into the crib and touched Ruthie's little hand. Her sister moaned in her sleep and snuggled deeper into the white sheet. Her breathing sounded a little labored, but she slept peacefully.

"*Willkumm heemet*, baby Ruthie," Lydia whispered. "*Ich liebe dich.*"

Ruthie twitched and then opened her eyes. "Lydia," she whispered.

"I'm so glad you're home," Lydia said softly. "You rest, *ya?*"

Ruthie nodded.

"Go back to sleep. I'll check on you later." Lydia kissed the tips of Ruthie's fingers and placed another kiss on her forehead. She then quietly stepped out of the room, closing the door behind her.

As she descended the stairs, a group of murmuring voices echoed throughout the lower floor. Reaching the bottom step, she was nearly knocked over as Amanda suddenly appeared and wrapped her arms around her.

"What a miracle!" Amanda said, her face glowing with joy. "Your family is back together!"

"I know," Lydia said with a smile. "I'm so very thankful. Our family is so blessed."

"I'm so *froh* for you," Nancy said, pulling Lydia into another hug.

Lydia looked around the family room, and tears filled her eyes at the crowd of family members and friends from her district. In the center of the room was Bishop Abner Chupp, an older gentleman whose gray beard seemed to personify his years of work in the community and his wisdom as the head of the church. He was also Barbie Chupp's great-uncle.

He cleared his throat, and the voices around him softened and ceased. "Let's have a prayer," he said.

Everyone bowed their heads. Lydia wiped the tears that trickled from her eyes as the bishop thanked God for the healing hands he'd divinely laid upon Ruthie. Then he blessed the feast awaiting them in the kitchen.

Once the prayer was concluded, Amanda bumped Lydia's arm with her elbow. "Let's eat," she whispered before taking Lydia's hand and tugging her toward the kitchen.

Lydia, Amanda, and Nancy moved outside after filling their plates and sat under a cluster of oak trees. Lydia lowered her plate onto the ground and a warm breeze blew back the ribbons of her prayer covering.

"It's a *schee* evening, *ya*?" Amanda asked.

Lydia lifted a fork full of chow-chow. "It is."

Nancy popped a potato chip into her mouth. "Have you heard what the follow-up will be for Ruthie?"

Lydia shook her head. "I haven't heard it officially. But when I talked to my *mamm* a few days ago, she said Ruthie would have follow-up appointments after she came home. I just hope the appointments will be local so she and my *mamm* can stay home. It was rough without them here."

Nancy touched Lydia's arm. "Maybe now you can join us for youth gatherings."

"*Ya!*" Amanda's face brightened. "You missed some fun Sunday night." She laughed, and Nancy joined in.

"What do you mean?" Lydia looked back and forth between her cousins. "What did I miss?"

Nancy shook her head. "We had a gathering at Lizzie Anne's house again, and Mahlon sort of got caught."

"What?" Lydia gasped. "What do you mean?"

"He was gathering up his friends to go off on their own, and his father showed up," Amanda said while forking some chicken salad into her mouth. "There was alcohol in his buggy. The bishop is going to discuss punishment with the church leaders this week."

Lydia frowned. "Oh."

"It's not going to just involve Mahlon. I think the bishop's grandson told him there have been more youths drinking with him." Nancy popped more chips into her mouth and then rubbed her hands together. "My *dat* told me the bishop also wants a list of whoever has been drinking with Mahlon."

Lydia's suddenly lost her appetite. "Is that so?"

"*Ya*, that's what my *dat* said. One of the deacons told him when they met at the farm supply store yesterday." Nancy shook her head. "He said if he hears I was involved at all that he'll take me out to the barn and whip me. Does he really think I would do something like that?"

Amanda guffawed. "You would never do anything like that. Why would he even think that?"

Worry mixed with guilt surged through Lydia while she pushed a blob of potato salad around on her plate. What if Mahlon had given up her name? Not only would she be punished severely, but her reputation would be damaged. Her family would be shamed for years to come.

Lydia swallowed hard, trying to find her voice. "Have you heard any of the names Mahlon gave?"

Amanda waved off the question while chewing a bite of her turkey sandwich. "You know. Just the same group as always." She rattled off the names of Mahlon's followers.

Nancy chimed in, adding a few more, and Amanda concurred with a nod.

"Anyone else?" Lydia asked.

Amanda and Nancy shook their heads in unison.

"Why?" Amanda asked, her eyes full of curiosity. "Is there someone who was left off the list?"

Lydia paused and then shrugged. "I was just wondering who might be absent from the next youth gathering."

"Will you be there?" Nancy asked, her face hopeful. "I think my *mamm* is going to let me host it."

"That would be *wunderbaar*!" Amanda said. "I love your huge pasture. We have so much fun there."

Her cousins prattled on about youth gatherings, and Lydia's shoulders tensed. She didn't know what upset her more—that Mahlon was giving up names of his entourage or that her cousins talked as if Lydia wouldn't attend the next gathering.

"Lydia?" Amanda asked. "Are you okay?"

"*Ya*," Lydia said, forcing a smile. "I'm fine." But she was far from being fine. Suddenly the joy she'd felt earlier evaporated into the spring air.

Ↄ

Later that evening, Lydia placed a washed dish on the towel beside her and glanced at her mother, who was leaning against the wall while yawning.

"Go to bed," Lydia said. "I'll finish cleaning up."

"Are you certain?" *Mamm* asked between more yawning.

"You look as if you've pulled a buggy full of people from town back to our house," Lydia said. "Please go to bed. I promise I'll finish up the kitchen and then make certain all of the lamps are snuffed out."

With a smile, *Mamm* stepped over to Lydia and pulled her into a hug. "It's so *gut* to be *heemet*." She kissed her cheek.

"Now, go to bed before I get *Dat* in here to send you himself," Lydia said, holding her tight before letting go.

Mamm laughed and then headed for the door. "*Gut nacht*."

Lydia hummed to herself while she finished up the dishes and then wiped down the table. She was pushing the broom across the floor when the door opened and slammed shut.

She glanced over as her father shucked his work coat and tossed it onto the peg by the door.

"It's cooling off out there," he said, rubbing his arms as he crossed the kitchen. "It's not summer yet."

Lydia grabbed the dustpan from the corner. "Yes, but warmer weather will be here soon," she said.

He fetched a glass from the cabinet and filled it with water. "The gathering was nice tonight, *ya*?"

"*Ya*," she said. "The food was *appeditlich*."

He finished the water and then leaned against the counter. "It's a relief to have them home. But we're not out of the woods yet with Ruthie."

Lydia swept up the dirt and then held up the dustpan while studying her father. "What do you mean?"

He set the glass on the counter and crossed his arms over his wide chest. "She still has to go to monthly appointments and may need more treatments. This was only the first round. The doctors will follow her for a few years to be certain she's cancer free."

"Oh." She dumped the dirt into the trash can.

"I wanted to ask you about something," he said. "Let's talk for a minute."

Dread filled Lydia as she met his serious gaze.

"I was talking with your *onkel* Robert," *Dat* began. "And he mentioned that there has been some inappropriate behavior at the youth gatherings." He tilted his head in question. "Did you know anything about this?"

Lydia took a deep breath as alarm shot through her, causing the hair on her arms to stand up. Hoping her expression didn't give away her anxiety, she nodded.

"What did you know about it?" he asked.

"Mahlon and some friends were known to go off on their own," she said.

"What were they doing?"

"As far as I know, they were drinking," she said.

Dat rubbed his beard while studying her. "Were you involved in this in any way?"

"No," she said, her voice sounding small and foreign to her.

He stood up straight. "*Gut.* If you had been, you would suffer severe consequences." His expression softened. "I knew in my heart I could trust you, but Robert said he asked Nancy about it. I thought I should ask you as well. You need to tell the adults when inappropriate behavior is going on. We want to avert tragedy and keep our *kinner* safe. Bad things happen when *kinner* operate machinery or try to drive when drunk."

"Of course," Lydia said, her voice still meek. "I understand, *Dat.*"

"You should head to bed. It's getting late." He started toward the door. "*Gut nacht.*"

Lydia breathed a deep sigh of relief as she put the broom back in the corner. Moving to the sink, she stared out the window at the dark pasture as guilt weighed her down like a one-ton anvil on her shoulders.

Closing her eyes, she sent up a silent prayer to God:

Lord, forgive me for my sins. I know that lying is a sin, but the consequences of the truth terrified me more than the consequences of lying. I promise from this day forward to be truthful, but I'm afraid of the repercussions if my parents find out what I did. Please forgive me, Lord. I'll do better. I promise.

Snuffing the light, she headed toward the stairs and up to bed.

16

On Friday, Lydia rushed past Tristan's house, hoping to get to the other side of his family's driveway before he spotted her.

"Lydia," a voice said.

Startled, she flinched and turned, finding him leaning against the back end of his car. "Tristan," she said. "I didn't see you there."

"How could you see me?" he asked sarcastically. "You were studying the sidewalk and walking as if you were trying to outrun a fire."

She hoisted her heavy tote bag farther up on her shoulder while considering how accurate his words were. She didn't want to fuel any more possible rumors about her and Tristan, however. She already had to defend their friendship to her aunts, Barbie, and Joshua. Although she missed Tristan, it seemed to be in her best interest to not talk to him.

He stepped toward her and lifted his arms in question. "Why are you avoiding me?"

"I'm not avoiding you." *There I go, lying and sinning again.* She frowned. "I've just been busy."

"Busy?" He gave a bark of laughter. "Let me guess. You've been washing your hair?"

"Excuse me?" She shook her head with confusion. "What does that mean?"

The corner of Tristan's mouth tilted upward. "Sorry. It's an expression that non-Amish girls use often as an excuse. Mostly, they tell boys that when they don't want to see them or talk to them."

"Oh." Lydia hugged her arms to her chest. "I've been busy with my family. My mother and sister came home on Tuesday."

Tristan's eyes lit up and her heart swelled with renewed friendship. She'd wanted to tell him the news since she found out they were going to come home. Why couldn't she enjoy their innocent friendship without being criticized?

"That's wonderful, Lydia." He reached for her and then pulled his arm back. "I'm really happy to hear it. What a blessing for you."

"*Ya,*" she said. "We're so happy to have our family back together."

"God is so good," he said.

"He certainly is," she agreed. "That's very true."

Tristan's expression darkened slightly. "Why didn't you tell me they were coming home?"

She shrugged. "I just told you. I've been busy and I hadn't seen you, and I—"

"I don't believe you." His expression challenged her.

"What do you mean?" Lydia asked. "You don't believe what?"

"That you've been too busy." He gestured toward the garage. "I've been out here working on my car nearly every day for over a week. You've been deliberately rushing past my house so you didn't have to talk to me. I planned to stay out here today and wait for you so I could stop you. That's why I've been standing here for twenty minutes watching for you."

She studied his sad face, and she knew she had to stop lying to him. Perhaps if she told him the truth, he would understand. "You're right."

He raised his eyebrows with surprise. "I am?"

"*Ya*," she said. "I've been avoiding you because I have to."

"What do you mean?"

"Our friendship is frowned upon in my community. I had to avoid you to stop rumors from spreading and ruining my reputation and my chances of being the full-time teacher next year."

Tristan's expression transformed from shock to disbelief. "You've got to be kidding me." He gestured between them. "Our friendship would ruin your reputation? Why? Because we were alone for ten minutes in your schoolhouse?"

"Yes," she said, dropping her bag to the ground to stop the pain of the weight from shooting through her shoulder. "That's part of it." She glanced over her shoulder to see if Deborah, Tristan's Amish neighbor, was standing on her porch. Thankfully, there wasn't any sign of her. "Friendship between an Amish girl and a non-Amish boy is forbidden because it is considered inappropriate."

"How can a friendship between neighbors be inappropriate?"

"Those are the rules." She reached for her bag. "I really have to get home. Please tell your family—"

"No," he said, glowering. "I can't accept that. How can the Amish call themselves Christians if they don't allow friendships outside of their tight-knit group? That seems elitist to me. I thought the Amish were supposed to be humble and God-fearing."

"We aren't elitist. We're humble, and we're all trying to do the right thing in God's eyes." Lydia wished he didn't look so hurt, because it was breaking her heart. "We don't profess to be perfect Christians or perfect in any way. We're all trying to live by God's words and follow his commands, and we know our actions have repercussions. If I don't follow the rules of my community, my family will be frowned upon."

"The rules of your community?" Tristan looked confused. "You mean like wearing the right clothes and being obedient?"

"It's more than that. It's a way of life that is engrained in us from birth. This is our culture. It's the way we choose to live." She shook her head, knowing the conversation was hopeless and was not going to get any better. "You don't understand." She hefted the bag onto her shoulder, and the pain began anew in her shoulder. She needed to clean out her bag before she wound up with serious shoulder and back problems.

"No, apparently I don't understand." He folded his arms across his chest in defiance. "You're a teacher's assistant. Educate me."

Lydia frowned. "I don't like your tone. I'm not attacking you, so why are you attacking me?"

He gestured widely. "Jesus told us to love one another. He accepted all people, even thieves and paupers. Why can't I be friends with you?"

She paused and hoped she'd choose the right words. "Amish girls are supposed to be chaste and pure, and we're not supposed to mingle with any boys alone. I was wrong to give you a tour of the schoolhouse. If the school board finds out I did that, I might lose my job."

"I think that's a little extreme," he said, "but all right. So what's wrong with standing here in my driveway and talking? We're not alone in a closed room, and we're only talking."

"The perception could be ..." She paused, struggling for words.

"Lydia, that's just plain dumb. You can't do something because of what people might think." He shook his head.

She threw up her hands. "This is hopeless. You're not listening to me. There's a reason my community has these rules, and I have to follow them. That's just how it is."

"No, you're not listening to me. I never had any bad intentions toward you. I told you I have a girlfriend, and I'm loyal to her. Besides, doing something inappropriate with you never even entered my mind." Tristan's frown deepened. "I thought you were my friend. In fact, I considered you a good friend, and Michaela did too. She's been asking about you nearly every day."

Lydia sighed. "I'm sorry."

"Yeah," he said with an emphatic nod. "Me too."

They stared at each other, and the tension in the air around them intensified.

Lydia needed to get home before she was seen with him. If the word got back to her parents, she would definitely be in trouble. She started to back away. "I have to go."

"Sure," Tristan said. "Whatever." With a wave of his hand, he turned around and started up the driveway.

As she hurried toward her house, she held back threatening tears. It didn't seem fair that Lydia had to walk away from a good friend like Tristan. Why couldn't her community accept that she and Tristan shared a perfectly pure and innocent friendship? As she moved toward her driveway, she couldn't stop the heartache that gripped her.

CB

"I'm glad you can walk with us," Irma said, skipping alongside Lydia on Monday afternoon. "It's fun when you walk us home from school."

Lydia smiled. "I'm glad I can too. Barbie said I should go and she'd clean up today. She said she knew we'd want to get home so we could help *Mamm* with Ruthie and make supper."

Titus pointed toward the end of the road. "I see Michaela in the driveway. I wonder if she lost her dog. She looks like she's looking for something."

Lydia's stomach tightened. Her disagreement with Tristan had echoed through her mind all weekend, and she dreaded facing him.

"Michaela!" Irma shouted.

Before Lydia could grab her arm, Irma took off running toward the little girl, who grinned and waved as Irma approached. When Lydia reached them, the girls were hugging.

"Today's my birthday!" Michaela said. "I was hoping to see you when you walked home."

"Happy birthday!" Irma said, and Lydia and Titus echoed the wishes.

"Would you come in and have a cupcake with me and my mom and my brother?" Michaela asked. "My mom made them, and they're my favorite — vanilla cake with chocolate icing and rainbow sprinkles."

Lydia turned to Irma. "We really need to get home. *Mamm* was up most of the night with Ruthie, and I'm sure she's tired."

"Please," Irma said, giving them her best puppy dog eyes, as their father called it.

"*Mamm* won't be *froh* if we're late," Lydia repeated. She turned to Michaela. "I'm very sorry, but we must get home. Our baby sister is very ill and—"

Michaela's big, blue eyes filled with hope. "Please, Lydia. I haven't seen you in forever."

"Please, Lydia?" Irma chimed in. "Just one cupcake? I promise I'll eat fast, but I won't get a bellyache."

Lydia blew out a sigh and looked at Titus, who offered a noncommittal shrug. The girls continued to beg until Lydia finally gave a quick nod.

"One cupcake," Lydia said. "Then we must hurry home."

The girls cheered and skipped up the front walk while holding hands.

Lydia and Titus walked side by side up to the house and followed them into the kitchen. Mrs. Anderson stood at the counter shaking a container of rainbow sprinkles over the cupcakes, causing the flakes to fall onto the pastries like colorful snow.

"Why, hello!" she called. "I'm so glad you could join us. Michaela had a party at her preschool class today, but she wanted to have a party at home too and hoped you could come." She picked up the tray full of cupcakes and motioned toward the table. "Please sit down."

"Thank you," Irma said, sitting next to Michaela.

"How is your sister doing, Lydia?" Mrs. Anderson asked.

"She's doing better," Lydia said, moving to the table. "She and my mother just got back from Hershey last Tuesday. Ruthie's chemotherapy went pretty well. We're happy to have them back home."

"I bet you are." Mrs. Anderson smiled. "It's really good to see you again. I've been praying for your family."

"Thank you. We have to be home soon, but I told the

girls we could have a quick cupcake." Lydia wondered where Tristan was and hoped he was not at home. Sinking into a chair by the window, she looked out and saw him in the garage. The hood of his car was up, and he stood looking down at the engine.

Then Lydia noticed Titus was looking at her awkwardly from the other side of the kitchen. Patting the bench, she motioned for him to sit with her. With a reluctant expression, he joined her.

"Here we go," Mrs. Anderson said, placing the cupcakes in the center of the table. "Let's sing."

"Wait!" Michaela hollered, holding her hands out in a dramatic attempt to garner attention. "What about Tristan?"

Lydia's shoulders tensed. *Please don't invite him in to join us.*

"Oh," Mrs. Anderson said. "I thought we were going to sing with Tristan and Daddy tonight."

Michaela frowned. "We can't leave him out. It'll hurt his feelings."

"All right." Mrs. Anderson pushed open the back door and the screen door leading to a porch that sat in front of the detached garage. "Tristan," she called over the blare of rock music emanating from the garage. "Please come in and help us sing to your sister."

Tristan said something in return and then wiped his hands on a red shop rag before heading toward the house. Lydia felt almost sick. Seeing him again would be uncomfortable.

"He's coming," Mrs. Anderson said as she crossed back to the head of the table.

The screen door opened with a loud squeak and then slammed shut. Tristan stepped into the room, stopping when he saw Lydia and her siblings. "I didn't realize we had company."

Lydia held her breath as awkwardness between her and Tristan filled the room like a thick fog. *This was a very bad idea*. She shouldn't be inside Tristan's house. She would run the risk of being spotted by Barbie's aunt when she left, and the consequences of arriving home late would be much worse than the rumor mill.

"Hi, Tristan," Titus said.

"Hi, there, Titus," Tristan said while moving to the sink. "How are you all doing?" He washed his hands with soap and water.

Lydia couldn't bring herself to force a smile. She absently ran her fingers over the wooden tabletop as she waited for the birthday song to begin. She had to keep her hands busy to prevent herself from bolting toward the front door.

"We're fine, thank you," Irma said with a grin.

Michaela wrapped her arm around Irma. "I invited them to come in for a cupcake since we haven't seen them in a while. I waited in the driveway until they walked by."

While drying his hands with a paper towel, Tristan met Lydia's gaze, and her cheeks heated. "That's a good way to see them," he quipped before sitting across from Lydia. "That way they can't sneak by, right?"

Lydia turned her gaze to the cupcakes and hoped Titus and Irma would eat quickly. *What am I doing here? We should've gone straight home.* But she knew why she'd come into his house—she couldn't disappoint Irma. She knew Irma had also suffered while their mother was gone. How could she not let her sister enjoy a quick cupcake with their friend?

Mrs. Anderson put a large candle in the shape of a five on top of a cupcake and pushed it in front of Michaela. She lit the candle with a match and raised her hands in the air as if she were conducting an orchestra. "Let's sing!" she called before starting a loud and off-key rendition of "Happy Birthday to You."

Once the song was over, the children each snatched a cupcake from the tray, and Mrs. Anderson handed out paper plates featuring animated female characters dressed like princesses, along with matching napkins.

Lydia did her best to avoid Tristan's gaze while she picked at her cupcake. She was thankful the girls talked loudly about their cupcakes. Once they finished discussing the delicious icing, Michaela recited a long list of all the gifts she hoped to receive this evening when her family celebrated her special day with her.

When they were finished eating, Lydia glanced at the clock on the wall and realized that they'd been at the Andersons' home for nearly an hour. Her stomach tightened at the thought of her mother's anger and disappointment when they arrived home later than expected.

"I'm sorry," Lydia began loudly in an effort to get the girls' attention. "We have to head home. It's been nearly an hour since we left school, and our mother is going to worry about us."

"Oh, dear." Mrs. Anderson popped up from her chair. "May I put a couple of cupcakes in a container for your folks?"

Lydia hesitated, but Irma piped up.

"My *mamm* and *dat* love cupcakes," Irma said. "Would you also include one for our baby sister?"

"Of course. I bet your sister would love a cupcake," Mrs. Anderson said. "I'll be certain to pick one with extra icing just for her."

After putting the cupcakes into a plastic container, Mrs. Anderson and Michaela led Lydia and her siblings to the door. Irma thanked them both and hugged Michaela before skipping out toward the sidewalk. Titus mumbled a thank-you and happy birthday before sauntering after his sister. Lydia wished she could run after her siblings to avoid more awkward moments with Tristan.

Mrs. Anderson handed the container of cupcakes to Lydia. "Thank you for coming in. I know Michaela was thrilled to see you all."

"Thank you for having us," Lydia said, hefting her bag onto her shoulder and taking the container in her hands. "My family will extend a thank-you for the delicious cupcakes too." She looked at Tristan leaning against the banister and gave him a halfhearted smile.

"Good to see you," he said with a wave. "Don't be a stranger."

Lydia hurried down the path, wishing her heart would stop thudding in her chest.

17

While Irma and Titus hurried ahead of her down the road, Lydia walked at a slower pace. Her stomach was in knots after seeing the hurt in Tristan's eyes, and her stomach fluttered more as her rock driveway came into view.

Irma and Titus hurried up toward the house. Balancing her heavy tote bag and the container of cupcakes, Lydia followed them. Her heartbeat accelerated when she saw her father and Joshua talking by the barn.

Clad in work pants and a blue shirt, Joshua's brown hair stuck out from under his straw hat while he leaned against the barn. His eyes seemed a deeper shade of blue due to the color of his shirt, and his face displayed serious concentration while her father talked. Somehow he seemed taller and more muscular than before. His shoulders and chest filled his shirt and his arms were bulkier. How long had it been since she'd seen him? Had he grown and bulked up within the past week or had she not noticed him at the last Sunday service?

"*Dat*!" Irma yelled as she approached him. "You're home early." She hugged him. "We just went to a party."

Oh no. Lydia groaned to herself. *Irma needs to stop talking!*

"A party?" *Dat* looked from Irma to Lydia as she moved toward them.

"*Ya*!" Irma pointed toward the road as if in the direction of Tristan's house. "Our *freind* Michaela's birthday is today, and she invited us in for cupcakes. They were *appeditlich.*" She looked at her brother. "Right, Titus?"

"*Ya*," Titus said. "They are almost as *gut* as the ones *Mammi* and *Mamm* make for our birthdays."

Lydia bit her lower lip. *Not even Titus knows when to stop talking!*

Dat's frown deepened and his eyes met Lydia's, causing her shoulders to tense and her heart to jump to her throat.

Unaware of the disapproval in her father's eyes, Irma continued to talk. "Lydia brought home cupcakes for you, *Mamm*, and Ruthie." She frowned. "I wish we had one for you, Josh. Maybe we can cut one in half? *Mamm* always says she's watching her weight."

With each of her sister's words, Lydia wished she could disappear into the barn. Did her sister know how much worse she was making this situation?

Josh gave her a tentative smile. "*Danki* for thinking of me, but a cupcake would ruin my supper."

Dat looked at Titus and then Irma. "Go in the house, *kinner*, and start your chores. Be sure to keep quiet. Your *schweschder* may be sleeping. She had a rough day." He turned to Lydia. "You went to a party?"

"No." She shook her head. Although her eyes were focused on her father, she was aware of Joshua's probing stare, causing her heart to thud in her chest even more. "We were walking home, and Michaela invited us in. She begged us to come, and Irma also begged me. I couldn't bring myself to say no and disappoint them." She knew her excuse was lame, but it was the truth. She'd only had the best intensions.

"You were worried about disappointing two little girls?" *Dat's* scowl deepened. "Lydia, you know that your *mamm* has been struggling to care for Ruthie." He pointed to her. "You're the oldest. You had the authority to tell the *kinner* that a party is out of the question and to bring them straight home after school." His voice rose and shook with his growing anger. "Did you even think of your *mamm*? Did you even think about starting supper for the family? You have obligations *here*." He jammed his finger toward the ground for emphasis.

"I know, but I didn't think we'd gone so long. We lost track of time." Lydia took a deep breath to try to stop the lump in her throat from swelling. Why did her father have to explode and humiliate her in front of Joshua?

"We will finish discussing this in private." *Dat* looked at Joshua. "*Danki* for coming over. I'll speak with you later about working for me." He turned to Lydia. "Let's go inside and finish our conversation."

Lydia hesitated. She couldn't let Joshua walk away without talking to her after witnessing this embarrassing scene. "May I have just five minutes with Joshua? Please?"

Her father touched his beard while considering the request. "Five minutes. Then you'd better be in the kitchen." He stalked toward the house without another word.

Lydia's thundering heartbeat echoed in her ears, and her shoulders tensed even more. She waited until he was out of earshot and then shook her head. "I'm in a lot of trouble," she said, cupping her hand to her neck in an effort to relieve the stress building there.

"What did you expect?" Joshua asked with a palms-up

gesture. "Did you think it was smart to detour at the *English-ers'* house instead of coming home to your sick *schweschder?*"

Lydia glared at him and her anger flared. "How dare you judge me, Joshua Glick? Where have *you* been through all of this? I haven't seen you in weeks, except at church. You haven't offered my family any support at all."

"Whoa!" He held his hands up to stop her from speaking. "You're the one who made a lousy decision. Don't take it out on me."

"Excuse me?" She placed the container and tote bag on the ground and slapped her hands on her hips in defiance. "I thought we were *freinden*. I thought you were one of my best *freinden*, yet I haven't seen you come and visit once. Today is the first time I've seen you offer to help my *dat.*"

Lydia was on a roll, and she couldn't stop the words from flowing from her mouth. She gestured toward her house with one hand. "Where were you when my sister came home from the hospital? Most of the community was here, but you were nowhere to be found. You used to act like you cared about my family. Now I never see you. You say you're busy, but can you possibly be that busy, Joshua? It sounds more like you don't care about us anymore."

He scowled. "I do care about your family, and I've prayed for you, your *schweschder,* and the rest of your family. But we couldn't make it over the night your *schweschder* and *mamm* came home. We had to go to my grandparents' house, but my *mamm* sent a dish over with your *mammi.* She stopped by the bakery to give it to her."

"Oh." She felt bad for a second but then her anger began anew. She continued her rant, now gesturing toward his house. "You said you'd come visit me over a month ago, but you never did."

He shook his head. "Maybe I've had problems of my own."

"What does that mean?" she demanded, crossing her arms across her chest and glowering.

"My *daadi* fell and hurt his back about a month ago," he said. "My *dat* and I have been spending a lot of time over at his farm helping him with his chores. He lives on the other side of Gordonville. That's why I haven't been here. I really have been busy, Lydia. I'm telling you the truth."

Lydia blinked. Now she remembered his telling her he'd been helping his grandfather. Still, her heart sank. *Gordonville*. Did that mean he was also visiting Mary?

"He's feeling better, so I stopped over today to see if your *dat* needed anything," Joshua continued. "I'm going to start helping Titus with his chores tomorrow. Your *dat* said he still needs to work long hours and take on more jobs because of the medical bills."

"Oh," Lydia said, feeling a mix of guilt and anger. But she couldn't stop wondering about his relationship with Mary. Although Joshua said he cared about her family, he never said he wanted to be more than friends with Lydia. *He must be dating Mary. He likes her more than he likes me.* "I bet you like going to Gordonville." She felt tears fill her eyes, and she hoped she wouldn't cry in front of Joshua. She'd been humiliated enough for one evening.

He raised an eyebrow. "What does that mean?"

"Nothing," she mumbled. "I pray your *daadi* is better very soon."

He shook his head and crossed his arms over his muscular chest. "What's going on with you?"

"What do you mean by that?" She studied his face, wondering what he was thinking about her.

"What's going on with you and this *English bu*?" Joshua

asked, pointing toward the road. "You're celebrating his sister's birthday now. You're getting pretty cozy with his family, *ya*?"

"No," she said shaking her head. "I've already told you, Josh. Tristan and I are *freinden* and nothing more." She paused and considered the heated conversation she'd shared with Tristan, and her frown deepened. "Actually, I'm not sure we're still *freinden*."

"What?" Joshua looked confused. "Now, you're really not making sense. You're *freinden* with him, but you're not *freinden* with him. Yet, you share cupcakes for his sister's birthday. What is it then, Lydia? What's really going on between you and him? Do you have feelings for him?"

"No," she said. "Like I've said over and over, we were *freinden*. That's it."

"I heard you were alone in the schoolhouse with him," Joshua continued, his eyes flashing with something that resembled jealousy. "Are you sneaking around with him?"

"What?" She shook her head with disbelief. "No. I was never sneaking around with him. He wanted to see the inside of the schoolhouse because he'd never been in an Amish school. He's *English*, and you know the *English* are fascinated with us. I showed him the schoolhouse and he walked home. That was it."

He studied her. "Who have you become, Lydia?"

"What are you saying, Josh?" She eyed him with suspicion. "You've known me my whole life. Doesn't our friendship still mean anything to you? I thought what we had was special." Her voice was thick, and she wished she could keep her composure. She didn't want him to know how much this conversation was hurting her.

Joshua was silent for a moment as if considering his words.

"I talked to Mahlon." His eyes were accusing. "I found out why he's so interested in having you come to the youth gatherings with him."

The words were simple, yet the insinuation ran deep. Lydia studied his eyes, wishing she could read his thoughts. Did he know the *truth* about that night?

"What do you mean?" Her voice and her hands trembled with worry.

He leaned in close to her, and she could smell his musky scent. "The bishop asked Mahlon for a list of youth who have been drinking with him."

She cupped her hand to her mouth in an attempt to stop the gasp bubbling up from her throat.

"He told me about you." His glare sent a shiver up her spine.

Lydia challenged him with her best steely eyed look. "What are you saying?"

Joshua shook his head. "You were never a very good liar."

"I have no reason to lie," she said, her quaking voice betraying her attempt to defend herself. Joshua was right—she was a terrible liar, especially when she knew she'd been caught.

"He told me everything," Joshua said, whispering in her ear. "I know you went out behind the barn with him and his buddies and drank too much. When he took you home, you couldn't walk straight."

She stared at him. "He told you that? You don't believe him, do you, Josh?"

Joshua nodded. "I know it's the truth, Lydia. Your eyes and your expression confirm it. You can stop trying to talk your way out of it."

"Lydia!" Her father's voice bellowed from the door. "*Kumm! Dummle!*"

Joshua jammed a thumb toward the house. "You'd better go."

Lydia stood cemented in place, wondering what to say to Joshua. By continuing to deny it, she would only get herself in more trouble for lying. Yet, she needed to know if Mahlon told the bishop. She had to find out if the bishop was planning to visit her parents.

And the bishop wasn't her only worry. Now that Joshua knew the truth, he saw her in a different light. She was no longer the sweet, innocent girl who lived next door. She had a reputation, and he would never consider courting her or marrying her. She could see her dreams of being his wife and the mother of his children evaporating right before her eyes.

All she'd wanted her whole life was what every Amish girl wanted: to get married and have a family. By making one stupid mistake late one night, she'd lost her chance with the one person she wanted to share that life with. She'd also lost trust and friendship with Joshua. She had nothing left. Her heart twisted with a renewed dread at the thought.

"Lydia," Joshua said, his expression softening. "Go. *Now*. Let me help you with your bag." He reached for it, but she grabbed it before he could help her.

"Lydia Jane!" Her father's voice was laced with anger. "Are you disobeying me?"

Carrying her bag and the container full of cupcakes, she started toward the house with her heart in her throat and her body shaking with fear. Glancing down at the container, she could see the outline of the sprinkled cupcakes. How ironic that she was bringing happy birthday cupcakes into the house where her father waited to berate her.

She knew she was going to face the worst punishment of her life when she walked through the back door. But what would her punishment entail? Did her father know the truth about the night she was with Mahlon and his friends? Was he going to take her out behind the barn or would he simply ground her? Or could the punishment be worse, such as sending her away to live with relatives in another state to save her reputation? She'd heard of youth who had committed indiscretions and been sent away to mend their ways in a new community. Would her father do that to Lydia and ruin her life in the process?

"Lydia," Joshua called, jogging up beside her and wrenching her from her upsetting thoughts.

She faced him as they stood a foot from the porch, where her father was glaring down at her.

"Mahlon didn't give your name," Joshua whispered. "I told him not to. Actually, I sort of threatened him, and he promised that he didn't."

Before she could respond, Joshua trotted across the pasture toward his house. She watched him, wondering why he would defend her if he said he didn't know her anymore. Suddenly a glimmer of hope swelled deep inside of her as she wondered if his actions meant he could possibly still care for her.

"Lydia Jane," her father snapped. "Get up here on the porch. *Now.*"

Lydia pushed any possible happy thoughts away as she stood at the bottom of the stairs, ready to face her father, no matter what the repercussions could be. She'd lost her friendships with Joshua and with Tristan. What would it matter if she were grounded for the rest of the year or if she were sent away? She didn't have any reason to go to singings if she had no chance of being with the boy she'd loved since childhood and would love the rest of her life.

Climbing the stairs, her feet moved slowly as if she were fighting her way through quicksand with the weight of the world resting on her shoulders.

Dat stood in front of her, his expression full of fury. "What do you have to say for yourself, Lydia Jane?"

Angry tears collected in her eyes. While a million excuses floated through her head, she couldn't form a coherent response. Instead, she looked toward the pasture, where Joshua was nearing his house.

"Lydia!" Her father bellowed again. "Not only are you ignoring my question, but you're not even acknowledging my presence. Where does this blatant disrespect and disobedience come from? You were disrespectful the night you demanded to know why you couldn't go to the singing. And now you're disrespecting me again."

Facing him, she squared her shoulders and angled her chin with a sudden surge of confidence. "I've done nothing wrong."

He raised his eyebrows in surprise. "Is that how you feel? You think you can run around with your *English freinden* and skip your chores at the house? You have responsibilities. You know that your *schweschder* is ill, and your *mamm* has her hands full. It's your job to come home at night and make supper and complete your chores. I resent your teaching your siblings that it's okay to do what you wish without consequences."

She wiped away a frustrated tear as rage pooled within her.

"Are you going to answer me?" he demanded, folding his arms over his chest. "What do you have to say for yourself?"

"I'm tired of this," she said. "I want our normal life back. I want to be a normal sixteen-year-old *maedel* who works, does her chores, and spends time with her *freinden*. I don't want to be accused and scorned when I want to have a life beyond this *haus*."

Shaking his head, he glowered. "That is not for us to decide. We have to follow God's plan, and his plan is for us to care for Ruthie. You can't run off whenever you please."

"I don't want to carry the load for this family anymore," she blurted out, her voice trembling and pitched higher than usual. "I want to live my life, not a life that is dictated to me. I want to be like Nancy and Amanda and go to youth gatherings and laugh with my *freinden*. I'm missing out on too much, and it's not fair!"

"You're out of line!" His voice shook. "I don't know where this attitude has come from, but I feel like I don't know you anymore. What's happened to you? Who have you become, Lydia? You're not the *maedel* your *mamm* and I raised."

She gasped. His words stung as much as Joshua's.

"You would break your *mamm's* heart if she heard this disrespect," he continued.

"Maybe she should know," Lydia continued. "Maybe she should hear me say that I'm tired of not being appreciated."

"You're tired of not being appreciated?" He gave a sarcastic snort. "Do you know how hard I've been working? I've been taking triple shifts installing floors. Our hospital bills for Ruthie are piling up, and I'm breaking my back trying to pay some of them. But no matter how much I work, it's never enough money. Do you know how that feels?" He pointed toward the house. "Do you know why I'm home early today? Did you even think to ask?"

She shook her head.

"Your *mamm* called me because she was worried about Ruthie. She was running a high fever, and *Mamm* was worried sick." He motioned toward the house again. "Have you thought about how all this is affecting your *mamm*? Do you ever think of her?"

"I do," Lydia said, her resentment mounting at his accusations. "I worry about *Mamm* all the time. I pray for her and also for Ruthie and the rest of our family. I worry about everything."

"You do?" he asked. "I thought you only cared about going out with your friends. That's what you said."

"That is *not* what I said!" Lydia insisted, her body trembling. "You're not listening to me, *Dat*. You order me around but don't listen to how I feel."

"Fine," he said. "Tell me how you feel, Lydia. I'm listening now."

"I'm missing out on all the things the youth do," she began, but the words felt insignificant and weak after his accusations. "The *buwe* and *maed* are dating, but I'm always here at home. There's no reason I can't get away sometimes and be a normal sixteen-year-old. When I wanted to go to that last gathering, you wouldn't let me!" She pointed at him, even though she knew it would only anger him more. "You wouldn't give me a reason."

"I don't have to give a reason," he fired back with fury sparking his brown eyes. "I am your *daed*, and I am the head of this household. I don't need a reason for my decisions. It's not your place to question me. According to the *Ordnung*, you're to obey your parents and not question them. Don't you remember all you've been taught? You're a teacher at the school. You should know the teachings."

She blanched at his words. "I know the *Ordnung*."

"Do you?" he asked. "You act as if you can just do whatever you please and not live within the rules of the *Ordnung*. Are you above it all? Are you too *gut* for the Lord's teachings?"

"No," she said, her tears flowing with full force now. "I just want to be a normal sixteen-year-old. That's all I want."

"We all have things we pray for, but we have to follow the Lord's plan," he said. "Our life and our future aren't for us to decide."

She shifted her weight and wished her tears would stop flowing. But she was sobbing now and couldn't stop.

"You don't deserve to be a part of this family if you hold such resentment about your role in this *haus*." He pointed toward the door. "Go! Go to your room. You're grounded."

She opened her mouth to protest, but he continued, his voice echoing off the porch.

"Don't even think about going to a youth gathering," *Dat* ordered, his face contorted with anger. "You will go to school and the bakery and then come straight home. You'll have no contact with that *English* family or your *freinden*, except at church services. You want to be on your own? Well, you'll be alone as much as possible. Consider it done."

Lydia stared at him and wiped more tears.

"Go!" he said. "Stay in your room. I don't want to see your face."

Lydia marched into the house, dropping her bag and the cupcakes by the back door. Irma looked up from sweeping the kitchen floor with a shocked expression.

Lydia rushed through the family room past her mother, who was rocking Ruthie in a chair.

"Lydia?" her mother whispered. "*Was iss letz?*"

Lydia ran up the stairs without responding to the question.

"Lydia?" she heard her mother call. "Come sit with me in the *schtupp*."

Lydia stomped into her bedroom, where she dropped on her bed and sobbed. Once she was out of tears, she flopped onto her back and stared up at the ceiling as the conversations with her father and Joshua swirled through her mind. In a matter of days, she'd managed to destroy almost every relationship she had.

"What's happening to me?" she whispered. "Are Joshua and *Dat* right? Have I changed? Am I no longer a *gut maedel*?"

She knew she needed to pray, but she couldn't form the words. She knew she'd been disrespectful to her father, and she was ashamed—so, so ashamed. How could she possibly take back her horrible, self-centered words?

Lydia knew in her heart that her father was right—it would have broken her mother's heart if she'd heard what Lydia had said.

"I'm so sorry," she whispered. "Lord, I'm so very sorry. Help me make this right. Give me the words to make my family realize that I do want to be here, and I do love them. Guide me with my friendships with Tristan and with my precious Joshua. Help me find my way back to you and your path, God."

Closing her eyes, she continued to pray. "Lord, please heal Ruthie and give my parents strength. Please make me a good example for my siblings."

Lydia rolled to her side and closed her eyes. She hoped she could dream now and wake up to find a new day and not this nightmare in which she was trapped.

18

The following Wednesday, Lydia stood at the stove cooking eggs and fried potatoes. She kept glancing toward the doorway, awaiting her father's arrival.

"I can't believe the last day of school is Friday!" Irma said as she finished setting the table. "It's almost summer. I'm so *froh*!"

"Me too," Titus agreed. "It's about time." He started toward the door. "I'll be back."

"I already fed the animals and got the eggs," Lydia announced, scraping the potatoes onto a large dish. "You don't need to worry about it."

Titus looked shocked. "You did?"

"*Ya*." She began cutting up another potato, which was already peeled. "You can go tell *Dat* that breakfast is almost finished." She turned to Irma. "Would you please run down to the basement and get a couple of jars of *Dat's* favorite preserves?"

"*Ya*," Irma said and then headed toward the basement door.

"Why are you doing extra chores?" Titus asked, moving next to Lydia. "Are you trying to get back on *Dat's gut* side?"

Although Titus's observation was correct, Lydia ignored the question. Ever since her heated discussion with her father the previous week, she'd gone out of her way to be pleasant and helpful. Her parents, however, had been reticent in her company. She'd hoped by doing her best and taking on more chores, they would forgive her and their home would become a more relaxed and pleasant place.

Yet, her father seemed to either ignore or not notice all the extra things Lydia had been doing to try to make amends. Twice she'd tried to open a conversation with him about their argument, and he walked away from her, leaving her feeling cold, alone, and ostracized from her own family. After praying about it, she decided not to give up. She would keep going above and beyond with her chores and also continue to pray for reconciliation with her father.

Lydia pointed toward the counter. "Titus, would you please grab a loaf of bread from the pile I made yesterday? Also, please get the butter out and set them both on the table. There's a basket for the bread over there."

Shaking his head, Titus grabbed the bread and then fetched the butter from the refrigerator. "You know doing extra chores won't make it better. You need to apologize and prove to him that you won't be disrespectful again." He put the bread into the basket.

Lydia faced him. "I've tried to apologize, but he won't respond."

"Keep trying," he said with a shrug. "You know how stressed out he is. Did you hear him that night he cried a few weeks ago?"

Lydia placed the spatula on the counter. "*Ya*, I did."

Frowning, Titus shook his head. "I've never seen him that upset."

"I know," Lydia said softly. "I realized I was wrong to behave like I did, and I just want to make it better."

Her brother tilted his head while contemplating something. "Do you want me to help you? Maybe I could talk to *Dat* and tell him you're really sorry."

Reaching over, Lydia touched his arm. "*Danki*. You're a *gut bu*, but I have to handle this myself. It's my mess, and I need to fix it."

He placed the bread and butter on the table. "*Gude mariye, Mamm*," Titus said as their mother appeared in the doorway.

The dark circles under their mother's eyes indicated she'd had another sleepless night with Ruthie. "*Gude mariye*," she said with a yawn. "Everything smells *appeditlich*." She looked at Lydia with surprise. "You've been busy."

Irma appeared from the basement with two jars of preserves. "*Gude mariye, Mamm*." She placed the jars on the table and kissed her mother's cheek.

"*Danki*," *Mamm* said.

"Have a seat, *Mamm*," Lydia said. "Everything is almost ready." She brought the plates of eggs and potatoes and set them down in front of her mother, then went back to the stove. "I thought I'd make *Dat's* favorite this morning."

"She's trying to get back in *Dat's* favor," Titus mumbled.

"Titus," Lydia said. "That's not nice."

While Irma prattled on about her excitement for their upcoming summer break, Lydia made three more plates of eggs and potatoes. She was placing the last plate on the table as her father entered. "*Gude mariye*," Lydia said, trying her best to sound chipper.

Dat mumbled a response and sat at the head of the table. Lydia sat down in her usual seat next to Irma and bowed her head for the silent meal blessing. When prayers were complete, she lifted her head and reached for the basket of bread in the center of the table. "Would anyone like some bread? It's freshly baked from yesterday."

Irma smiled. "I'll take some."

Lydia began to cut pieces and distribute them around the table. Her father took a piece and mumbled a thank-you under his breath.

Dat turned to Titus. "Are your chores done outside?"

Titus pointed to Lydia. "She did them already."

Dat shot Lydia a look of disbelief. "You did Titus's chores?"

"*Ya.*" Lydia scooped some potatoes into a spoon. "*Ya.* I fed the animals and fetched the eggs."

Her father studied her for a moment while chewing, then turned to *Mamm.* "Are you prepared for Ruthie's appointment today?"

"*Ya,*" she said, lifting her glass of water. "I think so. My *mamm* will be here in an hour to pick us up. The driver is going to get her first and then come here to get Ruthie and me."

Dat shoveled more eggs into his mouth while he asked Irma and Titus if they were ready for school. Lydia wished he would ask her if she was ready for her day at school, but he didn't. She felt invisible. How long would he treat her this way? What more could she possibly do to show him that she did love her family and wanted to be a help to her parents?

Once breakfast was complete, *Dat* kissed *Mamm* and headed outside to catch his ride. Lydia's heart sank when her father left without saying good-bye to her.

While Irma and Titus went to brush their teeth and retrieve their school bags, Lydia began cleaning up the dishes. She felt a hand on her shoulder and turned to see her mother's sad smile.

Amy Clipston

"He does love you, Lydia," *Mamm* said as if reading Lydia's thoughts. "He's just hurt. You need to give him time to get over it."

"What about you?" Lydia asked. "Are you still angry with me?"

"No." *Mamm* pulled her into a warm hug. "I understand how you feel."

"You do?" Lydia asked, searching her mother's face.

"*Ya.*" She touched Lydia's prayer covering. "You've had to shoulder a lot of the stress with Ruthie's illness, and I'm very proud of you for how well you handled things while I was gone. You're sixteen, but you're still young in my eyes. You're too young to run a family on your own, but you did it well."

"*Danki,*" Lydia whispered. For the first time since her argument with her father, Lydia felt hope swell within her. Maybe things could return to normal.

"What you said to your father hurt him, but I realize you only said it out of frustration. I know your father realizes that, but he's still upset. He can be very stubborn and set in his ways, and you have to give him time to work through his feelings."

"I don't know what to do or how to handle it all." Lydia gestured toward the table. "I've cried and I've prayed every night, asking God what to do. I've made his favorite dishes and handled all of the chores I could. I did Titus's chores this morning thinking it might get *Dat's* attention. But he still won't talk to me or look at me except to frown. I've even tried to talk to him, but he either doesn't answer or walks away. What else can I do besides get down on my knees and beg for his forgiveness?"

Mamm gave her a little smile. "Just keep being yourself and helping out as much as you can. He will forgive you and talk to you in his own time."

210

"Yes, *Mamm*."

"I've spoken to him about it, and he told me to worry about Ruthie and let him work through this with you." She shook her head. "I can't force him to talk to you, but I will keep reminding him that the way he's treating you is causing more anxiety in this *haus* than we need."

"*Danki, Mamm*." Lydia hugged her again.

"Go get ready for school and I'll finish up the dishes," her mother said.

"But what about Ruthie?" Lydia asked. "Don't you need to get her ready for the doctor?"

"I have time," *Mamm* said, carrying the dirty dishes to the sink. "She was up most of the night, so I'm letting her sleep. I'll go up in a little bit to get her dressed and bring her down for some breakfast." She gestured toward the door leading to the family room. "Go or you'll be late to school."

As she climbed the stairs to gather up her bag, she sent up a silent prayer, asking God to please soften her father's heart toward her.

❧

"The *kinner's* play was *wunderbaar*," Anna Glick said Friday while standing by the folding table and unwrapping the lunchmeat. "I can't believe the school year is over."

"I know," Lydia agreed. "It's gone by so quickly." She opened a jar of pickles. "It seems like only yesterday I was helping Barbie dust off the desks in preparation for the first day."

A crowd of children and parents milled about on the lush green pasture next to the schoolhouse to celebrate the last day of school. Lydia had helped Barbie write the skits the children had practiced and presented to the parents. Although

Lydia was still stressed about the situation with her father, she'd enjoyed helping the children prepare for the play. She'd smiled and laughed along with the parents while the children performed. Watching the children show off all they'd learned was Lydia's favorite part of teaching.

"*Ya*." Anna frowned. "I'm sorry that your *mamm* couldn't make it."

"*Danki*," Lydia said as she straightened the utensils. "Ruthie has been running a fever, so she was afraid to bring her out." She forced a smile. "But I'm certain Irma will provide her every detail of the day."

Anna chuckled. "*Ya*, she will do that for certain!"

"Thank you all for coming today," Barbie called while standing near the crowd. "We've had a *wunderbaar* year here at school, and I want to thank you for allowing Lydia and me to teach your *kinner*." She motioned for Lydia to come stand next to her.

Lydia felt her cheeks heat as she moved over to Barbie, who placed her arm around Lydia's shoulders.

"Lydia and I are very blessed to be your *kinner's* teachers," Barbie began. "I want to thank Lydia for her hard work this year. She was a *wunderbaar gut* helper, and the *kinner* love her, right, scholars?"

The children cheered, and Lydia felt her eyes fill with tears. She nodded a thank-you to the children.

Barbie turned to the bishop. "Would you please say a blessing so we can enjoy the food everyone brought to share?"

Bishop Chupp gave thanks for the food and the beautiful weather. Once he was finished, the children and parents made their way through the line, loading up their plates with food before taking a seat on quilts spread out on the ground for their informal picnic.

Lydia filled her plate and sat on a blanket with Titus and Irma. She was surprised when Barbie joined them since Barbie normally liked to mingle with the parents to avoid showing favor to any one family.

They talked about the weather and the speed at which the year passed. Irma shared her assessment of the year and Titus rolled his eyes while she spoke.

Once the children were finished eating, they deposited their used plates and utensils in a trash can and ran off to the playground.

"How's Ruthie?" Barbie picked up a handful of chips from her plate.

Lydia shook her head. "To be honest, I'm not certain. She's been to the doctor's twice this week, but she's still running a fever. My *mamm* is very worried, and she's in constant contact with the doctor. I fear Ruthie will be headed back to the hospital soon."

Barbie frowned with concern. "I've been thinking of Ruthie and your family. I'll continue to keep her in my prayers."

"*Danki*," Lydia said with a sigh. "I appreciate it very much."

"Does she have to have more treatments?" Barbie asked, lifting her cup of water.

"*Ya*," Lydia said. "She will have to go back to the hospital soon for another round of treatments, but she has to be well enough to get them."

"I'm sorry to hear that," Barbie said. "I'm also sorry your parents couldn't be here today to see the *kinner* perform."

"*Ya*, I was too, but they'll get an earful from Irma tonight," Lydia said with a smile. "My *dat* has been working long hours, and my *mamm* doesn't want to leave Ruthie with anyone since she knows her moods best."

"I understand." Barbie moved closer and smiled. "I want to speak with you in private later. I have something to share."

"Okay. That will be fine."

Barbie stood. "I'm going to go talk with the other parents. We'll catch up after everyone is gone."

Lydia finished her lunch and gathered up the dirty plates she found sitting on neighboring blankets. Then she moved to the food table where she wrapped up leftovers.

She made small talk with parents for the next hour, but her mind was stuck on Barbie's request to speak to her alone. She had a feeling she knew what the news would be — Barbie must've gotten engaged and was going to tell Lydia to request the position as the full-time teacher.

Her stomach knotted at the thought. Was she ready to be a full-time teacher? But what about helping out at the bakery? Her grandmother counted on her to help on her days away from the classroom. Lydia felt stuck between two opportunities, almost as if she were at a crossroads. Part of her wanted to bake full time and not be cooped up with two dozen children all day, every weekday. And yet, another part of her was excited about the idea of being in charge of the classroom. Where did she belong?

She looked around the playground where the children played softball, swung on the swing set, laughed in groups, and whipped down the slide. Was she even the right candidate to teach these children? They depended on her to teach the *Ordnung* and morality, along with reading, writing, and arithmetic. What did she know about morality when she'd gotten drunk with Mahlon and his friends, lost her friendships with Tristan and Joshua, and caused heartache for her parents?

The questions continued to haunt her while she helped the mothers clean up the picnic luncheon and then bid them good-bye. Once everything was straightened, Lydia and Barbie moved into the schoolhouse, where they finished preparing to close the school for the summer.

"I've spoken to the school board about the roof and how it leaks during a bad rainstorm," Barbie said while gathering up her books and placing them into her bag. "They said they will repair it over the summer."

Lydia smiled. "That's *gut*."

Barbie motioned toward the first row of desks. "Let's sit and talk for a moment."

Lydia sank into a desk chair next to Barbie and her anticipation swelled. "What did you want to discuss?"

"Stephen asked me to marry him last night!" Barbie's grin was wide, and her cheeks flushed a bright pink.

"Oh, Barbie!" Lydia exclaimed, hugging her. "That is *wunderbaar gut*! I'm so *froh* for you!"

"*Danki*," Barbie said, wiping tears from her eyes. "I can't believe how *froh* I am." She cleared her throat. "It's a secret right now, but I wanted you to know so you can talk to the school board when you're ready."

"Okay. I'll start thinking about what I want to do."

Barbie looked surprised. "I thought we talked about this, and you decided you want to be the teacher."

"I know, but I'm still having some doubts."

Barbie touched Lydia's arm. "You'll be a *wunderbaar* teacher. Don't doubt yourself so much. The scholars love you, and it would be easier for you to transition in than for someone from another district." She glanced at the clock and then jumped up. "I didn't realize how late it is. I need to get home. I'm making supper for my grandparents tonight." She grabbed her bag and started for the door. "I'll see you Sunday at service."

Lydia smiled. "I'll see you. Go on, and I'll lock up. Congratulations again. Please tell Stephen congratulations for me."

"*Danki*. I will." Barbie waved and then headed out into the sunshine.

Standing, Lydia moved to the front of the classroom and imagined herself as the teacher, calling the students up to complete math problems on the board and teaching the first graders how to write in English. Her shoulders tensed, and her stomach ached at the thought of being responsible for the children and their education. How could she possibly take that on?

She gathered up her supplies and headed home. She was relieved when she found her grandmother sitting on the porch and drinking meadow tea.

"*Wie geht's?*" *Mammi* asked as Lydia sank onto the swing beside her.

"I'm fine," Lydia replied, dropping her bag onto the porch with a thud. "I'm surprised to see you here this afternoon."

Her grandmother smiled. "Your *mamm* used the phone in your family's phone shanty and called me at the bakery. She said she really needed to take a nap and asked me to come watch over Ruthie. She was afraid she wouldn't wake up if Ruthie needed her. They're both sleeping now, and Irma and Titus are taking care of their chores."

"That's *gut*," Lydia said with a yawn. "I wish you could've been there today to see the *kinner's* play. It was really cute."

"I know," *Mammi* said with a frown. "I'd hoped to come and surprise you and your siblings, but I couldn't leave your *mamm*."

"I understand." Lydia smoothed her blue dress over her legs. "The weather is *schee*."

"*Ya*, it is," *Mammi* said, her expression turning more serious. "You look like you're carrying the weight of the world on your slight shoulders. Would you like to discuss something while your siblings are occupied?"

"That would be nice." Lydia stared off across the pasture at the dandelions dancing in the gentle breeze. "I'm conflicted about something, and I don't know what to do."

"Go on."

"How do you know if you're on the path God has chosen for you?" She turned to her grandmother. "I've been contemplating it and praying about it, but I'm still confused."

Mammi rubbed her chin while deep in thought. "I would say that you know you're on the right path when what you're doing feels right."

"That makes sense," Lydia said, nodding slowly. "But I'm not certain I would know if it felt right. I keep wondering if I'm missing that feeling. How do I know for sure?"

Mammi tilted her head in question. "Does this have anything to do with being a teacher?"

Lydia bit her bottom lip and considered sharing all her thoughts. "Can you keep a secret, *Mammi*?"

"Of course I can." She placed her glass of meadow tea on the table beside her. "You can tell me anything and it will be kept between me and God."

"Barbie told me Stephen asked her to marry him," Lydia said. "She wants me to talk to the school board about being their teacher next year. Even though the board normally chooses a new teacher from another district, she thinks they will seriously consider me. But I don't know if I'm the right person for the job."

"Why not?" *Mammi* asked. "You love teaching, don't you?"

"But I love working at the bakery too, and you need me there." Lydia folded her hands in her lap. "I don't want to leave you when you need the bakers to keep up with the tourists."

Mammi touched Lydia's cheek. "You're such a sweet *maedel*. You don't have to turn down a full-time teaching opportunity for the bakery. I'll make do. Of course we'll miss you, but I can find another baker to take your place if the Lord leads you to the teaching position."

"That's not all," Lydia said softly. "I don't think in my heart that I'm the right person for the job."

"What do you mean?"

"I just don't know if I would be the best role model for the scholars," Lydia said.

Mammi chuckled and swatted Lydia's leg. "Oh, you're so *gegisch*, Lydia. You're a fine role model. You're just *naerfich*, but you'll know what to do. You've been the assistant for two years now. Teaching will be as familiar as putting on an old sweater after a month or two. It will come naturally to you."

Lydia gazed toward the pasture and considered telling her grandmother about her indiscretion with Mahlon, about how she'd ruined her friendships with Tristan and Joshua, and about hurting her parents. But she knew it would break her grandmother's heart to know she'd strayed so far from the *Ordnung*.

Turning back to her grandmother, Lydia rubbed her neck where the tension seemed to gather.

"You should pray about it," *Mammi* said, and Lydia could feel the knot in her neck tighten. "The Lord will give you the answer, and you'll suddenly wake up one day knowing you're meant to be the teacher or that you're meant to work in the bakery. God will present the response to you when he's ready, and you'll know."

"Okay," Lydia said. "I will." *I just hope God gives me a clear answer.*

"I came across a verse this morning when I was reading," *Mammi* said. "It's from Hebrews and it goes like this: 'Therefore, since we are surrounded by such a great cloud of witnesses, let us throw off everything that hinders and the sin that so easily entangles. And let us run with perseverance the race marked out for us.'"

Lydia let the Scripture roll through her mind. "God chooses our path, and he will reveal it to me when he's ready and I'm ready to know it."

"That's right," *Mammi* said, patting Lydia's hands. "Don't be so hard on yourself, Lydia. Just open your heart in prayer, and let him guide you."

"I will, *Mammi*," Lydia whispered. "I will."

19

Sunday morning, Lydia stood in the doorway of Ruthie's room and watched her mother rock her baby sister while she coughed a deep, barky cough that seemed to originate down by her toes.

"Go on to church," *Mamm* said, waving toward the door. "I told your father we will be just fine, and I meant it."

Lydia hesitated and gripped the doorframe. "I don't feel right about leaving you, *Mamm*. Ruthie doesn't sound well, and you were up all night with her. I heard her coughing and you talking to her. Why don't you let me call a driver, and we'll take her to the emergency room? I'll go with you and help."

Mamm shook her head. "I know you're worried, and I appreciate it. But we'll be fine. She has a scheduled doctor's appointment tomorrow. We'll keep that appointment instead of paying for an ER visit. We simply don't have the money for both."

"Lydia!" Titus called from downstairs. "Are you coming to service? *Dat* says we need to leave."

"Go on," *Mamm* repeated. "You can come check on me after the service, *ya*?"

"*Ya*," Lydia agreed, although she still had a bad feeling creeping up her spine. "I'll pray for you and Ruthie." She hurried down the stairs and found Titus, Irma, and her father standing by the door. "I was just checking on *Mamm*. I'm worried about her and Ruthie. I tried to convince her to let me call a ride and take her to the hospital, but *Mamm* refuses."

"I know," *Dat* said, sounding frustrated. "Let's go before we're late."

"At least we only have to walk across the pasture for the service," Irma said as they descended the porch stairs. "It's fun to be only next door."

"I agree," Lydia said. "We can check on *Mamm* after the service."

"That's a *gut* idea," *Dat* said.

Lydia couldn't stop her smile. For the first time since their argument, her father had complimented her and acknowledged her opinion. Was he finally softening toward her? Had the prayers asking God to change her father's heart finally paid off?

They approached Joshua's house and the sea of buggies parked by the pasture came into view. A line of horses and buggies still moved up the rock driveway from the main road, crunching their wheels on the rocks on their way toward the barn.

As Lydia and her family moved toward the driveway, she saw familiar faces she'd known since birth. She greeted family members and friends on her way to the barn, where the service would be held since the weather was warm.

Glancing up at the sky, she saw foreboding dark clouds gathering in the distance. She hoped that it wouldn't rain and limit the fellowship to inside the barn after the service.

She heard the rocks crunch as someone ran up behind her. "*Wie geht's!*" Amanda called, coming up behind Lydia.

"I'm fine," Lydia said with a shrug. "How are you doing?"

"I'm well. *Danki.*" Amanda hugged Lydia. "It's so *gut* to see you." Her smiled faded. "*Was iss letz?*"

Lydia shook her head. "It's Ruthie. She had a very bad night. My *mamm* was up with her, trying to settle her down all night long. I never slept either, thinking about them." She looked over at a group of young children playing outside the barn. "I just wish she was healthy and life could return to normal."

With a sad smile, Amanda touched her shoulder. "I know. I'll pray with you today."

"*Danki.*" Lydia said. "I'm so blessed to have you in my life."

They greeted more friends and family members, and Nancy approached them with a few of her friends. Joining Nancy and her group, Amanda and Lydia headed toward their section of the congregation. Lydia sat between Amanda and Nancy.

Glancing across the barn, Lydia wished she could see her mother sitting with her aunts. She missed having her whole family at the service.

The congregation began singing the hymns, and Lydia joined in, doing her best to focus on the words. Then the minister began the first sermon, and Lydia tried to find meaning to comfort her heart. His holy message, however, was lost to her. All she could contemplate were her worries for her sister and mother.

A tap on her shoulder startled her. Glancing over, she found Nancy leaning in close with a concerned expression on her face.

"Was iss letz?" Nancy whispered. "You look so distressed that your knuckles are turning white."

"I've been praying for Ruthie," Lydia said softly. "She had a very bad night."

Nancy frowned. "I will pray extra hard too today and tonight as well."

"Danki," Lydia said.

Amanda leaned over and whispered in Lydia's ear. "Remember what *Mammi* always tells us when we're worried or upset." She squeezed her hand. "Trust in God's will. He'll take *gut* care of her. Put all of your burdens on him."

"I will," Lydia said, closing her eyes again. She tried to lay her burdens on God, but the tense feeling never left her shoulders.

The first sermon ended, and Lydia knelt in silent prayer along with the rest of the congregation. After the prayers, the deacon read from the Scriptures and then the hour-long main sermon began. Lydia felt someone staring at her, and she looked across the barn toward the young unmarried men. Her gaze scanned the sea of faces until they focused on Joshua, who was studying her while sitting between his brother, Joey, and her brother, Titus. Joshua's eyes were full of an intensity that caused her stomach to flip-flop.

Lydia wondered what Joshua was thinking and what had caused him to stare at her that way. Was he still angry with her? She'd spent nights thinking of him and wishing she could redo the conversation they'd shared in front of the barn more than a week ago.

Then another thought struck her: Perhaps the intense stare meant something completely different. Maybe he wanted to apologize and work to rebuild their friendship. Maybe he missed her as much as she missed him. She hoped he could find it in his heart to forgive her. Her cheeks flared with embarrassment, and she turned her eyes toward the deacon while he continued his sermon.

Lydia tried in vain to force her focus onto the sermon, but her thoughts wandered from her sister to her mother to Joshua and then to Tristan. She missed Tristan's friendship and hoped that someday they could be friends without the negative consequences of her community.

The deacon wrapped up his sermon and directed everyone to kneel for the prayer. Opening her heart, Lydia did her best to lay her burdens at the feet of God, asking him to relieve all of the stresses that were knotted in her shoulders. When the prayer was over, Lydia and the rest of the congregation stood for the benediction, and the closing hymn was sung.

While the men began converting the benches into tables for lunch, Lydia, Amanda, and Nancy followed the rest of the women headed into the house to gather up the food from the kitchen and bring it to the barn for the lunchtime meal.

As Lydia walked, friends and relatives stopped her to ask how Ruthie was and to ask why her mother didn't make it to the service. Lydia tried to sound upbeat and hopeful, and breathed a sigh of relief when she made it to the kitchen and was able to fetch a tray filled with condiments, including mustard, mayonnaise, and relish. But when she delivered it out to the tables filled with food in the barn, she was subjected to more questions.

"Are you okay?" Amanda asked, placing her homemade bread next to Lydia's tray. "You looked upset while you were telling everyone about Ruthie."

"I'm fine," Lydia said, pushing the ribbons from her prayer covering behind her shoulders. "Did I really look upset? I was trying my best to seem positive."

Amanda touched Lydia's arm. "You weren't ever a very good liar."

Lydia snorted. "I've heard that a lot lately," she muttered.

Amanda glanced around the barn and her expression turned devious.

"What are you thinking?" Lydia asked with interest.

"No one is paying any attention to us, right?" Amanda asked.

"Right," Lydia said.

"Why don't we quickly make our plates and go find a quiet place to sit away from everyone?" Amanda suggested. "No one has to know that we didn't serve the food. Plenty of young women are around to help the men get what they need. You look like you really need to just relax."

"That sounds *wunderbaar.*" Lydia started for the food table. "Let's do it."

They filled their plates and headed outside, moving toward a spot under some trees next to a small pond. They sank into the green, lush grass, and Lydia breathed a sigh of relief. This was exactly what she needed.

Amanda bit into a piece of cheese. "Now, tell me everything that's upsetting you."

"There's so much," Lydia said with a sigh. "I've been so worried about Ruthie, but that's not all. I had a horrible argument with my *dat* last week."

Amanda's eyes rounded. "You didn't tell me."

"I was too embarrassed," Lydia said. "The argument is why I can't go to youth gatherings anymore. I'm grounded for the rest of my life, I think."

"I'd wondered why you didn't make it to the gathering last Sunday. I had assumed Ruthie was sick, and your *mamm* needed your help." Amanda shook her head while looking surprised. "What happened with your *dat?*"

Lydia bit into a pickle and then told Amanda how she came home from Tristan's house and argued with Joshua and then her father. But she left out the part where Joshua shared that he found out about her secret from Mahlon.

Amanda listened silently, her eyes wide with shock.

"That's why I've been so upset lately," Lydia continued. "I feel as if in the last week I've lost my father, Joshua, and my friendship with Tristan."

Looking empathic, Amanda lifted her cup of meadow tea. "I'm so sorry to hear all of this. I had no idea you were going through so much. Have you apologized to your *dat*?"

"I've tried," Lydia said lifting her cup. "Nothing has worked." She took a drink and then put the cup back on the ground beside her.

"That has to hurt your feelings," Amanda said between bites of a peanut butter sandwich.

"It has," Lydia said, forking her red beets. "But I spoke with my *mamm* about it, and she suggested I just keep doing what I'm doing, and let him come around in his own time. I've been praying about it, which is helping me work through my guilt."

"Praying is likely the best thing for you and your *dat*," Amanda said. "It sounds like he was very upset, so it may take him longer to get over it."

Lydia chewed her beets. "My *mamm* said the same thing, and I think you're both right. In fact, this morning was the first time he treated me normally. I think maybe the Lord is softening his heart."

Amanda picked up a pickle. "That's *gut* news." She tilted her head. "What about Joshua?"

"I haven't seen him or spoken to him since our argument." Lydia sighed.

"You're always so negative." Amanda wagged a finger at her. "Maybe you cleared the air on some things that needed to be said. Just give him time to think about it."

"It's not that simple, Amanda." Lydia shook her head. She wished she could tell Amanda the whole truth and share about the night with Mahlon, but she worried about what Amanda thought of her. Also, if Amanda felt the obligation to tell an adult, then Lydia would be in more trouble. If the secret got out, it would cause more stress for her father. Although Lydia knew she would deserve the punishment, she couldn't add to her parents' problems.

"Like I said earlier," Amanda began with a mouth full of pickle, "you're always so negative. You look for the worst possible scenario and go with it." She smiled. "If your parents let you go to a youth gathering, maybe you can get him to drive you and take you home. That would give you plenty of time to talk in private and work through the things that upset you both, *ya*?"

Lydia shrugged. "Maybe, but I'm grounded, remember? I don't see how I could convince my *dat* to let me go to a gathering after the awful things I said to him."

"We're taught to forgive," Amanda said. "Your *dat* will forgive you."

Lydia glanced toward her house. "I really should go check on my *mamm* and Ruthie."

"Finish your lunch first," Amanda said. "Once we're done, I'll walk over with you. I'd love to see your *mamm* and Ruthie. It's been awhile."

"Okay," Lydia said, chewing a piece of peanut butter and fluff. "But we should hurry up."

"So, you aren't talking to your *English freind* anymore?" Amanda asked.

Lydia shook her head. "We had words a couple of weeks ago. I told him the perception of our friendship wasn't *gut* for me. He was really offended, and I can't blame him. The *English* don't need to worry about perception as much as we do. They don't have all the pressures either."

Amanda looked at Lydia with a curious expression. "How close were you to Tristan?"

Lydia shrugged. "We talked occasionally, but Barbie warned me to stay away from him. She said it might ruin my chances of becoming teacher next year."

"Next year?" Amanda grinned. "She's engaged?"

Lydia groaned and covered her face with her hand. "Oh no. I wasn't supposed to tell anyone."

"Don't worry," Amanda began with the wave of her hand. "Your secret is safe with me. You must be so excited! You could be a teacher."

"I *could* be," Lydia emphasized the word. "There's a chance that I won't be. They may want someone from another district, and I'll either have to stay on as assistant or go to another district. On top of that, I don't know what I want to do."

Amanda's expression changed to surprise. "Don't you want to be teacher? I thought that was your goal."

Lydia hesitated. "I'm not certain what my goal has been. I just knew I wanted to help out at the schoolhouse and work in the bakery." She placed her plate with half of her lunch uneaten onto the grass beside her. "I'm just not ready to make that decision."

"You should be ready because Barbie has made her decision." Amanda glanced across the pasture. "There's the volleyball net going up. The *buwe* are so predictable."

Lydia studied Joshua and again wondered what his intense stare had meant during the service. He looked over at her, and she quickly looked away, focusing on Amanda's clean plate. "Are you done? Can we go check on my *mamm*?"

"*Ya*," Amanda said, standing. "That's a *gut* idea."

They brushed off their skirts, picked up their plates and cups, and headed toward the trash cans lined up by the barn.

"Lydia! Lydia!" A voice hollered. "Lydia, *dummle*!"

Turning, Lydia found Irma running toward her at top speed. Her face was panic-stricken when she reached her. "Lydia, you have to come fast," she said while panting. "*Dat*, Titus, and I went to check on *Mamm*. We couldn't find you to ask you to come with us. We got to the house, and we found *Mamm* in the bathroom running the hot shower trying to help Ruthie breathe."

Lydia gasped and her heart thudded in her chest. "Ruthie can't breathe?"

"No," Irma said, grabbing her hand. "*Kumm*. Titus ran to the phone shanty to call nine-one-one. The rescue squad is on the way. We need you to come home now. *Dummle*!"

"Go!" Amanda said, taking Lydia's plate. "I'll go tell *Mammi* and my *mamm* and *dat*. We'll meet you there."

With her heart in her throat, Lydia took Irma's hand and ran across the pasture, pulling her little sister along beside her.

20

The rescue squad should be here soon, *ya*?" Titus asked while pacing on the front porch.

"*Ya*," Lydia said, doing her best to hold back tears. "They will be. Why don't you sit down?" She patted the swing beside her. "The best thing we can do is stay here while *Mamm* and *Dat* hold Ruthie by the shower."

"I can't sit," Titus said through gritted teeth while he continued to walk back and forth in front of the railing. "I just can't."

Irma sniffed and climbed onto Lydia's lap. "I'm scared, Lydia. What if the rescue squad doesn't get here in time? *Mamm* said that Ruthie's lips were turning blue."

"She'll be just fine," Lydia said, even though she was inwardly frantic about her sister. *She has to be okay. She just has to!* Glancing behind her, she saw a large group of friends and relatives heading across the pasture toward her house, and her heart warmed.

Sirens blasted in the distance and quickly came closer and closer.

"They're here!" Titus yelled, starting for the stairs as the ambulance rumbled up the driveway with the lights flashing but the sirens now turned off.

"Wait!" Lydia said, putting Irma down and following him to the steps. "We have to stay back and out of their way, *ya*? We have to let them do their job."

Her father rushed out the door and down the steps to the ambulance. Titus ran after him, but Lydia held Irma back.

"Why can't I go see the ambulance?" Irma asked with a scowl.

"We have to let *Dat* talk to them," Lydia said, keeping her voice calm despite the worry surging through her. "It's best if we stay up here."

Her father spoke to the driver and then pointed toward the other side of the house. The driver nodded and the ambulance rumbled forward.

Her father then climbed the steps, his eyes full of distress. "I told them to come to the back of the house. I think it will be easier for them to bring their equipment in and out through the back door." He gestured toward the group of church members heading up the driveway to the porch. "Please ask everyone to stay in the kitchen and out of the way of the EMTs. I don't want anyone getting in their way, *ya*?"

"I understand," Lydia said. "I'll keep everyone back."

Dat disappeared through the front door, and Titus stayed behind, nervously twisting his straw hat in his hands.

"Let's go into the kitchen," Lydia told her siblings. "But remember what *Dat* said—we don't go any farther than the kitchen doorway."

They waited in the kitchen, standing near the doorway, while four men and women in matching uniforms filed into the house and followed their father into the bathroom. Lydia stood with her arms around Irma and Titus while one of the EMTs talked to her parents and then performed tests on Ruthie. Then they left and came back with a gurney and asked more questions.

Lydia's body trembled with fear for her baby sister. She felt as if her life was being turned upside down again. Just when she thought things would get better, her sister's illness was tearing their house apart once more. *Will this ever end? Will Ruthie ever be healed? Will life ever be normal?*

"How are you?" a voice asked in Lydia's ear.

Turning, she found her grandmother standing with her arms open. Lydia launched herself into her arms and held on tight.

"She's going to be fine, Lydia," *Mammi* said softly in her ear. "Just have faith."

Her grandmother's words gave her a momentary feeling of solace. She hoped her grandmother was right.

"*Mammi!*" Irma called.

Lydia stepped back and her grandmother hugged Irma and then Titus. Looking behind her, Lydia saw a group of family members filing into the kitchen, including her aunts, uncles, and cousins.

"Lydia," *Mammi* said. "Please come here. Your mother is asking for you."

Lydia rushed into the family room, where she found her mother looking jittery.

"Lydia," *Mamm* said. "I need you to listen to me carefully. They're loading Ruthie into the ambulance right now. She has an oxygen mask on." She took Lydia's hand. "Your *dat* and I want to ride in the ambulance with her to keep her calm so that she can breathe better. I need you to get a ride and bring Titus and Irma to the hospital. Go ask your *onkel* Daniel to call his driver right now. Ask your *mammi* to ride with you. Do you understand?"

"*Ya*," Lydia said. "Of course."

"Daniel is already calling a driver," *Mammi* said, standing behind Lydia. "Beth Anne, you and Paul go to the hospital. I'll make sure Lydia, Titus, and Irma make it there." She hugged her daughter and whispered something in her ear, and tears splattered down *Mamm's* cheeks.

Lydia sucked in a breath to prevent herself from crying. She had to be strong for her parents and for her siblings, but inwardly she was falling apart. *When will I wake up from this nightmare?*

"Beth Anne!" *Dat* called from the front door. "We must go now."

"Go," *Mammi* said, squeezing *Mamm's* hand. "We'll be there soon."

Mamm rushed out the front door, and Lydia moved to the window to watch her parents leave. The sight of their climbing into an ambulance with her baby sister on a gurney was completely surreal.

Soon the ambulance pulled out of the driveway and its sirens blared as the vehicle reached the road at the end of the driveway.

"The driver is on his way, but he was on the other side of town running some errands," her uncle Daniel called. "He's going to be delayed, but he said he'd rush over."

Lydia looked up at her uncle. "I know how to get us a ride right away. My *English freind* lives down the street. I bet he could give us a ride right now, and you could come later in your driver's van."

"That's a *wunderbaar* idea," Daniel said. "Let's go ask him."

Lydia and Daniel hurried down the road toward Tristan's house. She spotted Tristan in the driveway under the hood of his car, and she rushed to him.

"Tristan," she called. "Tristan, we need help. It's an emergency."

Tristan looked up with a surprised expression. "Hey, Lydia. What's up?" He looked at her uncle. "What's wrong?"

"My sister ... " Lydia worked to calm the quiver in her voice. "An ambulance just took her to the hospital, and my uncle Daniel and I need someone to drive me and my siblings there to meet them. Can you help? We'll pay you for your gas and time. Please, Tristan. We're desperate." She folded her hands as if to beg.

"Of course we'll help you. That's what neighbors are for." Tristan dropped the tool in his hand onto a nearby work-bench and grabbed a red rag. "Let me go talk to my father. He has a big SUV that would hold quite a few people. I'll be right back."

Tristan hurried into the house, and Lydia and Daniel stood in the driveway. She hugged her arms to her chest. Her body shook with worry.

"Ruthie will be fine," Daniel said. "I believe the doctors will take *gut* care of her, and God is watching over her."

Afraid she might cry, Lydia looked up at him and nodded.

The back door opened and slammed shut as Tristan and an older man with the same dark hair and eyes rushed down the stairs.

"Lydia, this is my father, James Anderson," Tristan said. "And this is Mr. Daniel ...?"

"Kauffman," Daniel said, holding out his hand. "It's nice to meet you. We appreciate your help very much."

Mr. Anderson shook his hand and then motioned toward a large SUV parked in front of the garage. "I'd be happy to take you and your family to the hospital. Let's climb in."

Tristan, Lydia, and Daniel headed toward the truck.

"Dad," Tristan said. "Should I wait for Mom and drive her car up to Lydia's house so we can help take their other family members to the hospital?"

Lydia smiled. *How thoughtful of Tristan to offer another car to help my family.*

"That's a good idea," Mr. Anderson said. "Or wait." He handed Tristan the keys. "You take Lydia and some of her family, and I'll wait for your mother and bring the car up to the house to make another trip."

Tristan's eyes widened in surprise. "You're going to let me take your truck?"

"Yes." James nudged Tristan toward the SUV. "Now go."

Lydia climbed into the backseat while Daniel hopped into the front passenger seat. They drove in silence to her house, and she rushed out of the truck to the back porch where her siblings and family members were waiting. Daniel also exited the truck and stood by the porch.

"Tristan is going to take us to the hospital," Lydia said to her siblings. "Quick, get into the truck." She looked at her grandmother. "Will you come too? There's plenty of room."

Her grandmother, her grandfather, her aunt Kathryn, Amanda, Irma, and Titus all piled into the SUV, and Lydia sat up front in the passenger seat by Tristan. While they drove to the hospital, her grandparents spoke encouraging words quietly to Titus and Irma.

Lydia glanced over at Tristan, who kept his eyes focused on the road. "Thank you for helping us," she said. "I'll make sure you're paid for your time. You're truly making a sacrifice by dropping everything to help my family."

Tristan gave her a sideways glance. "I won't accept your money, Lydia. I meant what I said before—we help our neighbors. That's how I was brought up and I believe every word."

"Thank you," Lydia said, wiping a stray tear that had escaped her eyes.

"You're welcome," he said, stopping at a red light. "I'm just glad my dad allowed me to take his Excursion. He's very protective of it, but I know he would do anything to help a neighbor in need too. And my mother should be home soon—she took Michaela into town for new shoes. I think she could get four people comfortably into her car."

"We appreciate that very much," Lydia said. "When my uncle's driver was delayed, I thought of coming to ask you for help. But I never expected you to help this much."

"What happened to your sister? If you don't mind my asking, that is," Tristan said as he accelerated through the intersection.

"We're not certain what's wrong, but she had trouble breathing," Lydia said. "Her lips turned blue."

Tristan's expression was solemn. "I'm so sorry. I hope she's better soon."

"Thank you," Lydia said.

They drove in silence for the remainder of the ride to the hospital. When they reached the hospital parking lot, Tristan pulled up to the emergency room drop-off.

Lydia turned to Tristan as she unbuckled her seat belt. "Thank you again. You've really helped my family today."

"You're welcome," he said.

Lydia's grandfather, Eli, came around to Tristan's window and tapped on the glass. "Thank you, young man, for the ride." He held up a few bills. "This is for your time and gas."

"I can't accept that, sir," Tristan said, shaking his head. "I'm just happy I could help you out."

Eli shook his head. "I would like you to take the money."

"I can't," Tristan said. "I don't charge friends."

Her grandfather shook Tristan's hand. "Thank you, son." He looked at Lydia. "You have a *gut freind*."

Lydia smiled. "*Ya*, I do, *Daadi*." She opened the door. "Thank you again."

"Lydia!" Amanda called from the sidewalk. "*Dummle*!"

Lydia jumped down from the seat, took Irma's hand, and fell in step with Amanda and Titus as they moved through the whooshing automatic glass doors into the large waiting area. Her aunt and grandparents followed closely behind her.

A large desk sat in the middle of the room, where a woman in a uniform sat next to a phone that seemed to ring nonstop. Groups of people and children sat in the clusters of chairs spread around the large, open area, and flat television screens hung from the walls.

Lydia scanned the sea of people for her parents and found them sitting in a secluded corner, talking quietly. She rushed over to them, pulling Irma alongside her. "How's Ruthie?"

"We don't know yet," her mother said with a frown. "They're running some tests and will call us in when they're done."

Her grandfather touched *Mamm's* arm and gave her an encouraging nod. "I'm certain everything will be just fine, Beth Anne."

Lydia sat down and spotted a children's storybook on the small table in front of her. "Irma," she said. "Grab that book and I'll read it to you while we wait."

Irma retrieved the book, and Lydia pulled the little girl onto her lap. She began reading a story about a little bear that was afraid to go to school.

Soon a woman in pink scrubs came over to their group.

"Mr. and Mrs. Bontrager, would you please come back with me? Ruthie is asking for you. You can be with her while we're waiting for the results of the tests."

Lydia's parents stood, and her mother looked over at Lydia. "Will you be okay?"

Mammi touched Lydia's arm. "We'll take *gut* care of the *kinner*. You just go care for Ruthie."

Lydia bit her lip while she watched her parents disappear through the double doors with the nurse. Then she continued reading to Irma to try to relieve the tension.

Amanda dropped into the chair beside her and rubbed Irma's arm once the story was over. "What can I do for you, Lydia?"

Lydia shook her head. "I don't know." Her world was spinning out of control and she had no idea what would make it any better other than good news about her sister's condition.

Kathryn stepped over to them. "What if we went to get something to drink? You must be thirsty after rushing around."

"I don't want to leave," Lydia said. "I don't want to miss my parents if they come out and have news to share about Ruthie."

Amanda looked up at her mother. "We'll go get you something, right, *Mamm*?"

"*Ya*," Kathryn said. "That's a *gut* idea. We'll bring back something for everyone. Just let us know what you want to drink."

Titus looked up at their aunt. "You're going to the cafeteria?"

"*Ya*," Kathryn said, pushing his hair back. "I was thinking that you might be thirsty."

Titus looked hopeful. "Could I possibly get something to eat?"

"Didn't you have lunch?" Kathryn asked.

"*Ya,*" he said. "But I'm still hungry."

"*Ya,*" Kathryn said, touching his shoulder. "We'll get you something to eat." She turned to Lydia. "What can we bring back for you?"

Lydia shrugged. "I guess some iced tea or water."

"Okay." Kathryn looked at her parents. "What about you?"

After everyone had put in their requests, Amanda, Kathryn, and Titus headed toward the desk to ask where they could find the cafeteria, and soon they disappeared from the waiting room.

Her grandparents sat together on a small sofa and spoke to each other quietly while a news program sounded from the television suspended on the wall in front of them. Lydia rubbed Irma's back and hummed to her while she looked across the waiting room at the other groups of people. Her mind swirled with questions and worries for her sister.

Soon the doors opened with another *whoosh* and another group of friends and relatives stepped through the doors. Lydia saw her uncle David, her aunt Rebecca, and her cousins moving toward her. Her heart flip-flopped when she saw Joshua's face in the group. His eyes searched the waiting area and then settled on her, looking concerned.

Joshua crossed the waiting room and stood in front of Lydia. "How's Ruthie?"

"We don't know yet." Lydia fiddled with Irma's long braids. "My parents are back there with her, but we haven't heard anything yet. I know they've run some tests. We're waiting for the results."

He dropped into the chair next to Lydia. "I got here as soon as I heard the news. I'm sorry I wasn't there when the ambulance came. A group of us were playing volleyball and it took us awhile to notice everyone was leaving and heading to your farm."

"It's okay," Lydia said, looking down at Irma, who was squirming.

"I want to get up," Irma said, sitting up straight. "My back hurts." She looked across the waiting room and her eyes lit up when another group of relatives came into the waiting room. "Can I go over there and sit with them?"

"*Ya*," Lydia said. "Just listen to *Aenti* Sadie. Remember we need to behave in the hospital."

Irma nodded.

Their grandparents exchanged looks and then stood.

"Irma," *Mammi* began, "we'll walk over with you and let the adults know what's going on."

Irma took *Mammi's* hand and they headed over to the family and friends who were waving to them. They found a large open area of empty seats and sat down together while the children stared wide-eyed at the television.

Lydia was thankful the community had come to support her family, but she didn't feel like talking with them. Sitting alone with Joshua was all she craved at the moment instead of a barrage of questions she couldn't answer.

Joshua reached over and took Lydia's hand in his. "How are you?" His skin was rough from his hard work on his father's farm, but it was also warm and comforting.

Lydia shook her head with confusion. "I don't know how I am. I feel sort of numb while I sit here waiting to see what happens next. Lately my life is a series of stressful events tied together by the rising and setting sun." She studied his handsome face and longed for the air to be cleared between them. "Why are you here?"

His eyes studied hers. "Why do you think?"

"I didn't think you cared," she whispered.

"You're wrong," Joshua said, squeezing her hand. "I do care and I told you that the other night when we talked. I've always cared."

"I'm glad to hear that," Lydia said. "Who drove you here?"

"Daniel's driver brought a group in his van, and Mr. Anderson brought a few of us in his wife's car," Joshua said, leaning back in the chair. "Your *English freind* is bringing another group of church members out in his father's big truck. He went back to the house to pick up more people. He called his *dat* to tell him he'd be back to get another group."

"Tristan's making another trip?" Lydia asked.

"That's what I said."

She smiled. "He's a very nice person."

Joshua seemed to frown. "His *dat* wanted me to tell you that Tristan would be back to check on the family after making another run. I think he and his father are going to come up to see how everyone is."

"That's really thoughtful," Lydia said. Then they were silent, and she stared up at the television screen. But the news program was only background noise to her worries. She was thankful to have the reassurance of Joshua's warm hand.

Lydia looked across the waiting area. It warmed her heart to see members of her family and her church waiting for news of her sister. She studied Irma as she sat with her cousins, talking quietly and smiling. She hoped that someday she would see Ruthie at school, learning to read and write in the classroom and talking and giggling with her cousins and friends on the playground. Lydia wanted to see Ruthie in her classroom, smiling at Lydia from her little desk.

Then it hit her like a thousand bales of hay falling from the loft in the barn: Lydia *did* want to be the teacher. She could see herself in front of the class, leading them in their recitation of the multiplication tables. Although she'd doubted that she belonged in the classroom full time, she now knew she did want to be there instead of in the bakery every day.

The realization was overwhelming, causing Lydia to suck in a deep breath.

"Are you okay?" Joshua asked, his voice soft and smooth in her ear, sending warmth cascading down her spine.

"*Ya*," Lydia said. "I was just thinking about Ruthie and hoping she would someday be in school with the rest of the children."

"I think she will be," Joshua said, squeezing her hand again. "Just have faith."

"I do," she said. "I really do."

He sat up straight and gestured across the room. "Your parents."

Dropping her grip on his hand, Lydia jumped up and headed toward her mother and father, who stood with the large group of family members and friends in the center of the waiting room.

21

While her mother frowned, her father rubbed her back and spoke to everyone who'd come to offer support.

Lydia approached her parents with Joshua right behind her. "What's going on?" she asked, her voice sounding thin and foreign to her.

"Lydia," her mother said, turning to her. "*Kumm*." She took Lydia's hand and led her back toward the big double doors. "Ruthie has double pneumonia. It's a very serious case."

Lydia gripped her mother's hand. "What are they going to do?"

Mamm nodded at a nurse sitting behind the counter, and then the doors opened automatically. "*Kumm*," she said.

Her mother pulled Lydia into a busy hallway. Women and men dressed in similar nursing smocks and pants and clad in white coats with their names embroidered on them moved past each other, all rushing as if they needed to take care of a very important patient.

"How are they going to make her better?" Lydia asked.

Mamm kept her eyes glued to the hallway in front of

them. "The doctor has called Ruthie's cancer doctor, and he wants to move her to Hershey once she's stable."

"Stable?" Lydia asked.

"She's having a very hard time breathing," *Mamm* said. "They have her on oxygen and she's getting an IV of very strong medicine. Once she seems to be breathing better and has some medicine in her, they'll move her."

Lydia felt her lips tremble, but she willed herself to be strong for her mother. She didn't want to cause her mother more stress.

"This is her room," *Mamm* said, stopping in front of a doorway. "She's asked for you, which is why I came to get you. I need you to promise me you'll be as strong as you can be, *ya*?"

Lydia took a deep, cleansing breath while wondering if her mother had read her thoughts. "I'll do my best."

"*Gut.*" *Mamm* took both of Lydia's hands and squeezed them. "Ruthie is going to be okay. Just remember that and try your best to smile and act like you're certain she'll be just fine. This is the best way we can keep her faith strong."

"Okay."

Mamm pushed open the door, and Lydia stepped into the small room, finding her baby sister in the center of another bed that seemed too large for her tiny body. Even the prayer covering seemed too large on her fragile-looking, bald head. Lydia couldn't help thinking Ruthie resembled an old, worn-out rag doll. Her eyes were closed, and a tube was sticking out of her tiny arm. A clear mask was on her little face, and a machine hummed.

Trying in vain to stop her tears, Lydia lowered herself into a chair beside the bed and took Ruthie's hand in hers. Ruthie stirred but didn't wake up.

Mamm sat in a chair on the other side of the bed. "The doctor said she is very tired from the illness and the excitement of the ambulance ride."

Lydia again felt as if her world was coming apart as she studied her baby sister, who looked so weak. She stroked Ruthie's little hand.

"I think she wants to hear your voice," *Mamm* said. "She needs to know you're here with her."

"Ruthie," she began. "It's Lydia. *Mamm* said you wanted to see me. I hope you're feeling better. You gave us a real scare, but the doctor said you're going to be just fine. A lot of people are here in the hospital waiting room — they all came for you. All of our aunts, uncles, cousins, and most of our *freinden* from church are already here, and Joshua told me more people are on their way. You have to get better so you can visit with them when you feel up to it. You know they'll want to come by the *haus* and see you when you come home."

Ruthie turned her head toward Lydia and opened her eyes.

"Hi, there," Lydia said as a tear trickled down her cheek. "You need to get better, *ya?*"

Nodding her head, Ruthie weakly squeezed Lydia's hand.

Lydia sucked in a breath and smiled at her sister. They sat in silence for several minutes. The only sounds were the buzz and hiss of the machine and the occasional deep, barky cough from Ruthie's little mouth.

Lydia began to babble about everything she wanted to do with Ruthie when she was better, such as teaching her how to sew and how to write her name. She told Ruthie about the storybook she'd read to Irma in the waiting area. She prattled on and on until she was out of words.

Finally, *Mamm* leaned over. "Ruthie, I think you need to get more sleep. Why don't you close your eyes, *mei liewe*?"

Ruthie closed her eyes. Soon, her breathing changed, and she let go of Lydia's hand.

"Let's allow her to sleep in peace," their *mamm* whispered. "I think it helped her to see you and hear your voice. Maybe that will give her some strength to tell her body to get better." She gestured toward the door. "Let's head back out to the waiting area."

When they arrived, the group of family members and friends seemed to have doubled in size. She spotted more cousins, along with friends. Lydia hugged her mother and stepped farther into the waiting room, while her father took *Mamm's* hand and walked with her back toward Ruthie's room. Lydia wished her father would acknowledge her, but she had to let that worry go for today. Right now her focus was Ruthie.

"Lydia," Joshua said as he emerged from the sea of faces. "Let's go talk in private."

He took her hand and led her to a quiet, uninhabited area, around the corner and away from the group. They stood all alone, out of sight from the members of their community.

He opened his arms, and Lydia stepped into them, wrapping her arms around his neck and burying her face into his shoulder. With his strong arms around her, she let down her guard, allowing all of her stress and worries to pour out of her. She inhaled his musky scent and gripped him as if her life depended on his comforting embrace. She took deep breaths until she felt as if she was in control of her raging emotions.

"She has pneumonia," Lydia said, keeping her head on his muscular shoulder. "She looks so tiny and so pale."

Joshua rubbed her back. "I'm so sorry."

"She looks so *grank*. She's hooked up to an IV with medicine, and she has an oxygen mask on," Lydia continued, her voice trembling. "Her cancer doctor wants her at the hospital in Hershey, so they are going to treat her here and then move her. That means she'll be away from home again. I can't bear the thought of her and my *mamm* going away again. I know Ruthie has to go and stay there to get better, but we'll miss them so much." Her tears began to flow again, and she buried her face in his shoulder while he held her close.

"She'll be fine," Joshua whispered. "Keep your faith, Lydia. Don't let it go. You have to be strong for your parents and your brother and sisters."

"I know I have to be strong," she said. "Everyone tells me that all the time. But, honestly, it's just too much for me to handle anymore. Every time I think things are going to get better, something bad happens. I'm tired of trying to be strong when I'm dying inside. I feel like my world is upside down. Everything is crumbling around me."

"Your world isn't crumbling," he said. "I won't let it crumble. You have people to help you. I promise you I'll be by your side from this moment on."

She looked up at him and he wiped away her tears with the tip of his finger. She stared into his eyes, and her heart turned over in her chest.

"I've missed you," she whispered. "I'm so sorry for everything I said to you."

"Shhhh," he said, placing his finger on her lips. "Don't apologize. And I've missed you too." He frowned. "You were right. I've been a lousy *freind*. I haven't been around when you needed me most. I'm sorry for that, but I'm here now." He pointed to two empty seats by the window. "Let's sit."

Holding her hand, Joshua led her to the chairs, and they sat beside each other.

"I'm so sorry about everything," Lydia apologized again, still gripping his warm hand. "I was wrong to be so hard on you."

"It's all in the past," he said.

"No," she continued. "I owe you an explanation about the night I drank with Mahlon and his *freinden*. I never should've done it, but I was just so tired and stressed out about everything at home. Ruthie was getting sicker and sicker, and my parents were on edge all the time. You weren't there and neither was Amanda. And I missed both of you. Mahlon invited me to join him and his *freinden*, and I wasn't thinking clearly."

"I know," Joshua said. "I had assumed that's why you did it, because it wasn't like you at all."

"I felt horrible when I got home."

He looked at her with a curious expression. "Why didn't you tell me? Why did you keep it to yourself?"

Lydia frowned. "I was afraid to tell you. We used to share everything, but you stopped talking to me when Ruthie got sick. You were always too busy, and I felt alone."

He squeezed her hand. "I'm so sorry. I should've reached out to you, but after my *grossdaadi* injured his back, we were running over to his house all the time. I was exhausted from working on both farms. It's no excuse, but it's the truth."

She studied his eyes. "Why did you defend me to Mahlon?"

"Because I didn't want to see you get in trouble. You've been going through enough with your *schweschder* and so have your parents." His gaze was intense. "I wanted to believe you'd made a mistake but you were still the sweet, loyal, and innocent *maedel* I knew. I also wanted to believe that nothing was going on between you and Mahlon."

"I'm still that *maedel*," she said softly. "And nothing is going on between Mahlon and me—nothing at all. I promise you."

"*Gut*," Joshua said with a smile. "That's what I'd hoped was true."

"But I deserve to be punished," she whispered. "I was wrong and I should face the consequences."

"We can worry about facing consequences for your past mistakes later." He gently squeezed her hand again for emphasis. "Right now I'm just worried about Ruthie and I want to be here for you so you can be strong for your family."

Warmth gathered in her belly at the sound of the word *we*. Did this mean she had a chance with him? But what about the girl from Gordonville?

His expression remained intense. "Do you have feelings for Tristan?"

"No," she said with a shake of her head. "We're only *freinden*, and now that I'm going to apply to become the teacher, I'm going to be sure our friendship is inconspicuous. If I see him on the street, I'll say hello, but that will be it. I won't be spending any time with him at his *haus* again."

Joshua raised his eyebrows. "You're going to try to become the teacher? Is Barbie leaving?"

"*Ya*, but it's a secret. She's planning to be married in the fall, and she told me to talk to the school board about the job."

"That's *wunderbaar*!" Joshua said. "I'm so *froh* for you."

"*Danki*," Lydia said, studying his expression. "I have to ask you something."

"Anything," he said.

"Are you seeing a girl from Gordonville?" She bit her bottom lip while she awaited the answer.

"A girl from Gordonville?" he asked, looking confused. "Who are you—?" Then his eyes brightened with recognition. "Are you talking about Mary Fisher?"

"I don't know her last name, but Nancy and Amanda told me you'd been talking to a girl named Mary from Gordonville at a few youth gatherings. I felt so out of touch with everyone. I hate that I missed so many youth gatherings." *I was afraid I'd lost you.* Her heart pounded with worry as she awaited his response.

"No," he said. "I'm not seeing her. She talked to me a few times, and it turned out that I knew some of her friends, since I've met them at my grandparents' house. But I'm not seeing her or anyone else."

Lydia breathed a sigh of relief, and then her cheeks burned when she realized he'd seen it.

"We'd better get back before your cousins start looking for you." Joshua stood and tugged her hand as she stood up. "I'm sorry for giving you the impression that I didn't care."

"I'm sorry too."

He pulled her to him. "I promise I'll be a better *freind.*"

"I will too," she said, hugging him and enjoying the strength and comfort his embrace provided.

He put his finger under her chin, and lifted her face so she was looking up at him. Leaning down, he brushed his lips against hers, sending the pit of her belly into a wild swirl and rendering her breathless.

"We'd better go back before they come searching for you," he said, running his finger down her cheekbone.

Unable to speak, Lydia nodded with her eyes wide in surprise.

Taking her hand, Joshua led her back to the waiting room, where her friends and family members still gathered.

"There you are," Amanda said, sidling up to her and holding out a Styrofoam cup. "I've been looking for you. This is your iced tea."

"*Danki*," Lydia said, taking the cup.

Joshua leaned over. "I'm going to talk to my parents. They're over there with a few other friends."

"Okay," Lydia said. "I'll be here with Amanda."

Joshua headed over to where his parents were sitting.

"You two are getting awfully cozy," Amanda said with a grin.

Lydia sipped the cool beverage. *You have no idea.* "He's been really supportive."

Nancy stepped over to them. "I noticed you and Joshua are getting reacquainted. That's *gut* to see."

Lydia smiled. "*Ya*, we have. Things are going to be okay. I really believe that now."

Amanda hugged her. "*Ya*, I believe that too."

While talking to her cousins, Lydia felt a tap on her shoulder. Turning, she found Tristan standing behind her. "Tristan! You're back."

"Yeah," he said, folding his arms over his chest. "I made a few more trips to your house to bring more people out to the hospital. You have a big community."

"I appreciate your help so much today," she said, holding out her hand. "You really are a blessing to us."

"You're welcome." Tristan shook her hand. "I'm glad I could help. Your uncle told me Ruthie has pneumonia. I'm sorry to hear that, but I heard from another member of your community that the doctors here are very good. I bet she'll be just fine. We're going to add her to our prayer chain at church."

"Thank you," Lydia said. "I have faith too, and I know you're right." She introduced Tristan to her cousins, and the three of them sat and talked together for a long while.

CB

Later that evening, Tristan gave several members of the community a ride home while others called drivers or used taxis to get back to Joshua's house to collect their horses and buggies. Lydia sat on the porch at her house with Joshua while they watched the buggies in the distance move down his driveway toward the road.

"When are they moving Ruthie to Hershey?" Joshua asked.

"Tomorrow," Lydia said with a deep sigh. "My *mamm* is spending the night at the hospital and will travel with her."

"But the doctors said she was doing better, *ya*?" Joshua asked.

"That's what my *dat* said. Her oxygen level was much better, and she seemed to be responding to the medication." She gave him a weak smile. "It's the best news we could hope for. She's not home, but she's doing better. That's what I asked God for, and he answered."

"*Ya*, he did." Joshua stood and stretched. "I better get home before my *mamm* starts calling for me. I'll come by and visit you tomorrow night. Would that be okay?"

"That would be *wunderbaar gut*." She stood, hoping for a hug before he left.

Leaning down, he pressed his lips to hers, sending liquid heat through her veins. She held her breath, savoring his touch. *So much better than a hug!*

He touched her hand. "*Gut nacht, mei* Lydia."

"*Gut nacht*," she echoed. "See you tomorrow."

Joshua loped down the stairs toward the pasture. Lydia leaned on the railing and watched him disappear by the barn. She couldn't stop the smile forming on her lips. Never in her wildest dreams had she imagined Joshua would kiss her like that so soon, and he'd kissed her twice in one day. *Yes, things are definitely looking up!*

She started toward the front door, but stopped when she heard a horse clip-clopping up the driveway. She descended the stairs and walked over to the driveway to see who was coming for an unexpected visit.

The buggy stopped in front of her, and Lydia was surprised when Barbie climbed out from the passenger side.

"Lydia," Barbie said. "Stephen was just taking me home, but I was wondering if I could have a quick word with you."

"Of course." Lydia stepped over to Barbie and waved to Stephen, who sat in the driver's seat.

He gave a quick wave in response.

"I wanted to apologize to you," Barbie began. "I was wrong about your *freind*."

Lydia raised her eyebrows. "My *freind*?"

"*Ya*," Barbie said. "Your *English freind*, Tristan, drove me and a few others to the hospital, and I spoke to him in the car. He's a *gut* Christian *bu*, just like you said. He was very worried about Ruthie, and he spoke of God's love and having faith in his healing. I also spoke to his *daed* in the waiting room, and he too was very faithful to God and positive that things would be okay." She frowned. "I'm so sorry for assuming the worst about him. I was very wrong, and I feel just terrible about it."

Lydia hugged Barbie. "You don't need to apologize. We all make wrong assumptions at times."

"*Danki*," Barbie said. "I was hoping for your forgiveness."

Lydia smiled. "How could I not forgive you, my dear *freind*?" She took a deep breath. "I have something to tell you."

"What?" Barbie asked, looking excited.

"I've realized that I do want to be the teacher next year. I want to speak to the school board when the time is right."

"Oh, Lydia!" Barbie clapped her hands together. "That is *wunderbaar gut* news! We'll speak to the school board in a few weeks, *ya*?"

"That would be perfect," Lydia said.

"I better go," Barbie said, stepping toward the buggy. "We'll talk soon. *Gut nacht*, Lydia. Please tell your parents that I send my love and prayers for Ruthie."

"I will." Lydia waved to Barbie and Stephen as they drove down the driveway.

Lydia climbed up onto the porch and then looked back at the sun as it began to set in the sky. She smiled and headed into the house.

22

Lydia stood outside the one-room schoolhouse and smoothed her dark blue dress with her hands. The past six weeks had flown by at lightning speed. After spending two weeks in the hospital at Hershey due to her case of pneumonia, Ruthie had come home and then returned to the Hershey hospital for more treatments. When she and her mother had come home on Tuesday, Ruthie was tired, but she looked better than she had in months.

Lydia's mother wasn't quite as stressed out as she had been either. Their family was falling into a routine with Ruthie's illness. With school out, Titus and Irma were helping more around the house and the farm. Her father was still working long hours, but he was in the process of applying for state assistance with their medical bills, and he seemed more at ease with the debt they were facing. All in all, things were becoming more "normal," and Lydia was ready to look toward her future as the possible teacher.

Lydia touched her prayer covering and then smoothed her dress again.

"You look *schee*," Joshua said, touching her hand. "Stop fussing."

She looked up into his eyes and blew out a nervous sigh. "*Danki* for saying that I look *schee*, but I want to look better than pretty. I need to look grown-up, put together, professional."

"You're all that and more," Joshua said with a smile. "That's why I want you to be my girlfriend."

She gasped. "You do?"

He laughed. "You haven't figured that out already? I've been spending every moment of my free time with you. Wouldn't that give you a clue about my feelings? It won't be official until we join the church in the fall, but I wanted to ask you now."

"I'd love to be your girlfriend, and I'm really *froh*," she said, squeezing his hand. "But I'm about to ask the school board to consider me for the teaching position next year. I can't discuss my personal life or even kiss you in case they're looking out the window at me right now. They would be more than displeased if they saw me kissing my boyfriend out in public, in broad daylight, on a Friday afternoon."

"Then we'll save the kissing for later on your back porch." He touched her cheek. "I'll be happy to wait until then."

"*Gut*," Lydia said as she folded her trembling hands over her apron.

The door to the schoolhouse opened, and Barbie hopped down the steps with a smile glimmering on her face.

"I guess that went well," Joshua said.

"*Ya*," Barbie said. "They're ready for you. I told them you would be the best teacher for the class next year. They said they wanted to talk to you about it before they made a decision."

Lydia bit her bottom lip as doubt and worry coursed through her. "I can't do it. I'm not ready. I'll just work at the bakery. That's where I belong—with my cousins, my *aentis*, and my *mamm*."

"Stop being *gegisch*." Barbie touched Lydia's arm. "You're ready. You're a *wunderbaar gut* teacher. Now go in there and tell the school board how much you want this job."

Lydia turned to Joshua with a worried expression.

"You look perfect, Lydia," he said. "Go in there and show them why you'll be the best teacher our district can have, aside from Barbie."

With a chuckle, Barbie started toward the road. "I'll visit you later, and you can tell me how it went."

Lydia started up the steps and turned back to look at Joshua one last time.

He gave her a wave and his special smile, telling her she would do great.

Placing her hand on the doorknob, she sent a silent prayer up to God, asking him to continue blessing her and her family with his grace. As she moved into the schoolhouse, she knew she was taking a huge step toward her future as the new teacher for the district.

♋

"How'd it go?" Joshua asked as he took her hand while they walked down the road toward her house.

Lydia took a deep breath and tried her best to will her hands to stop trembling. "I think it went well."

"*Gut*." He raised his eyebrows. "Are you going to tell me what they asked or is it a secret?"

"I'll tell you." Her cheeks blushed. "I just hope you don't think I'm *gegisch*."

"Why would I think that?"

"I was so *naerfich* that I worried my answers would be

stupid." She shook her head. "They asked me why I wanted to be the teacher, and I said I felt as if God had chosen this path for me. I said that my *mammi* told me if the decision felt right then it was God's path, and this path feels right for me."

"Wow." Joshua looked impressed as he swung their entangled hands back and forth as they strolled. "That sounds like a perfect answer to me."

"They also asked me why I wanted to teach in this district instead of another one." She hesitated, wondering if she should share that answer with him.

"And . . . ?" He looked expectant. "What did you say?"

Lydia looked up at him. "Promise you won't think it's a *gegisch* answer."

"Lydia," he began, "nothing you can say would be *gegisch*."

She laughed. "You're *narrisch*."

"That may be true," he said with a grin. "But I don't think you could be wrong in anything you say from your heart."

"*Danki*," she said, feeling her cheeks flush again. "This is straight from my heart. I told them that deep in my heart I believe my baby *schweschder* is going to be well in the next couple of years, and she's going to go to school. I explained that I want to be her teacher. I want to have the joy of seeing her play on the playground and recite her multiplication tables at the front of my class. That would be a dream come true for me, and I believe it will happen very soon."

A glowing smile turned up Joshua's lips. "I think that is the perfect answer."

"*Danki*," she said as they turned up her driveway. "They also asked me to recite the *Ordnung* and they asked how I would deal with behavior issues. I think I answered those correctly, but I was so *naerfich*."

"I'm certain you did just fine," Joshua repeated. "You don't give yourself enough credit."

Lydia shrugged. "I guess I don't, but I don't want to be prideful. It's a sin."

"When will you know the answer?"

"I should know in a few days. Maybe they'll tell me at church on Sunday," Lydia said as they reached her porch. "I know I won't sleep until then."

"I'm very proud of you." Joshua smiled as they stood at the bottom of the steps.

"*Danki.*" She bit her bottom lip before sharing the thoughts that had been assaulting her mind since she'd spoken to the school board. "I made a decision."

He raised his eyebrows with interest. "What decision is that?"

She took a deep breath. "If I'm going to be the teacher, then I need to be a proper role model. I have to tell my parents the truth about what happened that night with Mahlon."

With a hesitant expression on his face, Joshua rubbed his chin. "Are you certain you want to do that?"

"*Ya,*" Lydia said. "I know that my *dat* just gave me permission to go back to youth gatherings, and I'll be okay if he takes away that privilege again. I'll even tell the bishop the truth if they ask me to." She felt queasy at the thought of facing the bishop, and she quickly pushed the thought away. "I just feel I need to be honest about who I am or I'm not a *gut* role model for my scholars." She smiled. "My scholars. I like the sound of that."

Joshua touched her cheek. "You will be a *wunderbaar gut* teacher."

A voice yelled Joshua's name from across the pasture.

"I better go," he said before kissing her cheek. "I promised my *dat* I'd be back in an hour." He started across the driveway walking backward. "I'll see you later tonight?"

"*Ya,*" Lydia said. "See you then." She gave a little wave and then hurried up the porch steps.

☙

Later that evening, Lydia took a deep, cleansing breath as she headed down the stairs to the family room, where her parents sat reading. Her hands trembled when she reached the bottom step, and they looked up with surprised expressions.

"Lydia?" her mother asked, placing her Bible on the table beside her. "Is everything all right? Are the *kinner* asleep?"

"*Ya,*" Lydia said, fingering her dress. "The *kinner* are fine. Everyone is fast asleep. I was wondering if I could speak with you for a moment."

"Of course you can," her father said, closing the *Budget,* their Amish newspaper, and removing his half-glasses. "*Was iss letz?*"

Clearing her throat, Lydia stood before her parents and hoped for the right words. "I need to tell you something important."

Now her parents exchanged concerned expressions before her father spoke. "Go on. We're listening."

"Today I stood before the school board and asked to take the role as the teacher for our district," she began. "When I did that, I made a commitment to the *kinner* in the community, and I feel that I should be the best role model I can be. If I'm not a *gut* role model, then I'm not a *gut* teacher."

Her parents nodded, still looking confused.

"When I made the commitment to the *kinner* and to the school board, I realized that I have to be honest with both of you," Lydia continued, still nervously fingering the skirt of her dress. "Therefore, I must confess something."

"Take your time," *Mamm* said.

"I did something very bad a few months ago, and I'm not proud of it." Lydia met her father's cautious stare. "In fact, *Dat*, you asked me about it, and I lied to you."

His expression grew grim.

"Do you remember when you asked me if I'd been out with Mahlon and his *freinden?*" she asked, her voice quaking as her nerves stood on end.

"*Ya*," her father said in a hesitant tone.

"I had. Once." She glanced at her mother, whose mouth gaped with surprise. "It was a stupid mistake, and I did it one night when I was very upset and worried about Ruthie. Josh and Amanda weren't at the youth gathering, and Nancy was busy with her boyfriend. I felt completely alone, and when Mahlon invited me to spend time with his friends, I wasn't thinking clearly. I drank beer, and I was tipsy."

Her mother cupped her hand over her mouth.

"I'm very sorry," Lydia continued, speaking faster and trying not to stumble over her words. "I know it was wrong, and it was even worse to lie about it. I've felt terrible about it, and I wanted to tell you the truth."

She turned to her father, whose expression was unmoving. "I've learned my lesson, and I understand if you want to punish me. Go on and ground me, and I'll stay home from youth gatherings until I'm eighteen. I'll even go speak to the bishop if you'd like since my name was never given to him. I understand if you're upset and disappointed. I'm disappointed in myself."

To her great surprise, *Dat* smiled.

Lydia gaped.

"I'm very proud of you, Lydia," he said. "What you just said has shown me that you're mature."

"It has?" Lydia asked.

He glanced at *Mamm*, who also looked surprised.

"You've shown me that you take the role of teaching seriously, and you're going to do your best for the *kinner* and the community. You're thinking of the *kinner* and not yourself. You've finally learned how to sacrifice for your community." He stood and hugged her. "I'm very proud of you."

"You are?" Lydia studied her father in disbelief. Was he ill? Was he joking? This was not the man with whom she'd argued only a month and a half ago. "*Dat*, I'm glad you're proud of me, but I don't understand. Why aren't you angry with me? Why aren't you yelling?"

Dat chuckled. "Lydia, you were wrong to drink, but you also know that it was wrong. You were very upset about your *schweschder* and how stressful things were at home, and you foolishly followed the wrong path. Now you realize your mistakes, however, and you're confessing your sins. You've grown up."

"That's right," *Mamm* chimed in with a smile. "I'm proud of you too."

"*Danki*," Lydia said with hesitation. "Are you going to punish me?"

Her parents looked at each other again and smiled.

"No," her father said. "*Danki* for telling the truth. But don't ever lie to me again."

"I won't," Lydia said quickly before they changed their minds. "I'm going to sit outside for a little bit. Joshua said he is going to stop by. I hope that's all right."

"Don't be long," her mother warned her, suppressing a knowing smile. "It's getting late."

"I won't be late." Stepping onto the porch, she heaved a sigh of relief that seemed to come from her toes. The discussion had gone much better than she'd ever imagined. She was so thankful she'd told the truth and elated that her parents forgave her. A huge weight had been lifted from her heart, and she felt renewed.

While Lydia awaited Joshua's visit, she hugged her arms to her chest, lowered herself onto the swing, and contemplated the past six months. Her life had been turned upside down by her sister's illness, but things were heading back to normal, or as normal as they could be when someone in your family has a chronic illness. In a day or two, she'd find out if she would be the new teacher, and she could now call Joshua Glick her unofficial boyfriend. Yes, things were definitely looking up.

She smiled as she spotted Joshua's lanky body loping toward her porch, glowing in the light of a battery-powered lantern. He hurried up the steps and stood in front of her.

Before she could greet him, he took her hand, pulled her up to him, and brushed his lips against hers. "I've missed you," he whispered.

She grinned as her cheeks flushed at the touch of his warm lips. "I've missed you too. We better start on our walk. I only have a few minutes. My *mamm* will probably come looking for me soon."

"That's okay," he said. "A few minutes with you will be *wunderbaar.*"

Holding hands, they crossed the driveway and sat on the ground. Above them, the stars twinkled in the clear night sky.

"It's the perfect night," she said.

"*Ya*, it is." He placed the lantern on the ground and

draped his arm around her shoulders. "Did you talk to your parents?"

"I did, and they were completely calm."

Joshua raised an eyebrow in disbelief. "Your *dat* was calm?"

"*Ya,*" she said with a shrug. "I was just as surprised as you are now. He even told me he was proud of me because I've shown him that I've matured and I'm no longer selfish. As a result I won't even be punished."

"Wow." Joshua gave a little chuckle. "I'm stunned."

"*You* are?" Lydia laughed. "I'm still reeling from the surprise of it. I'm glad I did it. God wanted me to, and I'm glad I listened." She snuggled into his side.

"I'm glad you listened too," he said, rubbing her arm. "It was the right thing to do."

She looked up at him. "Josh, I have one question that has been bothering me since that night we argued."

"What's that?"

"You said that you threatened Mahlon to keep him from giving my name to the bishop. What was your threat?"

Josh touched his chin, considering his response. "Let's just say I have a few secrets on him that could get him into even more trouble."

"Oh?" Lydia asked.

"I know who provides his illegal drugs," Joshua said. "He's seeing an *English maedel* who has connections through her *bruder.* I told him if he gave your name, I would give her name, which would cause even bigger problems for him."

"Oh, dear." Lydia gasped. "How did you know that?"

Joshua shrugged. "You'd be surprised by how much *buwe* talk while they play volleyball. We can be a lot like *maed* at quilting bees."

"*Danki* for protecting me," she whispered, moving closer to him and inhaling his musky scent. "You were there for me when I needed you most."

He kissed the top of her prayer covering. "*Danki* for being *mei maedel*."

"I'm so *froh*," she said. "After all of the scary and horrible things that happened this year, the summer is turning into a *wunderbaar* time in my life. I'm certain *mei schweschder* is going to get well, and I have you. I'm very blessed."

"I am too," he said. "*Ich liebe dich*, Lydia Jane Bontrager."

"I love you too, Joshua Glick," she whispered, closing her eyes and savoring the moment.

Chocolate
Peanut Butter Cookies

2 cups all-purpose flour
½ teaspoon baking powder

Cream together with:
½ cup shortening

Blend in:
½ cup sugar
½ teaspoon salt
½ cup brown sugar
¼ teaspoon baking soda
½ cup peanut butter

Add 1 beaten egg and mix thoroughly. Stir in flour mixture, alternately with ½ cup milk. Mix well. Fold in 1 cup of semi-sweet chocolate chips. Drop by teaspoon. Bake at 375 degrees for 15 minutes. Makes 3 dozen.

Discussion Questions

1. Throughout the book, Lydia feels the pull of two roles—being a normal sixteen-year-old girl and filling in as a mother and provider for the family. By the end of the story, she realizes it's her duty to fill in for her mother. If you were in her situation, which role would you have fulfilled? Would you have served as a mother and provider or would you have rebelled against the pressure?

2. Lydia's relationship with her father is strained near the end of the book. Despite her best efforts to work things out with him, their differences aren't resolved until after a scary medical issue with her sister Ruthie is overcome. Think of a time when your relationship with a close friend or loved one was strained. How did you overcome the issues in your relationship? How did you and that person find the strength to forgive? Or is this relationship still strained to this day? What Bible verses would help with this?

3. Lydia's grandmother, Elizabeth Kauffman, quotes Psalm 59:16: "But I will sing of your strength, in the morning I will sing of your love; for you are my fortress, my refuge in times of trouble." What does this verse mean to you?

4. Lydia feels caught at a crossroads when Barbie tells her she's not going to teach next year and suggests Lydia apply to become the full-time teacher. Although Lydia enjoys working as the teacher's assistant, she thinks she

may want to work full time at her grandmother's bakery with friends and family members instead. After praying and opening her heart to God, Lydia realizes teaching is God's path for her life. Have you ever found yourself at a crossroads? If so, how did you find your way to the path you were meant to follow?

5. At one point in the story, Lydia feels as if she's lost her relationship with three important people in her life: her father, Joshua, and Tristan. Think of a time when you felt lost and alone. Where did you find your strength? What Bible verses would help with this?

6. What role does the bakery play in the family unit and community? Can you relate this to your life and your family traditions?

7. At the end of the book, Lydia feels compelled to confess to her parents that she committed an indiscretion, which happened at the beginning of the story. Even though the news of her secret didn't leak out into the community, Lydia wants her parents to know the truth. She also felt that she needed to confess before taking on the role as school teacher. Have you ever felt compelled to tell the truth about a secret? How did you feel after you confessed? How did the person you told take the news of your confession? What Bible verses would help with this?

8. Lydia's grandmother recites Hebrews 12:1–2: "Let us throw off everything that hinders and the sin that so easily entangles. And let us run with perseverance the race marked out for us, fixing our eyes on Jesus, the pioneer and perfecter of faith." What does this verse mean to you?

9. Which character can you identify with the most? Which character seemed to carry the most emotional stake in the story? Was it Lydia, Joshua, Beth Anne, or even Ruthie?

10. What did you know about the Amish before reading this book? What did you learn?

Acknowledgments

As always, I'm thankful to my mother, Lola Goebel-becker, my best friend and plotting partner, who offers her unending support, love, and proofreading skills. I also appreciate my husband, Joe; my sons, Zac and Matt; my mother-in-law, Sharon; and my precious aunts, Trudy Janitz and Debbie Floyd, for their love and excitement about my books. Thank you also to my "aunt" Terry O'Brien for her love and her support of this story.

I'm more grateful than words can express to my awesome friends who tirelessly critique for me—Stacey Barbalace, Sue McKlveen, Janet Pecorella, and Lauran Rodriguez. I appreciate your email messages, pep talks, and hugs, both in person and virtual.

I'm very grateful to my special Amish friend who patiently answers my endless stream of questions. You're a blessing in my life.

I'm thankful for the medical professionals who gave their generous time to me and helped with my research, including Jerome Menendez, Nurse Practitioner at the Transplant Center in Levine Children's Hospital. I'm still convinced you're a superhero!

Thank you also to Kimberly Arnold, MSN, CPNP, in the Department of Pediatric Hematology/Oncology at Levine Children's Hospital for your research assistance with pediatric leukemia. I'm grateful to Kim Lassiter for introducing me to Christie Tucker, RN, MSN, whose generous time with my pediatric leukemia questions was invaluable. Thank you, Christie, for your patience and helpful phone conversations.

To my agent, Mary Sue Seymour—thank you for your unending friendship, support, and guidance in my writing career.

I'm grateful to my amazing editor, Jacque Alberta. I appreciate your guidance and friendship. Thank you also to Lori Vanden Bosch for her fantastic editing. Special thanks to every person at Zondervan who helped make this book a reality.

To my readers—I'm so honored you choose to read my books. As always, I appreciate the wonderful emails and your prayers for my husband.

Thank you most of all to God for giving me the inspiration and the words to glorify you. I'm so grateful and humbled you've chosen this path for me.

Special thanks to Cathy and Dennis Zimmermann for their hospitality and research assistance in Lancaster County, Pennsylvania.

Cathy & Dennis Zimmermann, Innkeepers
The Creekside Inn
44 Leacock Road—PO Box 435
Paradise, PA 17562
Toll Free: (866) 604–2574
Local Phone: (717) 687–0333

The author and publisher gratefully acknowledge the following resource used to research information for this book:
C. Richard Beam, *Revised Pennsylvania German Dictionary* (Lancaster: Brookshire Publications, Inc., 1991).